an
Honest
heart

an
Honest
heart

Richard M. Siddoway

Bonneville Books
Springville, Utah

ISBN: 1-55517-838-3
e.1

Published by Bonneville Books
Imprint of Cedar Fort, Inc.
www.cedarfort.com

Distributed by:

Cover design and typeset by Nicole Williams
Cover design © 2005 by Lyle Mortimer

Printed in the United States of America
10 9 8 7 6 5 4 3 2 1

Printed on acid-free paper

DEDIC*a*TION

To Janice and our children—Stan and Brenda, Derick and Bonnie, John and Sharlene, Christian and Rebecca, Brett and Melanie, David and Michelle, Matt and Sherri, and Kyle and Kati

*a*CKNOW*L*EDGM*e*NTS

No author works in a vacuum, and I am indebted to a supportive wife and family. I must also thank a dear friend, Mary Beth Clark, for telling me the story of the rice fields. The editors at Cedar Fort have done their usual exceptional work in making sense of the submitted manuscript and putting it in its final form. And most of all, thanks to you, the reader, for supporting my efforts to tell an uplifting and interesting story.

INVOC*a*TION

The window was directly behind Bishop Morgan, and the late afternoon sun backlit his white hair in a glowing halo. Jennica tried to see his face, but her eyes had adjusted to the brightness of the window, and all she could make out were indistinct blotches of shadow beneath the ring of fire around his head. He held the phone in his left hand while he took notes with his right. The question he had asked her before the telephone rang raced around inside her head like a child chasing dandelion puffs in the wind.

"Are you honest in your dealings with your fellowman?

She looked around the room. On the south wall were three small, framed pictures of the First Presidency. On the north wall was a picture of the Savior dressed in a red robe. The bishop's desk was cluttered with stacks of paper and half a dozen books. The credenza under the picture of Jesus was graced with a small tin can that had been covered with cardboard and which held a dozen handmade paper flowers, each with

1

the name of a Primary child written on the petals in childish scrawls.

"Are you honest in your dealings with your fellowman?

She interlaced the fingers of her hands and felt the sweat in her palms. Bishop Morgan spoke softly into the phone. *I wonder if I should wait outside,* she thought. But the bishop had made no suggestion that she leave. In fact, he seemed apologetic at the interruption. She pulled her hands apart and smoothed the wrinkles from her skirt. Her eyes were pulled to the picture of the Savior, and she stared at him, took a deep breath, and tried to relax.

How do I answer that question? Her mind flew back to the days when she was a tiny child.

ONe

"*Jennica, you quit* hittin' your brother," her mother shouted from behind the screen door.

"He hit me first," she pouted defiantly.

"Did not," her four-year-old brother replied. He lay on the ground trying to suppress tears.

"Did too," she said with all the power of her six-year-old voice. She placed her hands on her hips and thrust her chin forward toward Damon. "He started it."

"I don't care who started it," her mother said. "Both of you stop it. I don't want to catch you acting like heathens." Her shadowy form behind the screen door disappeared back into the kitchen, but over her shoulder she said, "Jenn, you help your brother up. And both of you say you're sorry."

Jennica sighed loudly and then extended her hand toward her brother.

Damon ignored it, stood up, and dusted off the seat of his pants. He was wearing a pair of hand-me-down striped overalls. The knees were almost nonexistent, and the back pockets were missing. He wore no shirt, and the button was missing from the left shoulder strap, causing the front flap to hang forward. Suddenly, he lunged at his sister, but she sidestepped his attack and shoved him back onto the ground.

"Sorry," she said. The sarcasm dripped from her lips like a Popsicle on a hot summer day.

Damon glared at her, holding back the tears. "Not either," he spat. "Neither'm I."

Jennica walked proudly across the backyard, throwing up cyclones of dust with her bare feet. She fought the urge to look back over her shoulder, though she was afraid her brother might launch another attack and catch her unaware. She reached the shade of the old pepper tree that stood in the southeast corner of their lot and scratched her back on the scaly bark. Her thin T-shirt offered little protection from the slivery gray toothpicks that split off from the chunks of bark. She reached up, pulled down one of the fernlike fronds, snapped it free, and sat down with her back against the tree. Absentmindedly, she began picking the pinnate leaves apart. Her brother had disappeared.

The afternoon was hot and still. No cooling breeze could be felt. The sun, a bronze ball, fought to reach her bare legs through the shifting shade of the pepper tree. Jennica scrunched her shoulders against the trunk and felt sweat gathering on the back of her head and sliding, serpentlike, down her pig tails. Bored, having pulled all of the leaves from the frond, she brushed them from her lap, stood up, and marched toward the back door of the house. She climbed the swaybacked wooden steps, pausing long enough to pull a sliver from the bottom of her left foot while balancing on her right. The screen on the door hung from its frame like the front flap on Damon's overalls. She heard her mother cursing softly in the darkness of the kitchen as she pulled open the door and padded across the worn linoleum.

"Mom, I'm bored."

Her mother stood at the stove, stirring a pot of soup. She glanced back over the top of the half-moon eyeglasses that perched low on her nose. The right lens was chipped and scuffed. She brushed a bead of sweat from the tip of her nose. "You know what?" she said. "So am I."

Jennica slid her feet across the smoothness of the linoleum until she reached the doorway into the living room, where a dirty, burnt orange, shag carpet covered the floor. She plunked herself down on one arm of the sofa. The couch had been gold velvet earlier in life but now was worn almost to its burlap backing. It had the mingled odor of cigarette smoke and ammonia imbedded in its stuffing. Jennica raised one arm straight above her head, clamped her nose with her other hand and fell backward onto the couch as if she were a scuba diver entering the sea. The frame of the couch squealed in protest.

"You quit jumpin' on the couch," her mother barked from the kitchen.

Jennica rolled dramatically onto the floor and lay as if dead.

"If you're just gonna hang around here, go down to the grocery store and get me a loaf of bread," her mother said.

Jennica opened one eye, "Do I hafta?"

"Yes, you hafta,'" her mother said sharply. She reached for her purse on the shelf above the stove, withdrew a worn coin purse and retrieved three quarters. She replaced her purse and held the coins in the palm of her hand. "Come, now. Get a move on it."

Jennica forced herself to her feet, walked slowly into the kitchen, feeling the strands of shag carpet between her toes, and took the money from her mother's outstretched hand. "Can I get a treat?"

Her mother shook her head. "Not today, toad. I just don't have any extra money until the check gets here next week." She brushed Jennica's hair back with her hand. "Now hurry. We'll have supper as soon as you get back."

Jennica moved slowly through the house and let herself out the front door. Damon was crouched in the shade of the porch steps, watching traffic go by on Keats Avenue. Jennica stepped majestically down the stairs and marched across the sparse tufts of grass toward the front sidewalk.

"Where ya goin'?" Damon asked as he bounded from his spot in the shade.

"None of your business," Jennica answered rudely.

"Can I come?"

"I don't think so," she replied. The sidewalk was so hot it burned the leathery soles of her feet, but she managed to walk tall and straight down

5

the street. Damon dogged behind her.

"Please," he whimpered.

Jennica sniffed, "Oh, all right. But only if you do what I say." He fell into single file in her wake. They traveled the two blocks to the corner grocery store, trying to take advantage of the sparse shade afforded by the struggling trees along the way. When they finally reached the market, Jennica turned to her brother. "When we get inside, I want you to go to the cooler where they keep the bottles of milk. Pull open the door and stand there. The cold air will feel good. Understand?"

Damon nodded his head. "I understand."

She pulled open the door of the store, and the two of them entered. Immediately, Damon scampered to the refrigerated dairy cooler and pulled open the door. Jennica hurried to the opposite side of the store and grabbed a loaf of bread by the twist-tied end.

"Hey, kid, close the door!" The teenaged cashier called across the store to Damon. The cooler door stayed open. Exasperated, the clerk left the cash register and hustled to the back corner of the store. "Kid," he said emphatically, "I said, 'Close the door.'" Damon let the door swing shut. "What do you want anyway?" Damon shrugged his shoulders.

"I came with my sister," he said timidly.

"Well, stay out of the cooler. Ya hear?"

Damon nodded his head and followed the clerk to the front of the store. Jennica stood at the side of the counter with the loaf of bread dangling from her hand. When the cashier approached, she placed the loaf of bread on the counter. The teenager rang up the purchase.

"That'll be sixty-seven cents," he said.

Jennica was barely taller than the counter, but she reached up and dropped the three sweaty quarters from her palm. The clerk swept them into one hand with the other, entered seventy-five cents into the cash register and punched a key. The drawer slid open with a chime. He threw in the quarters and retrieved a nickel and three pennies from the drawer. "Want a bag for that?" he asked as he handed Jennica her change.

"Yes, please," she said sweetly.

The clerk dropped the loaf of bread into a grocery sack, ripped the receipt from the cash register, and handed them to Jennica.

The two children hurried out the door and walked briskly down the sidewalk. Once they reached the shade of an oleander bush, Jennica pulled her brother off the sidewalk. She reached into the back of her shorts and pulled out an extremely soft Hershey bar, which she slipped into the bag with the bread.

"Where'd you get that? Do I get some? Gonna share?" Damon asked.

"At the store, stupid," she said haughtily. "Maybe I'll share, maybe I won't." She returned to the sidewalk and walked briskly home with her brother in her wake. They climbed the front stairs and opened the sagging screen door. Jennica reached into the bag and slipped out the Hershey bar. She looked quickly around the darkened front room and then settled on the book her mother had been reading before the accident. Swiftly, she slipped the chocolate bar between the pages of the book. Then she turned and continued into the kitchen. Her mother stood, sweating heavily, near the stove, stirring the pot of bean soup. Jennica handed her the plastic bag.

"Where's my change?" her mother asked.

Dutifully, Jennica opened her sweaty hand and dropped the coins into her mother's waiting palm. Her mother opened the tattered coin purse and dropped them in while Jennica retreated to the front room.

"Set the table," her mother commanded.

Without putting up her usual argument, Jennica carried three chipped bowls, each a different color, to the kitchen table, retrieved three spoons from the silverware drawer, placed them next to the bowls, and filled three glasses with water. Finished with the task, she returned to the comparative darkness of the living room. While her mother was busy ladling soup, she reclaimed the book-flattened Hershey bar and scooted furtively down the hallway to her bedroom. Quickly she placed the still-soft chocolate bar under her pillow and hurried back to the kitchen.

"Put some bread on a plate, toad," her mother said.

Jennica opened the loaf of bread and placed four slices on a saucer. She twisted the tie back on the bread wrapper, opened the refrigerator and removed the butter dish. There was nothing else in the refrigerator besides a half-empty gallon bottle of milk, a six-pack of beer, and a jar of mustard.

"Hurry up," her mother said. "I'm hungry."

Jennica and Damon plopped down on the wooden stools next to the kitchen table. Their mother placed a folded dish towel on the chipped

Formica top, lifted the simmering pot of soup, and placed it on the cloth. She stirred the steaming liquid once more before ladling it into the waiting bowls.

"More beans?" Jennica sniffed. "Why do we always have to have beans?"

"Don't smart-mouth me," her mother snapped. "You can go hungry if you don't like what we're having."

The girl sat sullenly, simmering like the soup in front of her. She then stood and walked proudly down the hallway to her room. Once there, she closed the door, lifted her pillow, and removed the Hershey bar. She slid the brown wrapper from one end of the foil lining and almost reverently peeled it back to expose the chocolate. She nibbled mouselike on one corner of the bar and let it melt on the tip of her tongue. She contentedly pulled her legs up against her frail chest and leaned against the wall behind her bed. She had almost consumed the candy when the door burst open and her mother strode into the room.

"What are you eating?" she demanded.

Jennica quickly stuffed the last square of chocolate into her mouth and turned her face to the corner, away from her mother.

"Don't you turn your back on me," her mother said furiously. "I want to know what you're eating."

Jennica hunched her shoulders and waited for the inevitable blow. Her mother reached for her shoulder, spun her around, and slapped her hard on her cheek. A splatter of tobacco-colored saliva burst from her mouth.

"I want an answer," her mother snarled.

Jennica began to sob uncontrollably, fell over onto the bed, and curled up in a fetal position. Drool ran from the corner of her mouth.

Her mother gave her bottom several quick slaps. "If you won't answer me, you can just stay in your room until you're ready to tell me what you're eating and where you got it." She spun on her heel and slammed the door behind her.

Jennica lay sobbing on her bed until the sun set and darkness stretched its comforting arms around her. Eventually, she climbed out of bed, opened the door as quietly as possible and made her way to the bathroom. Just as she reached for the doorknob her mother cleared her throat in the darkness.

"Ready to tell me?" she asked.

Jennica could smell the sour beer on her mother's breath before she could see her in the blackness of the hall. She turned to run, but her mother's hand shot out of the shadows and grabbed her by the shoulder. Her feet flew out from under her, and she fell wriggling to the floor. Her mother knelt beside her and pinned her frail shoulders to the threadbare rag rug.

"Where did you get the candy, Jenn?" she said menacingly. Jennica kicked her feet and arched her back, but her mother held her like a plucked chicken. "I ain't gonna letcha up till you tell me," she said, pressing her shoulders even harder against the rug.

Jennica began to cry. "You're hurting me," she snorted between sobs.

"I'll hurt you more, if'n you don't tell me."

In a spurt of defiance, the girl said, "I took it from the store. You never give me nothin', so I took it."

Her mother relaxed the pressure on her shoulders. "Now, that wasn't so hard, was it?" Jennica sat up against the wall and drew her knees up against her chest, just as her mother slapped her again. "I never want to hear of you stealing again. You understand?"

"Yes'm," the girl said through her tears. *I'll be more careful next time,* she thought angrily. *You'll never hear of me stealing again.*

"You kids'll drive me to drink." She lifted herself unsteadily to her feet and staggered down the hallway, while her daughter sat with her back against the wall and gulped huge bites of air.

T W O

Jennica glanced at the clock above the blackboard in the front of the room. There was less than ten minutes left until class was over. Miss Crawford was sitting at her desk in the front corner of the room next to the window. She had a stack of assignments sitting on the two-drawer file cabinet next to her desk, and she was correcting the papers while her class worked on the final examination of the year. Jennica had managed to get a seat next to Marcia Bell, the smartest girl in the whole fourth grade. Miss Crawford was intently reading one of the papers, so Jennica's eyes wandered over to Marcia's test paper. Quickly, she memorized the pattern of answers to the ten questions on the bottom of the page; then, with poised pencil, she filled in the little round circles on her paper.

The teacher stood up from her desk and walked to the back of the classroom. Jennica followed her out of the corner of her eye. When she thought she wasn't looking, she shifted her gaze to Marcia's paper.

Marcia had covered part of the answers with her arm, and Jennica had to crane her neck a little to see the last answers on the test. She sensed Miss Crawford even before she heard her and felt her hand on her shoulder.

"Jennica," she said in a whisper, "please follow me. Bring your paper."

Jennica felt as if every eye in the room was glued to her as she followed Miss Crawford into the hall. Her teacher closed the door behind her, turned to Jennica and said, "How many times do I have to tell you to keep your eyes on your own paper?" She extended her hand, and Jennica handed her the test paper. Miss Crawford rolled it into a tight little cylinder and tapped it gently on the girl's head. "Jennica, you're a bright girl, but you always seem to take the easy way out. I've warned you before about cheating, and now I'm going to have to invalidate your final test."

Jennica wasn't sure what "invalidate" meant, but she knew it wasn't good. "I wasn't cheating," she said defiantly.

"Oh?" her teacher replied. "Well, let's see." She unrolled the test paper. "Perhaps you could answer a couple of these questions for me, then?" Her eyes scanned down the paper. "What is the capital of Texas?" She looked at Jennica with hooded eyes.

"Uh . . ." Jennica tried to think of the answer. She thought of every Texas-sounding city she could. "San Diego?" she finally answered.

"Interesting," said Miss Crawford. "How about the capital of California?"

"That's easy—Los Angeles," the girl replied.

"I wonder why you marked Austin for Texas and Sacramento for California on your test paper?" She pointed one crimson-polished fingernail at the answers Jennica had filled out on the paper.

The girl shrugged her shoulders. "I dunno."

"You 'dunno'? Well, you just scoot down to Mrs. Hawthorne's office and wait for me there." She gently pushed Jennica toward the principal's office, turned, and went back into the room.

Jennica moved slowly down the hallway, as if her feet were stuck in soft tar. Eventually, she reached the principal's office and knocked softly on the door. There was no answer, so she pushed the door open gently. The room was empty. Without a second thought, she whirled and ran out the front doorway of the school, cut across the lawn, and scurried on home.

When she pushed the back door open, she could hear her mother on the phone.

"I'll take care of it," her mother muttered and then fell silent. "I said I'll take care of it," she repeated before she set the handset back on its cradle. Without turning around she said in a menacingly low voice, "What are you doing home?"

Jennica froze in place. "I dunno."

In a flash her mother spun around and grabbed her by her left arm. "Cheating? Why, Jenn? You're smart enough. Why cheat?" Her hand snaked out and hit the girl on the side of her head. "You go to your room—now! And I never want to hear of your cheating again. Is that clear?"

"Yes'm," the girl sputtered through tears. *You'll never hear nothing about me cheating,* she thought, *'cause I ain't never gonna get caught again.*

THRee

"*Will you clear* that table, Jenn?" Lorna said over her shoulder as she headed toward the front of the restaurant.

Jenn pushed her waitress cap down more tightly on her head and shoved the cart to the edge of the table. "What pigs," she said under her breath. A family with four small children had eaten in the booth, and crumbled crackers were strewn all over the floor around the table. The wooden high chair had root beer and macaroni and cheese plastered on the seat. Jenn removed the plates and stacked them in the plastic tub on the cart. She swiped at the tabletop with a damp rag that hung over the cart's handle bar and had reached in to wipe off the seat when she spotted the wallet on the floor. Carefully, she picked it up and stuffed it into the pocket of her apron. She looked furtively around to see if anyone had seen her. Confident that no one had, she finished cleaning the booth. Jenn pushed the cart toward the kitchen just as the father of the family who had been eating in the booth walked back into the restaurant and made his way to the now-empty booth. He squatted down and looked under the table. The man was wearing a faded T-shirt with a couple of small holes under his left arm, a pair of worn jeans held up by a tooled leather belt with an enormous oval belt buckle, and scuffed cowboy boots.

Jenn pushed the cart through the swinging door into the dish-washing area of the kitchen and began emptying the tub into the sink. The three cooks barely glanced at her, and the dishwasher was outside having a smoke. When she was sure no one was watching, she reached into her apron pocket, pulled out the wallet, and stuck it behind a box of plastic cup lids on the shelf above the sink. Then she continued emptying the dirty dishes into the sink.

Lorna pushed open the swinging door. "Jenn, you didn't find a wallet while you were cleaning 14, did you?"

Jenn slid the last of the plates into the dishwater before turning toward her supervisor. She shook her head. "A wallet? What kind of wallet?"

Lorna shrugged her shoulders. "I don't know. This guy out here thought he dropped his wallet when they were getting out of the booth. You didn't see it?"

"Not me," she said with a shrug.

Lorna let the door swing closed behind her. Jenn fought the urge to retrieve the wallet from its hiding place and waited a minute before following her supervisor back into the restaurant. Lorna was standing by the cash register writing down some information from the man who had lost his wallet. Jenn hurried past them and began clearing another booth. She struggled to keep from looking at him, bending to the task of wiping off the table. Finally, the tiny bell that hung above the restaurant door rang its silvery note, and she glanced over her shoulder in time to see the door closing behind the man. She followed him with her eyes as he crossed the parking lot to an ancient Volkswagen bus. He shook his head as he hoisted himself into the driver's seat, started the engine, and backed slowly out of the parking place. Jenn felt a pang of guilt as the bus passed by the window, and her hands shook a little as she rolled the cart away from the table.

"Might as well close down," Lorna said as Jenn pushed the cart through the swinging doors into the kitchen. "It's been a pretty slow night, and I think we've had our last customer."

Louis, the dishwasher, had finished his smoke and was scrubbing the dishes in the sink as Jenn began unloading the cart. "I hate mac and cheese," he said. "Sticks like glue." He scrubbed a spot on one of the plates.

"Lorna said we're going to close early," Jenn said as she removed four glass tumblers from the cart and slipped them into the soapy water. She felt Louis's hand grab her wrist, and she recoiled as if bitten by a snake. The soapsuds gave him a poor grip, and she was able to slip free of his grasp. "Don't you touch me," she said with disdain and anger.

Louis shrugged his shoulders. "Don't get yer back up, sweetheart," he sneered. "You're no better than the rest of us." He moved slowly toward her with his hands on his hips. Flecks of suds slid between his knuckles and onto the stained apron that hung nearly to the ground. "I could show you a real good time."

She backed up, keeping her eyes on Louis's face. She let her face become emotionless as she saw the curl of his lip. Without looking, she knew the cooks were watching this slow fox-trot with amusement, and she could expect no help from them. Jenn spun around, but before she could reach the swinging doors, Louis had enveloped her from behind and was running his hands over her. A cast-iron skillet rested on the edge of the stove. With one quick, catlike motion, she slipped her soapy arm free, grabbed the frying pan by the handle, ducked, and swung it over her head. She felt a satisfying clunk as the skillet met with Louis's head. Immediately, his grasp relaxed, and he let out a scream. Jenn ran through the doors into the restaurant. Lorna was finishing counting out the till and dividing the money from the tip jar. She glanced at Jenn as she ran into the room.

"Here's your cut of the tips," she said extending a handful of bills toward Jenn. "What's the matter?" she asked when she saw tears rolling down Jenn's cheeks. At that moment Louis, armed with a butcher knife, came screaming through the doors. He was holding a towel in one hand against the side of his head, trying to stop the flow of blood. "What is going on here?" Lorna yelled.

"She tried to kill me," he bellowed as Jenn cowered behind the manager. Louis waved the knife in front of him, "And now I'm gonna make her pay."

"No, you're not!" Lorna said. "Put that knife down and go wash off that blood," she said as she inched closer to the counter where the cash register rested.

"Fat chance," he said with a swipe of the knife a few inches from her face.

"Louis! I said put down the knife." Lorna's hand slipped into the shelf beneath the cash register, and when she withdrew it, she was holding an ancient .38 caliber Smith and Wesson revolver. She pointed it at Louis's head. "Now!" Lorna nodded her head slowly. "Put it down," she said with steel in her voice. "Then go get your things and get out!"

The man held the knife for a moment and then dropped it onto the linoleum floor. Holding the blood-soaked towel to his head, he backed through the swinging doors into the kitchen. "This ain't over," he snarled as the doors swung closed behind him.

"Oh, yes it is," Lorna said loudly.

Jenn slumped to her knees and sobbed. Lorna followed Louis into the kitchen and a moment later Jenn heard the back door slam shut before her manager reappeared. "I don't think he's going to give you any more trouble," she said, "but you'd better keep your eyes peeled on the way home." She crouched down beside Jenn. "Now, wipe your eyes, and let's get out of here." She patted the girl on her shoulder. Jenn sobbed inconsolably. "Come on, now. Go hang up your apron, and I'll give you a ride home." She lifted the girl to her feet.

Timidly, Jenn walked back into the kitchen. The cooks avoided her eyes as they finished cleaning the grills. She removed her apron, hung it on the hook next to the walk in refrigerator, and slipped on her jacket. Jenn glanced at the cooks, reached up to where she'd hidden the wallet, grabbed it, and stuffed it into her jacket pocket. Lorna was waiting for her by the cash register.

"I'm sorry about what happened, Jenn. I should have warned you about Louis. He . . . well, let's just say this isn't the first time he tried to make a move on one of my girls. But for sure it's the last time." Lorna locked the front door behind them. "Generally, I don't leave until the cooks have left, but I think you need someone to take you home. Tell me how to get to where you live."

Jenn slumped down on the front seat of the car. "Over on Keats," she said. "Just take a right at the next corner." A few minutes later she climbed out of the car and up the front steps of her house. Lorna watched until the door closed behind her and then made a U-turn and headed back toward the restaurant.

Her mother was sitting in the darkened living room. "You're home early. Get fired?" she slurred.

"No, Mom, just not much business tonight." She slipped past her mother and started down the hallway toward her room.

"Who gave you a ride home?"

"Lorna," she answered warily.

"How come?" Her mother took another drink from the bottle in her hand. "She don't usually give you a ride."

Jenn thought of what had happened. She could still feel the wetness from Louis's hands on her blouse, and she shuddered. But she feared that her mother would force her to quit if she told her what had happened. "No reason," she blurted out.

"Must be some reason," her mother pried. "You're sixteen years old, and you don't need no baby-sitting supervisor to chauffeur you around town."

"No reason, Mom," she reiterated. "I'm tired. I'm going to bed."

"Where's Damon?" her mother called through the gloom of the hallway.

"How should I know? I've been at work," Jenn snapped.

"Don't use that tone of voice with me," her mother said. "I work hard around here. If your father hadn't gone and got hisself killed . . ." Her voice trailed off.

It's always somebody else's fault, isn't it, Mom, she thought as she closed her bedroom door behind her. The wallet bounced against her hip as she removed her jacket, and she slipped it out of the pocket and laid it on her bed along with the money from the tip jar. Quietly, she slipped out of her clothes, grabbed the money and the wallet, and crossed the hallway to the bathroom. She locked the door behind her and sat down on the edge of the bathtub. With a practiced hand, she counted the handful of bills—eighteen dollars—and placed them on the toilet seat. Her hand trembled slightly as she opened the wallet and glanced over her shoulder, even though the bathroom door was locked.

The billfold smelled of sweat and mildewed leather. Inside were two twenty-dollar bills and two ones. Jenn added the money to the stack of dollars on the edge of the tub before she checked what else was in the wallet. There were no credit cards, just a driver's license and a laminated picture of a woman.

Jenn pulled out the license and turned it over in her hands. The picture under the peeling lamination made the man—Randall Grant—look even scrawnier than he'd appeared in the restaurant. Jenn read his name and address—543 Pine Street in Ten Sleep, Wyoming—then slid the license back into the billfold. She examined the picture. It was clearly the woman who had been with him in the restaurant but much younger. Jenn turned it over and read the message on the back of the photograph: "With all my love, Jan." She shoved it back into the wallet, stood, unlocked the bathroom door, and slipped quietly into her bedroom.

Jenn closed the door to her room and then removed the bottom drawer of her dresser. She had discovered many years before that there was a space beneath the drawer in which she could hide treasures. Furtively, she flattened the bills in her hand and added them to the other cash in the hiding place before replacing the drawer. She heard her mother's step in the hall, stuffed the wallet under her pillow, turned out the light, and slipped into bed. A moment later the door opened.

"I thought your light was on," her mother mumbled.

Jenn lay as still as a newborn fawn with her eyes closed. After a couple of minutes, her mother turned and made her way down the hallway. Jenn waited until she was sure her mother had gone into her own bedroom before she dared stir. She could smell the worn leather billfold, and her hand slipped almost involuntarily under the pillow and grasped it. She reached down and pushed it under the bed.

The next morning she slipped the wallet into her backpack and carried it with her to school. She was about to toss it into the garbage can outside the school office when she realized that it might be retrieved. Her mind churned through a possible chain of events. If the wallet were found, the owner would be contacted, he would report that he had lost it at the restaurant where she worked, and she would immediately become a suspect.

Jenn wondered if she had left fingerprints on the wallet or its contents. Nervously, she pushed it to the bottom of her backpack. After school she went into a stall in the girls' rest room and pulled the billfold out of its hiding place. She removed the driver's license and the picture and slipped them into a pocket on the side of the backpack. She then left the school and started for home. As she passed a construction project about a block from the school, she decided to toss the wallet into a dumpster that sat next to the sidewalk.

That night after work she added the photograph and license to the stash of bills in her secret place. But when she climbed into bed, she could still smell the lingering odor of the wallet as she tried to go to sleep.

FO*U*R

Rolayne beckoned to the other girls. She was partially hidden in the shadows in the alley that ran between the grocery store and the video rental shop. Jenn and her three friends crouched behind the low hedge that surrounded the parking lot. It was long after midnight, and there were but few cars parked on the asphalt. The summer was drawing to a close, and the night was chilly. Jenn spotted the old man pushing a grocery cart toward his Cadillac. He had parked the car under one of the lights that bathed the parking lot in a white blue haze. The man was perhaps slightly taller than Jenn's five foot five, but he was much thinner. A few sparse silver hairs stuck up like insect antennae from his otherwise bald head. He reached the Cadillac, opened the trunk, and began to transfer the plastic grocery sacks from the cart into it. He finished the task, closed the trunk, and pushed the cart to a cart return station.

Rolayne waved her hand furiously. Jenn and her friends stood, jumped over the hedge, and ran toward the old man. He was oblivious to their presence until Jenn was nearly at his side. She grabbed the car keys that dangled from his hand as the other three girls pushed him to the ground. Immediately, Jenn pushed the button on the key ring, unlocked the Cadillac, pulled open the door, and jumped in. Her friends jerked the back door open and slid into the car. The old man lay curled up on the ground with his hands over his face as Jenn started the car, shifted into gear, and spun across the parking lot to where Rolayne emerged from the alley. She flung open the passenger's door, jumped in, and slammed it shut. Jenn squealed across the parking lot and out onto the street. She had never driven a car before, and she swerved erratically across the pavement. In the rearview mirror she saw the old man struggling to his feet.

When they had driven for about ten minutes, Jenn pulled into the parking lot of a church and stopped the car. She popped the trunk open, and the five girls pawed through the bags of groceries. They found a box of ice cream sandwiches and ripped it open. A minute later they were lying on the church lawn eating the treat and arguing about who would eat the extra one when a police car cruised slowly by.

"Just lie still," Rolayne whispered loudly. "Don't make any quick moves."

The police car continued up the street nearly half a block before it stopped and began to back up.

"Run!" Rolayne yelled.

The girls leapt to their feet and ran. Jenn spotted a row of shrubs along the foundation of the church. Frantically, she pushed her way through them and lay down between the shrubs and the building. The other four girls raced down the sidewalk away from the chapel. A few seconds after Jenn found her hiding place, two policemen rounded the corner of the church on a dead run and pursued the girls. Jenn waited until she could no longer hear the sounds of anyone running. Then she cautiously stood up and slipped out of her hiding place. For a moment she considered taking the Cadillac but decided against it. She was only half a mile from home in the opposite direction from where her friends were running. She brushed the dirt and grass clippings from her shorts and walked quickly toward home.

Even though it was after one o'clock in the morning, Jenn was afraid her mother might still be up, so she opened the back screen door as carefully as possible. The hinges protested with a throaty squeal, but there was no sound from inside the house. Jenn twisted the doorknob and pushed the kitchen door open. A gust of stale hot air escaped around her into the cooler night like an errant spirit. She pulled off her shoes and tiptoed across the worn linoleum toward the hallway when she heard her mother's soft snores from the living room. In the muted glow of the streetlight coming through the front room window, she could make out the form of her mother asleep in her chair. Three beer cans at the side of the chair reflected sprinkles of light from their silver surfaces. Jenn continued down the hallway to her bedroom.

Just as she pushed her shoes under bed and slipped in between the sheets, there was a tapping on her window. Jenn heart fluttered wildly in her breast. She turned her head until she could see the window. A shadowy shape was barely visible in the weak moonlight. She saw it raise its hand and rap on her window again. Gathering her courage, she climbed out of bed and crept across the floor.

"Let me in," her brother whispered.

Jenn slid the window open. "What are you doing?" she hissed.

"I don't want Mom to catch me," Damon whispered in return. He hoisted himself up and slid noiselessly through the window onto her floor.

"Where have you been?" she demanded.

He shrugged his shoulders. "Just out with the guys." He started to leave the room but then turned and whispered, "Where have you been? I've been waitin' an hour for you to get home."

"None of your business," she snarled under her breath. "Besides, I'm nearly eighteen. I'm an adult." She tossed her hair.

Damon slunk across the hall to his bedroom as quietly as possible, and Jenn climbed back into bed.

The next morning the sun burned its way through the mist and struck Jenn full in the face. Groggily, she stretched and yawned before sliding out of bed. She pulled on an old pink robe that her mother had passed down to her as a present five or six years before, and then walked down the hallway to the kitchen. Her mother was still sleeping in her chair. Jenn picked up the empty beer cans and threw them in the trash.

She opened the cupboard door and saw there was no more cereal. *Just like Old Mother Hubbard,* she thought. *The cupboard is bare.* She pulled open the refrigerator, opened the nearly empty plastic gallon of milk, and sniffed. Sour! She recoiled and wrinkled her nose before pouring the little bit that was left down the sink. She could hear her mother stirring in the living room.

"Mom," she called out. "We don't have any more cereal or milk."

"And I ain't got no more money," her mother said through a yawn. "Any chance I can borrow some from you until the check comes?"

Jenn gritted her teeth. "Sure, Mom. I'll walk down to the store." She took a quick bath, combed her hair, and dressed in a navy blue halter top and white shorts. Jenn closed the door to her room, pulled out the dresser drawer, and retrieved two twenty-dollar bills from her trove. "I'll be back," she said as she walked past her mother and out the front door of their house. It was Sunday morning, and now that the mist had burned off, the air was clear and clean. Jenn walked briskly down the sidewalk toward the grocery store. She passed the little corner market that was closed on Sundays and continued another couple of blocks until she approached the church where she had hidden the night before. The Cadillac was nowhere to be seen, although the parking lot was beginning to fill with cars. A pair of young women dressed in ankle length skirts and white blouses were talking to each other in front of the church. One was a blonde, the other a brunette.

Jenn glanced at them as she approached. They each wore a little black badge, and as she began to pass by, one of them spoke to her.

"Good morning," the blonde said.

"Mornin'," Jenn replied almost under her breath.

"Have a nice day," the other woman said.

Jenn nodded her head and continued walking. Two blocks later she reached the supermarket, where she bought food for breakfast, lunch, and dinner for her family. She slipped the two plastic bags over the fingers of one hand, picked up the gallon milk jug with the other, and began her walk home. The two young women were still standing in front of the church building as she approached.

"Looks like you could use some help," the blonde said. "Can we help you carry your groceries?"

"You gotta be kiddin'," Jenn said. But she stopped and set the groceries down on the lawn in front of the church. The plastic bags were cramping her left hand, and her right hand was nearly frozen from carrying the jug of milk. "Why would you help me?"

"Because you look as if you need help," the dark-haired woman answered. "Isn't that enough reason?"

"Look, guys, I live nearly half a mile down this street," she said, pointing her finger in the direction of her house. "That means you'd have to truck nearly a mile. I don't think you wanna do that."

"Why not?" the blonde said.

Jenn was flustered. "I mean, don't you have church or somethin'?"

"We can catch another block," the brunette replied.

"Block?" Jenn said, wrinkling her forehead.

"Come on," the blonde said, picking up the gallon of milk. "You lead; we'll follow."

The brunette picked up both plastic bags and waited for Jenn to lead them to her house.

"I can take one of them," Jenn said.

"As you wish," the brunette replied. She handed Jenn the lighter of the two bags. "By the way, I'm Sister Sandberg. This is Sister Lingfelter."

"Sisters? You don't look much alike." Jenn neglected to tell them who she was.

Sister Lingfelter laughed and shook her blond hair. "We're sister missionaries, but we're not really sisters, except in the gospel."

Jenn wrinkled her brow. "We, I mean, I don't go to church much." She sounded slightly embarrassed. She glanced at the parking lot and was surprised to see nearly every slot filled. "But I guess those people do," she gestured with her free hand.

"Oh, but you're not alone," Sister Sandberg said. "There are a lot of people who haven't discovered the happiness of the gospel."

"Happiness?" Jenn snorted. "All I ever thought church meant was that you couldn't have any fun."

"I'm sure you're not alone in that thinking either," Sister Lingfelter chuckled. "There really is a lot of difference between happiness and joy."

Jenn shrugged her shoulders. "I guess." They walked nearly a full block in silence before Jenn said, "Why are you guys doing this? I mean, what's in it for you?"

"You mean carrying your groceries for you?" Sister Sandberg said.

"Yeah, and this whole sister bit. You make pretty good money at it?"

The two missionaries smiled at each other for a moment. Then Sister Lingfelter said, "The only thing that's in it for us is helping spread the gospel. We don't get paid anything except for that."

"But why help me? I'm nobody."

"Ah, but that's where you're wrong. You are a daughter of God."

Jenn exploded into laughter. "Me? Boy are you wrong."

Sister Lingfelter shook her head gently. "No I'm not. That's something I'm absolutely sure of."

Jenn continued to chuckle as they finally reached her house. Her mother was sitting on the front porch with a can of beer in one hand and a cigarette in the other. Jenn looked at the neatly dressed women who had helped her home and then at the shabbiness of her surroundings and felt uncomfortable.

"I can take them from here," Jenn said, reaching for the jug of milk and the second plastic sack.

"We've come this far, we might as well finish the journey," Sister Sandberg said as she walked briskly up the sidewalk toward Jenn's mother. She climbed the sagging wooden steps and extended her hand. "Hello, I'm Sister Sandberg," she said.

Jenn's mother reluctantly set down the can of beer and took hold of Sister Sandberg's hand. She turned to Jenn and said, "Where'd you get these two?"

"They offered to help me carry the food home," Jenn answered.

"What are ya—some kinda nuns?" She stubbed the cigarette out on the porch railing. "Some kinda religious nuts?"

Sister Lingfelter smiled, "No, just a couple of missionaries out trying to spread the word."

"Well, ya won't have much success here," Jenn's mother snorted. She struggled out of the chair, turned on her heel, and marched into the house. The screen door slammed behind her.

Jenn felt increasingly uncomfortable. "I . . . thanks for helping with the groceries. I appreciate it, even if . . ." she glanced at the screen door.

"Our pleasure. We'd be delighted to come and share our message with you, if you'd like."

"I dunno,'" Jenn stammered. "I mean, we're not very religious people."

She wished the two sisters would leave.

"I understand," said Sister Lingfelter with a toss of her blond hair. "Could I leave you our card, in case you change your mind?"

Jenn shrugged her shoulders. "Sure, I guess." She was holding the two plastic bags in her left hand and the milk jug in her right. "Just stick it in the waistband of my shorts."

Gingerly, Sister Lingfelter stuck one of her cards into the top of Jenn's pants. "Well, I hope we hear from you. Have a good day." The two sister missionaries walked down the steps and back toward the church.

Jenn watched them go and then turned to the screen door. Damon was standing behind it. He pushed the door open for her. "The blonde's pretty good-looking," he said. "Where'd you find them?"

"They followed me home," Jenn laughed, "but I don't think I'm gonna keep them."

F*i*V E

The telephone rang as Jenn put the milk in the empty refrigerator. Damon grabbed it. "Yo!" He listened for a minute before extending his hand to Jenn. "Rolayne, for you," he said flatly before slinking out of the kitchen.

"'Lo," Jen said into the phone. She looked around to see if she was alone. She could see her mother sitting in her chair in the living room.

"Where'd you go? Them cops nearly nailed us."

"I can't talk," Jennica whispered glancing at her mother. "Where'd you end up?"

"We ran into Albertson's," Rolayne replied. "We split up and kinda looked like we was shoppin'." She chuckled. "You have any idea how many people are walking around that store even at that time of night? Them dumb cops came in a couple minutes later and looked around for a few minutes before they left. All you gotta do is look cool, and they'll walk right past you. Just never let 'em see you sweat." She chuckled again, "We're meeting over at Charlie's about three o'clock. You comin'?"

Jenn glanced over her shoulder at her mother. "Sure. What's up?"

"I dunno, just hangin', I suppose." Rolayne coughed again. "Well, gotta go."

Jenn hung up the phone and started to fix herself a bowl of cereal. Her mother coughed in the living room. "Who was that?" she asked.

"Rolayne," Jenn answered. "I'm going to go over to her place this afternoon."

"You'd better fix dinner before you go." She yawned loudly. "I don't like you hanging out with that bunch all the time."

Jenn took a deep breath and exhaled slowly. "Right, Mom. Like there's anything going on here."

"Don't you smart-mouth me," her mother said from the gloom of the living room.

She turned her back on her mother, opened the box of raisin bran, and searched for a bowl. All of them were in the sink, waiting to be washed. Jenn rinsed out one of them, poured in the cereal and milk, and sat down at the table. She looked out the window toward the backyard and saw her brother pushing through the sparse hedge that separated their lot from the neighbor's. She finished the cereal, washed the bowl, and placed it in the cupboard next to the sink. Her mother had fallen asleep in the front room. Jenn walked quietly to her mother's side, removed the smoldering cigarette from between her fingers, took a quick puff, and then ground it out in the ash tray on the floor next to her mother. She glanced around at the clutter in the front room but decided she'd wake her mother if she started putting things away.

Her mother snored softly from her chair. A thin trickle of saliva slid down the corner of her mouth. Jenn looked at her and saw the thinness of her shoulders, the threadbare dress, and the gray-streaked unkempt hair. She shook her head. *I'm not going to end up like that,* she thought. She felt a welling of anger in her breast toward her mother and her father. Unbidden, a tear slipped down her cheek. She brushed it away and slipped silently out the screen door. She picked up the empty beer cans, threw them in the garbage can at the side of the house, and returned to sit in the discarded overstuffed chair that rested on the front porch. She propped her feet on the porch rail and looked, unseeing, toward the road. The odor of stale tobacco slithered out of the chair and embraced her. She picked idly at the stuffing that protruded like a bloated white thumb from the arm of the chair. She felt something stick against her stomach and removed the card the missionary had placed there. One side of the card showed a picture of a building with spires, obviously a church of some kind. The other side had an address and phone number. Jenn dropped the card onto the floor of the porch. *A daughter of God? Not me, sister,* she thought. A whisper of wind caught the card and blew it under the chair.

SIX

"*Like I said,* Jo-Jo runs into Albertson's and spots this old lady by the dairy case. She sidles up to her and says, 'Do you need some help pushing your basket?' and the old broad says, 'Why, thank you, young lady.' So there's Jo-Jo hangin' onto this old lady's basket when the cop comes up the aisle of the store, gives her a once-over, and then asks, 'You see three girls run in here?' Of course, Jo-Jo just shakes her head, and the old lady shakes hers, and the cop thanks her and keeps sniffin' around the store for a few minutes." Rolayne threw back her head and laughed a sound akin to a mule braying. "Them cops is so dumb," she coughed deeply. "So what did you do, girlfriend?"

Jenn sat cross-legged on the floor with her back against the wall. Rolayne was stretched out on the couch, and Jo-Jo was sitting on Charlie's lap in the rocking chair. "I hid," she said with a shrug of her shoulders. "I saw that little hedge in front of the church, and I dove behind it."

"Pretty smart," Rolayne said with a smirk. "Wonder what happened to the Caddy?"

"It wasn't there this morning," Jenn said with a shake of her head. "I walked by that church on the way to the store. I guess they 'pounded it."

"Don't matter," Charlie snickered as he nibbled on Jo-Jo's ear. "Always more where that come from. It ain't like you gonna go back and drive them wheels again."

Jenn wrapped her arms around her knees and drew them against her. "Where's Moana?"

"Her old man grounded her," Rolayne said huskily. "I suspect she'll get here soon as he's passed out."

Jenn heard the toilet flush down the hallway and knew that Rolayne's boyfriend, Miles, would soon join them. *Odd man out,* she thought. *Charlie and Jo-Jo, Miles and Rolayne . . . and me.* "I guess I'll head home," she said as she pushed herself to her feet.

"Don't have to leave on my 'count," Miles said as he strutted into the room while he cinched up his belt. He put his arm around Jenn and gave her a hug.

"Watch what you're doin'," Rolayne said from the couch. "You's mine, big boy."

Miles laughed. "There's enough of me for both of you." He swaggered across the room, sat down on the edge of the couch, and began tickling Rolayne. She fought back until the two of them wrestled to the floor. Jenn stepped over the writhing bodies and worked her way out the door of the apartment. The sun was setting and burned like an amber ball through the low-lying haze in the city. A light breeze drove a piece of paper across the street like the sail of a ghost ship. In the distance she could hear the sound of a siren as an ambulance screamed its way across town. She wrapped her arms around herself and walked dejectedly toward home.

Labor Day tomorrow, and then school starts—my senior year. For some reason a feeling of melancholy washed over her and tears formed in her eyes. She swiped them away with the back of her hand. She wandered aimlessly down the sidewalk feeling empty, old, and alone. Eventually, she reached her house and climbed the protesting steps to the front porch. The house was as dark as her mood.

Jenn pushed the front door open and stepped into the living room.

She flipped on a light switch, and the aged floor lamp dimly lit the room.

"Mom," she called out. There was no answer. She made her way wearily down the hallway to her mother's room, pushed the door open slowly, and peered in. It was empty. Puzzled, she walked back to the kitchen and turned on the light. The dinner dishes were still on the table. Almost without thinking, she carried them to the sink and began washing them. She placed them in the dish drainer on the edge of the sink and wiped off the table with a dishrag. Slowly, she pirouetted a full circle and looked at the kitchen. As if through new eyes she saw the tattered curtains that hung limp and listless, the chipped fronts of the cabinets, and the linoleum floor with the worn path from back door to living room. She sighed deeply.

"Maybe I should drop out of school," she said to herself. "Rolayne, Jo-Jo, and Moana aren't going back. I could work full time at the restaurant and get out of this dump."

The phone rang, and she picked it up. "'Lo."

"Where have you been?" her mother said. "Damon's been shot!"

Jenn's heart stopped. "What? Where are you?"

"At the hospital." Jenn could hear the strain in her mother's voice. "It's bad, Jenn. Real bad." Her mother burst into tears.

"Which hospital?" the girl asked.

"St. Agnes," her mother replied. "Hurry, Jenn. It's really bad."

"What happened?" she asked, but all she heard was the buzz of the phone line. Quickly, she went to her dresser, pulled out the drawer, and retrieved some money. She phoned for a cab and waited impatiently on the front walk until the taxi pulled up in front. She opened the back door of the cab and climbed in. "St. Agnes Hospital," she said to the driver.

He looked back over his shoulder. "I gotta see some money first," he said rubbing his thumb and index finger together. Jenn handed him a twenty-dollar bill and with a nod the driver pulled a U-turn and headed toward the hospital.

Her mother was waiting in the foyer when Jenn burst through the doors. She threw her arms around her daughter and hung like a rag doll on her shoulders.

"Where is he, Mom?" Jenn asked.

Her mother sobbed and pointed toward the elevator. Without saying a word the two women made it across the floor and into an open elevator car.

"What happened?" Jenn asked frantically.

Her mother gulped down her sobs and said, "Somebody shot him." Then she turned toward the chrome steel walls of the elevator and began hitting them with her fists. "Why, Jenn? Why?" The elevator came to a stop, the door slid open, and the two women exited. Jenn took her mother's arm and guided her toward a nurse's station.

"Can I help you?" The woman behind the counter was dressed in pale blue scrubs.

"Damon Cooper," Jenn said haltingly. "My brother."

The woman's face barely showed a flicker of change as she rose from her seat. "Perhaps you could wait in there," she said, pointing to a small room next to the elevators. "Dr. Broadhead will be here soon. He can brief you on your brother's condition."

"Is he all right?" Jenn asked pleadingly.

"Dr. Broadhead will be able to answer all your questions." She smiled frostily and gestured toward the room. "You'll probably be more comfortable in there."

"Thank you," Jenn said as she took her mother's elbow and led her toward the waiting room. The room was wallpapered with a repeating pattern of lilacs. Two fake leather couches faced each other across the room. A table at the end of each couch was covered with month-old magazines. The Coke machine hummed arthritically in one corner. They sank heavily onto one of the couches and waited. Nearly two hours passed before the door opened, and two policemen entered the room.

"Mrs. Cooper?" the older of the two officers asked. Jenn's mother nodded her head. "I'm Sergeant Hill, and this is my partner, Officer Cray." There was no response from either of the two women, so the two policemen sat down on the couch opposite them. Another hour passed before the door opened again, and a short, stocky man entered.

"Mrs. Cooper? I'm Doctor Broadhead. Your boy's still in the recovery room," he said softly. He was still dressed in blue scrubs, with tufts of silver hair sticking out from under the surgical cap on his head. "The next forty-eight hours are critical. The bullet entered his skull just above the right eye, and we're not sure how much permanent damage it did. We've removed the bullet and placed a shunt in the wound to reduce swelling in the brain." He spread his hands apologetically. "I wish I could tell you more." He turned slowly and faced the officers. "Anything else?"

Sergeant Hill shook his head. "No, I think that's all, Doc."

"Then I think I'll get back to the emergency room; it has been a busy afternoon." He turned to Jenn and her mother, "Your son will be moved to room 4 in the ICU as soon as he's stable. You can wait for him there, if you'd like." The door slipped shut with a pneumatic hiss as he left the room.

Sergeant Hill turned to the couch where Jenn and her mother were sitting. "Have any idea who could have done this?" he asked as he withdrew a small pad of paper from his breast pocket and flipped it open.

Jenn's mother shook her head. "He's a good boy," she muttered over and over.

Jenn saw the two policemen glance at each other. Sergeant Hill's left eyebrow rose like a tented caterpillar. "I'm sure he is, ma'am," he replied. "We're just trying to gather as much information as we can. Are you aware of any enemies your son might have had? Anyone who would want to harm him?"

Jenn shook her head and put her arm around her mother's shoulders. She could feel her shaking. "What happened?" she asked.

Sergeant Hill glanced at his partner. "I'm not at liberty to say much, at this point," he replied. "You have any idea who he was with this afternoon?"

Jenn shook her head again. "I saw him leaving the house about noon. I haven't seen him since." She studied the two policemen. "Look, I don't have any idea what happened. My mother's in no condition to tell me. I mean, can't you give me some idea?"

The two policemen exchanged glances, and then Sergeant Hill spoke. "We think it was a drive-by shooting. Apparently, your brother and some of his friends were over at the elementary school when a car drove by and your brother was shot. That's about all I can tell you."

"What about his friends. Can't they give you more information?"

"They all ran away," the policeman said. "The information we have is from a neighbor who was sitting on his front porch across from the school. He said that once your brother was hit, the others scattered." He shrugged his shoulders. "I'm sorry for your brother. I hope he recovers."

The policeman slipped the pad of paper back into his breast pocket, fished out a card, and handed it to Jenn. "If you need to get hold of me, here's my number." He and his partner stood up as if joined at the hip, patted Jenn's mother on her shoulder, opened the door, and left.

"Why?" the older woman sobbed. "Why? He's such a good boy. Why would anyone want to shoot him?"

Jenn pulled her mother closer to her. "I don't know, Mom." She had remained composed until that moment, but suddenly she began to cry. The sun had set hours before, and the small window in the room looked out over the parking lot. The only light through the window was from a streetlight that fought unsuccessfully to illuminate the street and sidewalk below. Jenn left her mother sitting on the couch, wandered to the window, and stared blankly into the darkness. Her reflection stared back at her as if she were a ghost imprinted against the outside world. Mist was curling across the parking lot in phantom tendrils, slipping under and around the few cars parked there. She sighed dejectedly.

"We might as well go up to his room," she said quietly. Jenn helped her mother to her feet and guided her out the door toward the elevator.

SEVEN

The chair was stiff, unyielding, and inflexible. Jenn shifted her weight, trying to find some position that afforded some comfort, but finally stood up and paced back and forth across the small room in the intensive care unit. Damon had not yet arrived, and her mother sat almost catatonic in the only other chair in the room. Occasionally, she moaned softly as tears ran down her cheeks.

"Why would someone do this?" she whispered.

Jenn shook her head. "I don't know, Mom. That's the most frustrating thing—I just don't have any answers." She continued to pace. "Maybe Damon can give us some answers if . . . when he wakes up."

"First your father, now this," her mother moaned. "What did I do to deserve this?"

"I don't know, Mom." Jenn walked out of the room to the nurses' station. An elderly woman dressed in a pink and white striped pinafore over a white blouse sat primly behind the counter.

"May I help you, dear?" she asked.

"Just wondering about my brother. We've been waiting here nearly two hours. I mean, they said he was in the recovery room and ought to be here." She gestured toward the room where her mother sat weeping.

The woman smiled. "Let me check for you, dear. What is the patient's name?"

"Damon Cooper," Jenn said quietly. "He was shot," she added as she tapped her forehead above her right eye.

The woman nodded her head, picked up the phone, and tapped in a number. After a brief pause she said, "This is Beatrice in ICU. Do you have any information on Damon Cooper?" She sat smiling for a moment as the person on the other end replied. "Thank you," she said and hung up. She looked at Jenn. "He should be down any minute."

"Thank you," Jenn said and wandered back into the room. "Mom, Damon ought to be here soon." Her mother nodded but said nothing. Jenn continued to pace back and forth, stopping each time at the doorway to peer at the doorway into the ICU. Nearly ten minutes passed until the doors swung open and a gurney was wheeled into the room where the two women waited. Damon's head was swathed in bandages, and tubes and wires seemed to emerge from every part of his body. The attendants efficiently transferred him to the bed, moved the bottles attached to IV lines to supporting posts, plugged wires into monitors, and punched codes into the computer keyboard at the left side of the bed.

One of the attendants turned to Jenn and her mother. "He's pretty heavily sedated, but he seems to be responding well." He turned and looked at the monitor. "I hope everything works out." He smiled and left the room. Almost immediately a nurse entered, wrote some notes on a chart, slipped it into a plastic pocket at the side of the door, and then left.

Jenn and her mother moved to opposite sides of the bed. They each took one of Damon's hands in theirs. Being careful not to dislodge the needle stuck in the back of his hand, Jenn stroked her brother's fingers. They lay limp in her palm.

"Why?" her mother asked again.

"I don't know, Mom. When Damon wakes up, we'll ask him. Maybe he knows, maybe he doesn't." She looked at the clock on the wall. It was nearly six o'clock on Labor Day morning. "Mom, why don't you go home and try to get some sleep. I'll stay here with Damon and if anything changes, I'll call you."

Her mother shook her head. "I can't leave him. You go home, Jenn."

"Are you sure?"

"Yes. I'll stay here." She continued to stroke Damon's arm.

"Call me. Okay?"

Her mother nodded her head. "You go home and get some rest."

"I'll be back this afternoon," Jenn said as she took a last look at her sleeping brother before walking quietly out of the ICU, down the hallway to the elevator, and out of the hospital. The sun was backlighting the hills to the east and giving notice that sunrise was not far away. The early morning air was cool, and the mist clung to the ground like a fuzzy blanket. Still dressed in her shorts and halter top, Jenn shivered and wrapped her arms around herself trying to keep warm while she called for a taxi from the pay phone outside the entrance to the hospital.

Five minutes later a cab pulled up in front of the building, and Jenn climbed into the backseat. She gave the driver her address, put her head back, closed her eyes, and wondered what had happened to her brother. She nearly dozed off by the time they arrived at her house. She paid the fare and dragged herself up the steps and into the living room. In the early morning light the house seemed as if all the life had been sucked out of it and a hollow husk left behind. She washed her face, walked sleepily to her bedroom, kicked off her sandals, and fell face down on her bed. A troubled sleep came almost immediately.

The phone rang, and Jenn awoke with a start. She pushed herself off the bed and scurried to the kitchen. "'Lo," she said.

"Jenn?" her mother's voice said.

"Yeah, Mom. How's Damon?" she said through a yawn. She glanced at the clock. It was nearly three o'clock in the afternoon.

"No change. They check on him all the time, but there's no change," she said dejectedly. "Are you coming back to the hospital soon?"

"Soon as I change clothes, I'll be there," she replied. "Then maybe you can come home and get some sleep."

"Maybe," her mother replied. "Hurry." She hung up.

Jenn showered, changed clothes, and called for a cab. She dipped into her hiding place and retrieved more money. Half an hour after her mother had called, she walked into St. Agnes. When she stepped off the elevator, her mother was waiting. She had circles under her eyes, and her whole body looked as if it were sagging, being pulled down by a great weight.

"How's Damon?"

Her mother shrugged. "The same."

A nurse was taking his blood pressure when Jenn walked into the room.

"How's he doing?" she asked.

"He seems stable," the woman replied with just a trace of a smile.

"How long do you think it will be before he wakes up?" Jenn asked.

The nurse shook her head slightly. "I have no idea, dear. With a head injury, sometimes it's a long time." She patted Jenn's shoulder. "But we'll give him the best care we can and hope for the best." She entered the blood pressure on the chart and left the room. The monitors behind Damon continued to beep regularly. More IV bottles hung from supports, and Jenn watched the hypnotic drip into the tube that ran into Damon's hand. She lifted it again. There was no more response that when she'd last touched it. The fingers felt like lukewarm, lifeless sausages.

"You go on home, Mom. I'll stay here," she said. She handed her mother a twenty-dollar bill. "That'll pay for the cab."

Her mother sank heavily onto one of the unyielding chairs. "I'll pay you back, when my check comes," she said lifelessly.

"Don't worry about it, Mom. Just go home and get some sleep." Jenn sat down on the chair and took her brother's hand in hers. She watched as he took rapid shallow breaths through his half-open mouth. After half an hour she ached from sitting in one position. Gently, she replaced Damon's hand by his side, stood, and paced back and forth across the small room. After a while a nurse entered, took blood pressure and pulse, recorded them, and left.

Jenn followed her into the outer waiting room. Someone had left a paperback book on one of the chairs. Jenn picked it up and carried it back into her brother's room. She sat down in the chair next to her brother and opened the book. After she scanned a half-dozen pages she realized she couldn't remember what she'd read and closed the cover of the book. She stood and looked out the window. Damon moaned softly.

"Damon," she said hopefully as she returned to his side. She took his hand in hers again but felt no more response than she had before. She sighed heavily. An hour later the nurse returned to check Damon.

"Would you like something to eat?" she asked. "They'll be bringing dinner to this floor in a little while, and I could order something for you."

"Thank you," Jenn said. "I'd appreciate that." She rearranged herself in the chair. "Is there any change with my brother?"

The nurse shrugged her shoulders slightly. "Not much change, but that's a good thing." She moved toward the doorway. "I'll order you some food."

Jenn opened the book and tried to read again. After a while the door swung open, and a tray of food was delivered. She picked at it, paced the floor, and sat back down. The tray was removed. The door opened, and her mother returned.

"Any change?" she asked wearily.

"He's holding his own," Jenn replied. "They say that's a good sign."

"I guess." She stroked Damon's cheek. "You go home and get some sleep. You have school tomorrow."

Jenn fidgeted. "Mom, I've been thinking maybe I wouldn't go to school and work full time instead. I mean, I could help with the bills and everything."

Her mother stiffened. "Jenn, honey, I don't need your money. You go to school. Education is your way out of . . . you know what I mean." She sank heavily into the chair at the side of the bed and turned her attention to her son. "Damon, why? Why?"

Jenn stood up. "Mom, this is gonna cost money. We don't have insurance, and I can work full time."

Her mother seemed not to have heard her as she gently rubbed Damon's arm. After some time she focused on Jenn. "Go home, Jenn. Get some sleep. School starts tomorrow. I'll stay here with your brother."

EI*g*HT

The days passed both quickly and slowly. At the end of each school day Jenn hurried to the restaurant, and when her shift ended she made her way to the hospital to relieve her mother. She had little time to waste and the days flew by, but the time at school and the hours at the hospital dragged as if she were treading oatmeal. Trying to sleep in a chair at the hospital was impossible. She couldn't remember ever having been so tired in her life. Saturday offered respite from her self-imposed schedule, and she collapsed on her own bed in an exhausted heap. Her mother had come to the hospital an hour before, and Jenn had left for home.

The telephone jangled her from sleep. "'Lo," she said stifling a yawn.

"Yo," Rolayne said. "Wassup?"

"Not much," Jenn replied.

"Where ya been? You ain't answered your phone all week."

"I've been at the hospital," Jenn replied weakly.

41

"How come? Who's sick? Your old lady?"

"Somebody shot Damon," she replied flatly. She felt anger welling up within her, although she was not sure at whom it was aimed.

"No way!"

"Yes," Jenn mumbled.

"Who?" Rolayne asked.

"We don't know."

"Man, what a bummer." Almost as an afterthought she said, "How's he doin'?"

Unbidden tears began to flow. "I don't know. They say he's holding his own, but I just don't know."

"Bummer." There was a pause before Rolayne said, "I don't suppose you wanna come over to Charlie's tonight?"

"I've got to go to the hospital," Jenn answer wearily. "Mom's there now, and I have to spell her off." She wiped her eyes with her sleeve. "I'd really like to, Ro, but I can't."

"Sure. I understand. I hope he gets better."

"So do I." She hung up the phone and sank onto one of the kitchen chairs. She folded her arms on the table and laid her head on them. *Why Damon? Why me?* Despair welled up within her. Nearly half an hour passed before she forced herself to stand and walk to the bathroom. She drew water into the bathtub and immersed herself in it. An hour later she awoke. The water had grown cold. Shivering, she toweled herself dry, wrapped the towel around herself, and wandered back to her bedroom, where she dressed in shorts and a T-shirt. She walked to the kitchen, opened the refrigerator, and found it was nearly empty. With a sigh she closed the door. *I guess I'd better go to the store.*

She slipped on her sandals, let herself out the front door, and walked toward the market. Her mood was the opposite of the sun that shone brightly through a scattering of marshmallow clouds. It seemed as if it took a long time to reach the store, but eventually she walked through the automatic door, dislodged a cart from the row of them resting against the wall, and like a robot pushed it through the aisles. When she had finished her shopping, she paid for her purchases, slung a plastic bag over each hand, and started walking home.

Jenn had walked a block and a half when an old black Chevrolet with heavily tinted windows pulled over to the curb. Miles leaned across the seat, rolled down the window and said, "Want a ride?"

Numbly, Jenn nodded her head. "Sure." She opened the back door, placed the plastic bags inside, and climbed into the front seat next to Miles. "Where's Rolayne?" she asked.

"Beats me," he said with a shrug of his shoulders. "Headin' home?"

She nodded her head. "Had to get some groceries so I have something to fix for lunch before I go back to the hospital."

Miles glanced at her. "Damon?"

She nodded her head again. "Yes."

"I heard he was shot pretty bad," he said as he pulled away from the curb. "He gonna be okay?"

Jenn could feel the tears starting to form. "Hope so." She wiped her hand across her cheeks. "How come Ro didn't know about him getting shot?"

Miles glanced at Jenn across the seat. "Don't know." They drove on in silence until he pulled up in front of her house. Jenn climbed out of the car and retrieved her bags of groceries from the backseat just as Miles rounded the back of the car. "Let me give you a hand," he said. He took the two plastic sacks from Jenn, carried them into the house, and laid them on the kitchen table.

Jenn began putting the groceries away while Miles leaned against the kitchen door frame. "I'm going to fix myself a sandwich, want one?"

"Sure," he said.

She fixed the food, and the two of them sat at the table and ate the sandwiches. Miles reached across the table and took her hand in his. "This week been tough?"

She nodded her head. "Real tough."

He rubbed his thumb across the back of her hand. "I heard it was the TCR that got him."

Jenn's eyes flew open. "The Tongan Crips? Where'd you hear that?"

"Just goin' round," he said defensively. "I hear they was gettin' back at the UVB."

Jenn's forehead wrinkled. "What does that have to do with Damon?"

Miles said nothing for a few seconds. "That's the gang Damon belongs to." He continued to rub her hand. "Didn't you know?"

Slowly she shook her head. "Damon? Why?"

"I dunno," Miles replied. "We all need to belong somewhere, I guess."

Jenn leapt to her feet. "I've got to call the cops."

"Whoa, sister. You do that and . . ." he shrugged his shoulders.

"And what?"

Miles laughed nervously. "They hear you fingered them. Well, they know where you live." He stood and put his arms around her. "'Sides, the word'll reach the cops. They ain't as dumb as some folks think." He hugged her tightly.

Jenn could feel the fury and impotence build inside her. She felt she had no control over the situation and wanted to lash out in anger. Miles continued to hold her tightly against him, and she felt conflict in that action as well. Suddenly she lost control and began to sob. Miles released his hold and led her to the couch.

"Come on," he said. "I'll give you a ride to the hospital. Go wash your face, little sister." He leaned over and kissed her on the forehead.

*n*INE

Jenn pushed the button to summon the elevator. The foyer of the hospital was bustling as usual. The lady at the information counter nodded at her in recognition. She leaned wearily against the wall until a chime announced the arrival of the elevator. The doors slid open, Jenn stepped inside, and the doors began to close. Suddenly an arm was thrust between the doors, and they slid back open. Four people hurried into the elevator, two young women and two young men. Jenn barely glanced at them. She closed her eyes and leaned against the cool, stainless steel wall as the elevator began its crawl upward.

Suddenly one of the women spoke. "You're the girl with the groceries."

Jenn's eyes opened. "What?" She looked at the black badge attached to the woman's pocket. "Oh, yeah, you're Sister Lingfelter."

"What brings you to the hospital?" the missionary asked.

"My brother, Damon. He's in the ICU."

"What happened?"

"He was shot." Automatically, Jenn tapped her right eyebrow as Miles's words rang in her head. She said nothing more.

Sister Lingfelter's face immediately registered concern. "How awful. How is he?"

Jenn's shoulders fell. "Okay, I guess. He doesn't seem to be getting any worse, at least."

Sister Sandberg said, "Is there anything we can do to help?"

Jenn shook her head. "Not anything anyone can do, I suspect." They rode on in silence until the car came to a stop and the doors opened. Jenn stepped out, and the doors closed behind her. She dragged herself into the now familiar room and found it empty. Frantically, she hurried to the nurse's station. "Where's my brother?" she asked in panic.

The nurse looked up. "They've moved him out of ICU to a regular room." She tapped on the computer keyboard. "Looks like he's in 409. That's a good sign, honey, when they take him out of ICU."

Jenn thanked the woman and then walked briskly to the elevator. She pushed the button and waited impatiently for the car to arrive. *Good news. We can use some good news,* she thought. The doors opened, she entered, and rode to the fourth floor. When the door opened she searched for room numbers and found room 409. She pushed open the door and entered the room. Her mother sat asleep in a chair beside Damon's bed. He looked unchanged.

Gently, she shook her mother's shoulder. "I'll take over, Mom. You go get some rest."

Her mother stood, stretched, and yawned. "I can't believe I fell asleep. This chair's no more comfortable than the one in his old room."

"They say this is good news, Mom. Is Damon getting better?" She looked at her brother and could see no change. She lifted his hand and it felt as if she were lifting a glove filled with sand.

"I guess," her mother said sadly. "I don't know. I can't see any change." She pulled a tissue from a box at the side of the bed and dabbed at a small trickle of saliva at the corner of Damon's mouth.

"I'll walk you to the elevator," Jenn said. She took her mother's elbow and led her from the room. They walked slowly past the nurses' station to the elevator. Jenn punched the down button. "I'll see you later," she said as the door opened. Her mother nodded slightly as she padded into the elevator.

As Jenn walked back toward Damon's room, she saw Sister Lingfelter leaving a room across the hall. The missionary spotted her and smiled.

"Your brother isn't in ICU anymore?" she said cheerfully.

Jenn shook her head. "I guess they moved him this morning. He's in 409."

Sister Lingfelter said, "That's good news. You probably remember Sister Sandberg?" Jenn nodded her head. "This is Elder Parker and his companion Elder Youngberg." Jenn looked at the two young men. They were both dressed in dark blue suits and white shirts. The black name tags hung on their breast pockets. Sister Lingfelter continued, "I don't think we ever learned your name."

"Jennica Cooper. I go by Jenn."

Sister Lingfelter extended her hand. "Nice to meet you, Jenn."

"How come you're here at the hospital?"

Sister Lingfelter gestured toward the two elders. "They were giving a blessing to one of our investigators."

Jenn looked bewildered. "If you say so." She walked toward Damon's room. Sister Lingfelter caught her arm.

"Would you like the elders to give your brother a blessing?" The two young men looked slightly uncomfortable at the suggestion.

"What does that mean?" Jenn asked puzzled.

Sister Lingfelter smiled, "Well, Elder Youngberg would anoint your brother's head with oil and Elder Parker would give him a blessing."

Jenn still looked puzzled. "Why?"

Sister Sandberg stepped forward. "Jenn, these elders hold the Melchizedek Priesthood, which has the power to heal. It is the same power the Savior had when he was on earth. They can give your brother a blessing to help him regain his health, if it is the Lord's will."

"But we're not even members of your church," Jenn said.

"I understand," Sister Sandberg said. "We aren't trying to force anything on you. But if you'd like your brother to have a blessing, the elders would be happy to accommodate you."

Jenn looked at the two young men. Elder Parker had a carefully combed thatch of red hair. His cheeks glowed pink and showed a sprinkling of freckles. He smiled timidly at her. Elder Youngberg was taller and darker than his companion. His eyebrows were bushy and nearly met above the bridge of his nose. His dark brown eyes bored into hers. Finally he spoke. "Miss Cooper, I can see you're not comfortable with this. The last thing we want to do is force ourselves on you. Perhaps another time." He bowed slightly and led his companions past Jenn toward the elevator.

"Strange bunch," Jenn said as she walked back into Damon's room. She settled herself on the chair at the side of his bed and tried to find a comfortable position without success. The only change she could see was that the nurses came less frequently to check on her brother. *What's an investigator? What is he investigating?* she wondered. An hour later Jenn stood, stretched, and yawned. She began to pace back and forth across the small room. She stretched again and wandered into the hall. She noticed that the doorway through which the missionaries had appeared was open, and she hesitantly crossed the hall and peered into the room. "Cornwell" was written on the plaque at the side of the door. An elderly woman lay in the bed. Her silver white hair surrounded her head like rays of sunlight.

"Come in, dear," the woman said.

Startled, Jenn backed up involuntarily into the hallway. "I'm sorry, I didn't want to disturb you."

"You're not disturbing me. I'm feeling much better. Please, come in." Jenn took a few steps into the room. "What brings you to the hospital?" the woman asked.

"My brother's across the hall," she said, pointing over her shoulder.

"I see. How is he doing?"

Jenn shrugged her shoulders. "I don't know. He doesn't seem to be getting any worse. I guess that's a good sign."

The old woman's eyes closed slowly and then suddenly flew open as she tried to focus. "They've given me a sedative," she explained. "I'm afraid I won't be much company." Her eyes slid shut again.

"Can I ask you a question?"

"Of course," the woman slurred.

"I heard you were an investigator."

There was no reply from the bed. The woman had fallen asleep.

TeN

"*Do you find Hamlet* boring, Miss Cooper?"

Jenn's eyes flew open. "What?" she said. There were chuckles from her classmates. Mrs. Parker stood near her desk. She was a tall woman with wrinkled skin. Her hair was tied back in a severe bun, and her eyeglasses hung around her neck on a beaded cord.

"I asked if you were bored." She tapped one long, red-polished fingernail on the corner of Jenn's desk. "Or perhaps you were dreaming about Queen Gertrude?"

"I'm sorry," Jenn stammered. "I'll try not to fall asleep again."

Mrs. Parker wheeled around and walked to the front of the room just as the bell rang. Jenn slid out of her desk and plodded toward the door.

"Jenn," Mrs. Parker called out. "Is there a problem?"

"My brother's in the hospital, and I'm spending the nights there watching him. I don't get a lot of sleep," she said.

"I'm sorry. I didn't know," said Mrs. Parker. "Is he sick?"

Wearily, Jenn set down her books on the corner of the nearest desk, "He was shot."

Mrs. Parker's hand flew to her mouth. "How awful. How is he doing?"

Everyone asks that, Jenn thought, *and I really don't have an answer.* "Okay, I guess," she said. "Guess I'd better get moving." She walked slowly out of the classroom, down the hallway, and out of the school. Rolayne was waiting for her on the front steps.

"You hafta go to work?" she asked.

Jenn nodded her head. "Till nine o'clock. Then I gotta go to the hospital."

"Bummer."

Jenn nodded her head again. "Man, I'm so tired. I just got chewed out by Parker."

"Why don't you quit school? It's a major bummer."

"Don't think I haven't been tempted," Jenn said as she dragged herself down the front sidewalk of the school.

"Why do you keep goin'? Ain't gonna do ya no good."

"Maybe you're right," she said. "At least I could get some sleep."

"Well see ya round," Rolayne said as she walked away from Jenn.

The restaurant was exceptionally busy for a Friday evening, and Jenn picked up nearly sixty dollars in tips. She caught the bus home, added the money to her cache, changed clothes, and caught the bus to the hospital. It was after ten o'clock when she walked into room 409 and awakened her mother.

"I'm here, Mom," she said with a barely stifled yawn.

Her mother's eyes flew open. "I was just resting my eyes," she said.

"How's Damon?" Jenn asked.

"No change," she replied heavily.

"Well, go on home and I'll keep watch." She replaced her mother in the chair at the side of the bed.

"You seem tired, Jenn."

"I'll catch up on some sleep tomorrow," she said, shifting her weight in the chair.

"I'll see you in the morning," her mother said as she headed out of the room.

Jenn passed the night struggling to get some sleep and finally gave up as sunlight fought its way through the mist and into the room. Mentally, she counted the seconds as the second hand on the wall clock moved in its inexorable path. Time moved slowly until it was nearly ten o'clock. She wandered into the hallway and to the rest room she'd become accustomed to using. When she started back to Damon's room she saw the silver-haired Mrs. Cornwell being brought out of her room in a wheelchair. When she saw Jenn's face her eyes lit up. "I'm going home," she said cheerfully. "This is my son, Paul," she said, indicating the man walking beside the wheelchair. "I'm sorry. I don't know your name."

"Jenn."

The woman smiled. "I hope your brother gets better soon." The nurse continued to push her toward the elevator.

"I hope so, too," Jenn called after her. She returned to Damon's room and sat looking out the window. She rested her hands on the sill and her chin on her hands. Her eyelids drooped as fatigue washed through her body.

"How's your brother?"

Jenn's eyes flew open, and she spun around in her chair and looked at the pair of women who were standing at the end of Damon's bed. "About the same," she said as she recognized the two sister missionaries.

"We came to check on Mrs. Cornwell. They told us she'd gone home today. That's great news," Sister Lingfelter said. "We just thought we'd check in on you." She extended her hand to Jenn. "Your brother looks peaceful," she said.

Jenn looked closely at Damon. "I guess," she said. "I just wish something would happen. He just lies there."

"Maybe he's gaining strength," Sister Sandberg said softly. "The body is a marvelous thing."

"I guess," Jenn said again.

"Well, we'd better be on our way," Sister Lingfelter smiled. "We need to go check on Mrs. Cornwell."

"What was wrong with her?" Jenn asked.

"She had pneumonia. At her age it could have been fatal."

"But she got better," Jenn said brightly. "I hope Damon gets better soon."

Sister Sandberg glanced at Sister Lingfelter, "Well, the blessing helped. She was going downhill fast until Elder Youngberg's blessing."

"I guess I don't understand all of that," Jenn said. "I mean, we're not a very religious family." She looked out the window. "I mean, I guess there's a God and all that, but we just don't go to church much," she babbled.

"Well, it would take a little time to explain it all, Jenn. And I suspect that this is neither the time nor the place. We'd be happy to come by your home and tell you about the gospel, at your convenience."

Jenn thought of the schedule she was keeping. "I'm pretty busy right now, with Damon and school and work."

"We understand. Well, we'd better be going."

Jenn walked with them to the elevator. "Do you think giving Damon a blessing would help him?" she asked.

A smile creased Sister Lingfelter's face. "It couldn't hurt. Would you like us to arrange for the elders to come by?"

"Can't you do it yourselves?" she asked.

Sister Sandberg smiled and showed a set of perfect white teeth. "I'm afraid not. We don't hold the priesthood."

Jenn's forehead wrinkled, "Why not?"

"It's part of that long story." Sister Sandberg said. "Would you like us to have the elders give Damon a blessing?"

Jenn thought for a moment. The elevator door opened, and Sister Lingfelter put her hand out to keep the door open. "Sure. Why not?"

"When would be a good time?" Sister Lingfelter asked.

"Anytime. He's not going anywhere," Jenn said with a sigh.

"Perhaps tomorrow morning after church," Sister Sandberg said. "About eleven thirty?"

Jenn nodded agreement. The two missionaries smiled at her and entered the elevator. "We'll see you in the morning." The elevator door closed. When it opened again, Jenn's mother walked out to relieve her.

ELEVEN

"*What she don't* know won't hurt her," Miles said. He slid his arm around Jenn's shoulders and pulled her close to him. They were sitting on the couch in her living room. "'Sides, like I told ya before, there's more than enough of me for two women."

Jenn rested her head on Miles's shoulder. She found comfort and warmth sitting with him. Her eyelids drooped, and she fought to keep them from closing. She could see the clock on the kitchen wall. It was barely ten o'clock. Still, she could barely keep her eyes open. She'd slept fitfully after getting home from the hospital and then had forced herself to make it to the restaurant for her three o'clock shift. She was grateful to see Miles's battered Chevrolet waiting for her when she got off work half an hour before.

"I've got to get some sleep," she said struggling to get out of Miles's grasp. "Besides, I'm not sure Ro would agree with you."

"Goin' to bed?" Miles chuckled. "Best offer I've had all day." He stood, pulled her to her feet, and crushed her body against his.

A small marble of panic began to form in Jenn's stomach. "I don't think so," she said as she tried to escape from his arms.

He pulled her tighter, and his voice became raspy. "Come on, baby, don' give me trouble."

The marble grew to the size of a baseball. "Miles! Please! Just go."

He began to stroke her back with one hand while he held her tightly with the other. "Jus' relax. You know you want me as much as I want you."

She struggled to free herself, but he was much bigger and stronger. He lifted her off her feet and carried her toward the hallway to her bedroom. She fought one arm free and began hitting him on the back of his head. Miles merely grunted and continued to carry her down the hallway. The baseball grew to the size of a basketball. Jenn balled her fist and hit Miles in the eye. He bellowed, let go of her, and grabbed his face. She ran screaming past him and out of the house.

There was no one in sight on Keats Avenue. Mist was beginning to swirl in tendrils across the street and onto the sparse lawn. Jenn raced around the back of the house and forced herself through the hedge into the backyard of the house behind hers. An aluminum fishing boat was resting upside down on cinder blocks. She threw herself on the ground and wiggled under the boat. She could feel her heart pounding so hard she was afraid it would burst through her chest wall. She strained her ears to hear any sounds that would tell her where Miles was, but she could hear nothing except the pounding of her heart.

The ground was damp beneath her, and soon she was shivering in the evening chill. She could not judge how long she had been there, but at last she thought she heard Miles's car start a block away and drive off. She waited, shaking with cold, for another thirty minutes. Then she slipped out from under the boat. The mist had thickened into a shadowy fog, and she slipped wraithlike through the hedge. There were no lights on in her house as she crept through the backyard. As quiet as a shivering shadow, she tiptoed down the driveway until she could see where Miles's car had been parked. It was gone.

Still vigilant, she entered the front door that was wide open. She inspected the house room by room. Miles had smashed the lamp in the living room and broken the mirror in the bathroom. Shaking uncontrollably, Jenn locked the doors and windows and lay down on her bed. She did not think sleep would come, but she drifted off into troubled dreams. The telephone awoke her, and she struggled to the kitchen.

"'Lo," she said.

"It's nearly ten o'clock," her mother said. "I just wondered when you were coming to the hospital."

Jenn looked into the living room at the smashed lamp. "I'm leaving in a few minutes," she said.

Her mother hung up without further comment.

Jenn swept up the shards of glass from the threadbare carpet and deposited them in the garbage can. There was nothing she could do to disguise the broken mirror in the bathroom. As carefully as she could, she removed the broken glass from the medicine cabinet door and carried all of it to the trash. *How am I going to explain this to Mom?* Memories of the previous evening caused her to shudder. She bathed, dressed, and prepared to leave for the hospital. Anxiously, she peered out the front window to make sure the Chevrolet was not in sight before she walked to the bus stop.

Her mother stood outside the hospital, smoking a cigarette, when Jenn arrived. Before she could ask, her mother said, "No change, Jenn. I just wish something would happen."

"So do I, Mom." She looked at the ground near her mother's feet. "Mom, there was a little problem last night," she began.

"What happened? Another shooting?" she said frantically.

"No, no, Mom," Jenn stammered. "I had some friends over and a couple of things got broken."

Her mother's eyes narrowed. "What happened?"

"The lamp kinda got knocked over." She glanced at her mother's eyes.

"Go on," she said. "What else?"

"The mirror in the bathroom kinda got broken," she said sheepishly.

"How did that happen," her mother demanded.

"I'm not sure," she stuttered. "I'll get it fixed, Mom."

Suddenly her mother burst into tears. "Jenn, I just can't deal with much more." She leaned against the stucco wall of the hospital. "I'm at the end of my rope." She sank to the ground and wrapped her arms around her knees. Jenn crouched down beside her.

"I'm sorry, Mom. I'll make sure it doesn't happen again." She helped her mother to her feet. "You go home and get some rest." She dug into her pocket and handed her mother some money. "Get something to eat on the way home."

Her mother took the money, wiped her nose on the back of her hand, and walked slowly toward the bus stop. Jenn watched her go. Then she walked into the too-familiar lobby of the hospital. A nurse was changing an IV bag when Jenn walked into Damon's room. "How's he doing?" she asked.

"Holding his own," the nurse said with a slight smile. She patted Jenn on the back of her hand before leaving the room. Almost immediately, there was a knock at the door.

"Come in," Jenn said. The door opened and four missionaries entered. Sister Lingfelter walked across the room and extended her hand to Jenn.

"I suspect you remember Elder Parker and Elder Youngberg," she said. Jenn nodded her head. "How's your brother doing?"

"No change," Jenn said. "At least as far as I can tell."

Sister Lingfelter nodded her head. "This must have been tough for all of you."

"More than you know," Jenn replied. She stood a little uncomfortably, not knowing what was going to happen next. Finally, Elder Youngberg spoke.

"I understand you'd like us to give your brother a blessing."

Jenn nodded in agreement. "I guess. I mean, I'm still not sure exactly what you do or what happens."

"We, that is Elder Parker and I, will place our hands on your brother's head and give him a blessing. Just as the Lord and his disciples did in the New Testament."

Jenn looked at the carpet, embarrassed. "Actually I've never read much of the Bible," she admitted.

"You're not alone," Sister Sandberg said with a slight smile.

"Is it all right if we proceed?" Elder Youngberg asked.

"I guess," Jenn replied.

"Would it be all right with you if we had a word of prayer before we give your brother a blessing?" Elder Youngberg's brown eyes searched Jenn's.

"Sure," she said. "I mean if that's the way it's done."

The four missionaries sank to their knees. Jenn was at first unsure what to do but finally knelt next to Sister Sandberg. "Sister Lingfelter, would you lead us?" Elder Youngberg asked.

"Thank you," she replied. She began a simple, poignant prayer. Jenn listened intently to the words she said and realized that she had never offered a vocal prayer in her life. In fact, she hadn't offered any prayers in many, many years, not since her father's death. Sister Lingfelter petitioned the Lord that Elder Youngberg would be guided and inspired in the blessing he was about to give. When she finished, the others said, "Amen." Jenn followed a second later. The two elders rose and helped the three women to their feet.

Elder Sandberg withdrew a small aluminum cylinder from his suit pocket, opened it, and then turned to Jenn. "What is his full name?"

Jenn was surprised. They were the first words she had heard him speak, and he had a deep, resonant voice that didn't seem to fit with his rosy cheeks and carrot red hair. "Damon Latrell Cooper," she replied.

"Thank you," he replied. He tipped the cylinder, and a single drop of oil fell onto Damon's head. He handed the cylinder to Elder Youngberg, placed his hands gently on Damon's head, addressed him by name, and offered a short prayer. When he finished, Elder Youngberg placed his hands beside Elder Sandberg's and began to seal the anointing. He offered words of comfort and words of encouragement and then fell silent.

Jenn noticed that the two Sisters had closed their eyes, so she closed hers partially but continued to watch the elders through hooded eyes. When Elder Youngberg stopped praying, she watched him closely. His forehead creased when he wasn't speaking, and then his face relaxed and the hint of a smile crossed his lips. He began to speak again.

"Damon, I feel inspired to bless you that you might heal completely and quickly, that you might return to your family, whole and well. This will be done as a testimony to the power of the priesthood and of a loving Savior." The words pierced Jenn as surely as a sword, and then she began to feel as if a warm, comforting blanket had been placed around her. For the first time in weeks a feeling of peace washed over her. Tears began to fall from her eyes. Elder Youngberg finished the prayer and turned to Jenn. He placed his hand on her shoulder. "Your brother is going to be fine," he said confidently.

She looked into his eyes and noticed that he too had been weeping. The tears made his chocolate eyes seem shining and incandescent. "Thank you," she choked out. And then Damon opened his eyes.

TWELVE

Jenn stood in front of the hospital with the two sister missionaries. It had been nearly two hours since Damon's eyes fluttered open, but he had not yet spoken. The doctor had been summoned and was checking him over. Jenn called home, but her mother hadn't arrived yet. Finally, Sister Lingfelter and Sister Sandberg offered to drive her home to wait for her mother, but Jenn called again and finally reached her. Her mother then returned to the hospital.

"What happened?" Jenn asked, pointing at the window to Damon's room.

Sister Lingfelter indicated some stone benches arranged around a small pond. "Perhaps we could sit there," she said. When they were seated, she continued. "Jenn, I don't have any idea what your religious background is, so I'm not sure how much you'll really understand. Your brother was healed by the power of the priesthood in conjunction with a loving Heavenly Father and his Son." She paused. "But let me ask you, What do you think happened up there?"

"I don't know. Maybe it was just a coincidence. I mean, maybe he would have woke up anyway." Jenn drew a circle in the gravel with the toe of her shoe.

"Maybe," Sister Sandberg said. "Is that what you believe?"

Jenn remembered the feeling that had come over her as Elder Youngberg was praying. "No. I don't know what happened, but I've never had a feeling like that before." Tears began to overflow again. "Is that what heaven's like?"

"Perhaps," Sister Lingfelter said. "What you felt was the Holy Ghost."

Jenn went on as if she had not heard Sister Lingfelter. "Because if it is, I've been in both heaven and hell in the past twenty-four hours."

"I can understand you feeling that way," Sister Sandberg said soothingly. "Not knowing what was going to happen to Damon must have felt like hell."

Jenn shook her head. "No! That wasn't it . . ." She began to recount what had happened to her the night before. Once the words began in a trickle, they opened into a flood. The missionaries listened without interruption until she finished.

"Who is this Miles?" Sister Sandberg asked. "How do you know him?"

"My best friend's boyfriend," Jenn spat out.

"Oh, really."

"Yeah, there's Miles and Rolayne, and Jo-Jo and Charlie, and Moana and Mike . . . and me."

"Tell me about them," Sister Sandberg said softly.

Jenn began to pour out her heart to the two missionaries. She told about the fun that she and her friends had had. She expressed how lonely she often felt when the other girls were with their boyfriends. She talked about the good and the bad. When she finished she said, "I'm really not sure why I'm telling you all this." She was obviously embarrassed.

Sister Lingfelter cleared her throat. "Jenn, do you know the story about the rice fields?"

Jenn shook her head.

"I heard this story in church some time ago. I've pondered it more than any other story outside of the scriptures. If you have time, I'll tell it to you."

Jenn realized how relaxed she felt with these two young women. "I'd like that," she said.

Sister Lingfelter began. "The story is told of a small Chinese fishing village that bordered the Yellow Sea. Most of the people in the village supported themselves by fishing, and they had built their simple huts on the beach. However, in order to supplement their diet, they had climbed the mountain that rose from the edge of the beach, terraced it, and planted rice.

"One family was chosen to take care of the rice terraces, and their home was built halfway up the mountain above the rest of the village. Each morning the father and his sons would climb the mountain from their home to the rice paddies where they would weed the fields and take care of the tender rice plants.

"One morning, late in the season, the rice was almost ready to harvest, and the man and his sons took their little teapot and meager lunch and climbed to the terraces. They started a small fire, placed their teapot above it, and went to work in the fields. The boys were encouraged with the bountiful yield they would reap from their labors.

"Lunchtime came and the father straightened up, rubbed his stiff back, looked down on the little town below, and felt pride in the harvest that was soon to come. He saw that the sea had become choppy, and all of the fishing boats had returned to the safety of the harbor. Then his heart leapt into his throat, for out on the horizon he saw an enormous tidal wave, a tsunami, heading toward the village.

"Quickly, he realized there was no time to race down the hillside and warn the people. They were too far away to hear his voice. He wrung his hands in anguish, thought for a moment, and then called to his sons, 'Burn the fields.'

"The boys looked at their father as if he was crazy. 'It is our food,' they cried.

"'Do not question me,' he said. 'Burn the fields.'

"The father and his sons grabbed handfuls of the ripened rice stalks, thrust them into the fire beneath the teapot, and set the fields on fire. Down in the village the people saw the column of smoke and the red tongues of flame over the lip of the terraces and ran—every man, woman, and child—up the path to the fields to fight the fire.

"Only when they had climbed high enough to be safe did they hear the angry howl of the tsunami and watch as their village was destroyed."

Jenn was enthralled with the story. When Sister Lingfelter finished, she looked Jenn straight in the face and said, "I think you need to burn a field."

THIRTEEN

Damon's recovery was remarkable, a miracle, everyone said, and two days later he was released from the hospital. He rested in the old rocking chair in their living room. There was a slight slur to his speech that was getting better with every passing day, but other than feeling weak, he seemed to be his old self. Daily he gained strength. Jenn had fished into her savings, purchased a new lamp and a new mirror for the medicine cabinet, and tried to put the episode with Miles behind her. Now that she no longer had to spend the nights at the hospital, she was beginning to catch up on her sleep. She had not yet told Damon or her mother about what had happened in the hospital, nor had there been any other contact from the missionaries.

Friday morning Jenn prepared to leave for school. She threw a backpack strap over one shoulder and settled it into place on her hip. Her mother and brother were still sleeping as she let herself out the front door of their house. A black Chevrolet with tinted windows was parked at the curb. Jenn's heart froze within her. Before she could move, the driver's door opened, and Miles stepped out of the car. He slicked back his hair with his hands. "Wanna ride?" he asked. There was still some puffiness around his eye.

"I don't think so," she said icily.

"Hey, I'm sorry 'bout the other night," he said, spreading his palms. "Let me make it up to you."

Jenn shook her head and began to walk silently down the sidewalk toward school. Miles caught up with her.

"Hey, little sister, I'm sorry. I don't know what got inta me," he pleaded.

"Miles, just leave me alone," she said firmly.

He reached out and grabbed her arm. "Look, I'm tryin' to be nice. But you're makin' it awful hard."

Jenn tried unsuccessfully to pull away from his grip. Panic began to rise in her breast. "Look, Miles," she said, "just leave me alone. Okay?"

"Come on. All I want to do is give you a ride to school." His grip tightened on her arm.

"Oh, all right," she said shakily. "But straight to school. Understand?" He nodded his head. "Promise?"

"Sure," he said as he guided her back up the walk to his car. He opened the door and ushered her inside. He then moved quickly around the car to his side. Jenn placed her backpack between them on the front seat. The car was idling, and as soon as Miles sat down he screeched away from the curb, slamming his door shut. Jenn leaned against the passenger door, as far away from Miles as she could get. Suddenly two arms shot around her from behind, pinning her to her seat. She screamed.

"Shut up!" Charlie said from the backseat. "Unless you want to get hurt."

Jenn struggled against his embrace. "Let me go," she screamed. Charlie squeezed her harder.

"I'm not kiddin'," he said. "You keep that up, and you're gonna get hurt."

"You promised. Straight to school," she spat at Miles.

"I lied," he chuckled. Then his face hardened. "We're gonna finish what we started the other night."

Jenn's heart beat wildly against her breast as Charlie continued to hold her in his grip while the streets flew by. She could hardly breathe. The car bounced over a curb and spewed a plume of dust as it raced across an abandoned lot and came to a stop near a small grove of trees. Miles jumped out of the car, pulled Jenn's door open, and grabbed her by both wrists. Finally, Charlie let go. She gulped air and began to cough from the cloud of dust. Miles dragged her toward the trees with Charlie following behind.

"Bring the blanket from the backseat," Miles commanded. Charlie turned back toward the car.

Jenn struggled against his grasp, but he was much stronger than she was, and the harder she pulled, the tighter he gripped her wrists. She looked vainly for a weapon of any sort, but Miles continued to drag her toward the grove of trees. "Don't do this, Miles," she begged. He dragged her into the shade of the trees.

"Hurry up!" He yelled to Charlie. "Now, little sister," he said menacingly, "we can do this the easy way or the hard way. It's up to you." A fallen tree had formed a natural bench on the east side of the grove. He forced her onto the log while he still grasped her wrists. Charlie came puffing into the clearing, carrying the old khaki green blanket over his arm.

"Spread it on the ground," Miles said with a shake of his head. "Over there."

Charlie shook out the blanket and spread it on the ground. He moved next to Jenn on the log and put his arms tightly around her. Miles let go of her wrists, stood, and backed up next to the blanket. "Your choice. Hard or easy, what's it gonna be?" Charlie squeezed her so hard she was afraid he was going to break her ribs. She reached back with her hand and steadied herself against the ground. She felt a rock about the size of a brick stuck in the dirt.

"I can't breathe," she managed to whisper. Charlie relaxed his grip slightly. Jenn wiggled the rock with her hand and freed it from the soil that held it in place. She grasped the rock with her fingers and said softly, "Have it your way, Miles." At that, Charlie released his hold on her. She swung the rock into the side of his head. He let out a sound like a wounded bagpipe and slumped to the ground. Miles took three steps to reach her, and as he groped for her hands she kicked him viciously in the shins with the heels of her shoes. He fell to the ground, screaming. She leapt to her feet and threw the rock into the pit of his stomach while he lay writhing on the ground. She then sprinted to the car, climbed into the driver's seat, and locked the doors. The key was still in the ignition. Jenn started the car and drove away just as Miles staggered out of the trees.

In cold fury she contemplated turning the car around and running Miles down, but instead she bounced across the lot, over the curb, and down the street. She was shaking uncontrollably, sweating, and gasping for breath. As she approached the high school, she spun the car into the parking lot of a strip mall a block away, pulled on the emergency brake, grabbed her backpack, and locked the keys in the car with the engine running. She could not keep from looking over her shoulder as she hurried up the steps of the school. No one was in sight.

She scurried down the hallway to her first period class, pulled the door open slowly, and slipped into the room. The other students were silent, taking a quiz, and all of them looked at her in mute unison.

"Well, Miss Cooper, it's wonderful that you could join us today," Mr. Balderson said. His half-moon glasses perched on the end of his bulbous nose, and he peered at Jenn over the top of them. His few strands of gray hair stuck out in porcupine fashion. He handed her a sheet of paper. "Take your seat and do this quiz." He glanced at his watch. "There's about ten minutes left. I'd suggest you hurry," he said with a slight smirk.

Jenn sat down and tried to concentrate on the math problems on the sheet of paper, but her heart was still racing and she was finding it hard to control her breathing. She closed her eyes, swallowed, and tried to calm herself. Suddenly she slid to the floor.

When she opened her eyes she was lying on a cot next to the assistant principal's office. Miss Hardy, her counselor, was sitting on the chair next to the bed holding a cold damp compress on Jenn's forehead.

"How do you feel, dear?" Miss Hardy asked.

"Dizzy," was all that Jenn could croak out. Her throat felt as dry as week-old oatmeal. Miss Hardy handed her a cup of water and helped her sit up.

"I think you hyperventilated. You gave Mr. Balderson a scare," she said with a slight snort. The counselor looked at Jenn's wrist. "What happened?"

Jenn pulled her hand away. "Nothing."

Miss Hardy's eyebrow lifted. "It doesn't look like nothing to me. It looks as if someone tried to take the skin off your wrists."

Jenn pushed herself into a sitting position and swung her legs over the side of the cot. "It was nothing, Miss Hardy. Can I go to class now?"

The counselor folded her hands in her lap. "Jennica, if there's some problem at home . . ." She left the sentence hanging expectantly.

Jenn shook her head and felt the room begin to spin. "No. Can I just go to class?"

Miss Hardy exhaled. "I suppose so, if you feel all right."

"I'm fine." She pushed herself to her feet and felt her knees buckle. She sank back onto the cot.

"Why don't you lie here for a few minutes? I'm going to give your mother a call."

Jenn tried to protest, but the counselor closed the door behind her, leaving Jenn in the darkened room. She closed her eyes and tried to keep the room from spinning around her.

FOURTEEN

"*Don't tell me* nothing happened," Jenn's mother snapped. "Just look at your wrists!"

The two of them sat in the sick room at the high school. Jenn tried unsuccessfully to pull the cuffs of her blouse over the bruises. "Mom, there's nothing you can do about it. Just forget it." She stared out of the darkened room into the lighted hallway. "Let's just go home."

"Jenn, why won't you tell me what happened?"

"Mom, it won't do any good. I'll take care of it." She stood and closed her eyes against the dizziness she felt. She blinked her eyes slowly. "Come on, Mom, let's go home." She walked a little unsteadily from the room. Her mother followed as Miss Hardy walked out of her office.

"Are you all right?"

"I'm fine," Jenn replied, "but I think I'll go home for the rest of the day." She walked out of the office, her mother following a step behind her. They reached the front door of the school, and Jenn looked down the street to the strip mall where she had left the Chevrolet. It was still there, but she couldn't tell whether the motor was still running or not. The fresh air revived her, and she led her mother at a brisk pace away from the car and toward their home.

"Jenn, why won't you tell me what happened?" her mother gasped, a little out of breath.

"Mom, it's nothing you can solve. I'll take care of it." They turned the corner and saw the police car parked in front of their house. Jenn's heart leapt to her throat, and almost involuntarily she began to run down the street. Her mother struggled to keep up with her. Jenn bounded up the front steps, threw open the front door, and flew into the room. Sergeant Hill and his partner were sitting on the couch. Damon sat quietly in the rocking chair. "What's going on here?" Jenn said loudly.

The two policemen struggled to their feet. "Good afternoon," Sergeant Hill said with a brittle, toneless voice. "We were just talking to your brother about the . . . the incident." Jenn's mother came through the door, gasping for air. Sergeant Hill nodded in her direction. "Just trying to gather some information," he said in a clipped tone. Damon sat mutely in the rocking chair.

Jenn's mind slipped back to the warning Miles had given her. Her stomach churned as his image sprang unbidden into her mind. She looked at her brother, rocking slowly and saying nothing, and realized that she had information that might help, but at what cost?

Sergeant Hill and Officer Cray sat back down on the couch. "Well, Damon, are you sure you have no idea who might have shot you?" Damon shook his head slowly as if in a trance. "Have you had any problems with anybody previously?" Damon continued to shake his head soundlessly.

The two policemen looked at each other. "Do you think this was just a random act? Somebody just taking a pot shot without any motive or justification?"

Damon continued to rock. "Man, I don' know nothing," he said sullenly. "Ain't nothin' you can do about it anyhow." Sergeant Hill closed his little pad of paper and slipped it into his breast pocket.

"How about you, Mrs. Cooper? Do you have any idea as to the responsible party?" He retrieved the pad of paper.

She shook her head. "I can't imagine anyone wanting to hurt Damon.

He's a good boy," she said. Her voice was almost manic and popped from her mouth in staccato bursts.

"I'm sure you're right," Sergeant Hill replied before turning to Jenn. "What about you?" He flipped through his notebook. "Ah, yes, Jennica, I believe. Do you have any idea who might done this?" He pointed toward Damon. "Any ideas at all?"

Meekly, Jenn shook her head. "I'm afraid not, Sergeant. I don't have any information that I could give you."

"I see," he said as the two of them struggled to their feet again. "Well, we don't have much to go on, quite frankly, and if you don't have any ideas . . ." He looked at Damon, who quickly averted his eyes. "We'll keep you posted if anything new happens." The two policemen bowed slightly and walked across the room and out the door to the car.

Jenn looked through the sagging screen door toward the police car where the two men sat and talked. Occasionally, one of them would glance toward the house before continuing the silent conversation. She watched and waited until Officer Cray started the car and drove off. She turned to where Damon sat in the rocking chair, walked to his side, and sank to the carpet next to him. Their mother had wandered into the kitchen.

"Damon," she whispered, "Miles told me it was the TCR that shot you." She waited for confirmation, but there was none. She reached up and placed her hand on top of his. His hand was warm and alive, unlike the waxen mannequin hand she had held in the hospital. "Are you involved in a gang?" she queried.

Damon continued to rock silently and then he looked at her hand resting on his. "What happened?" he said, stroking her wrist with the forefinger of his other hand.

"Nothing," she replied as she pulled her hand away from his.

"Don't lie to me," he said through clenched teeth. "Who did this to you?"

"There's nothing you can do about it," she said in low tones. "Don't upset Mom."

He sprang to his feet. "Maybe it's time we upset Mom," he said with a slight slur. "Maybe it's time we got honest about what's going on here." He grabbed her hand. "Tell me what happened," he demanded.

Jenn tried to pull her hand out of her brother's grasp. "Damon, let it go. There's nothing you can do. I've already taken care of it." She struggled, but he continued to hold her hand. "Besides, if we're going to get honest, why don't you tell me who shot you?"

"Look, Jenn, I don't care much what happens to me, but nobody's going to hurt my sister. Understand?"

Their mother called out from the kitchen, "Are you two fighting?"

"No, Mom," they replied in unison.

"Jenn, I've got friends who can take care of whoever's bothering you."

"I'm sure you do," she said coldly. "But I don't need your help, little brother. Let me go!"

Damon let go of her wrist and sank back down onto the rocking chair. His eyes were like brittle anthracite staring out the window. Absently, he rubbed the scar on his forehead. "Nobody better hurt you," he said through his teeth as he began to rock slowly.

Jenn pulled away from him and walked woodenly into the kitchen to help her mother prepare dinner. She was washing a potato in the sink while she stared sightlessly out the window. "Mom, I'll do that," she said. "You go sit down and rest."

"You're the one who's sick," her mother replied.

"I'm fine, Mom. You go relax."

Her mother dropped the potato into the sink and walked like a zombie down the hallway to her bedroom. Jenn peeled the potato, opened the cupboard beneath the sink, and looked for another one. The bag was empty. "Damon, I'm going to get some potatoes," she said to her brother as he rocked in the living room. He nodded slightly. She checked the refrigerator and mentally made a note of the groceries she needed to buy. Jenn went to her room, closed the door, slid open the dresser drawer, and retrieved some money. She stuffed the bills into the pocket of her jeans, closed the drawer, and made her way out of the house. Her stomach clenched as she opened the front door. She studied the road in front of the house to make sure that no black Chevrolet was lurking before she walked down the street toward the grocery store.

Half an hour later she climbed the bowed front steps of the house and opened the sagging screen door. Damon was still sitting where she'd left him. "You okay?" she asked. He nodded his head slightly. Jenn carried the groceries into the kitchen and put them away. She peeled more potatoes and put them on the stove to boil and then began to set the table for dinner. There was a knock on the front screen door. Warily, she peeked around the corner of the doorway. Damon sat, unmoving except for the gentle rocking, and two figures were silhouetted against the screen.

Jenn walked gingerly across the room to the front door until she recognized the two sister missionaries. "Oh, hi," she said shyly through the screen.

"Hello, Jenn," Sister Lingfelter said. "We were in the neighborhood and thought we'd drop in and see how your brother is doing."

Jenn looked at Damon. "He's doing fine," she said somewhat timidly.

"May we come in?"

Jenn surveyed the shabby front room quickly. "I suppose," she said as she pushed open the door. The two missionaries walked in and shook her hand. Sister Sandberg spotted Damon in his chair, walked to him, and extended her hand.

"I'm Sister Sandberg," she said with a smile. Damon ignored the outstretched hand. "This is Sister Lingfelter," she said, glancing over her shoulder. Damon continued to rock silently. Finally Sister Sandberg turned and walked to her companion's side.

Jenn stood uncomfortably near the front door. "Would you like to sit down?" she said.

"Thank you," Sister Sandberg replied, and the two women sat down softly on the couch.

"As I said," Sister Lingfelter smiled at Jenn, "we were in the neighborhood and wondered about Damon. She glanced in his direction.

"He's doing really good," Jenn said.

Damon suddenly pushed himself to his feet and walked down the hallway. "I'm doin' fine," he said curtly. Jenn seated herself in the rocking chair Damon had left.

"Well, he certainly seems to be getting better," Sister Sandberg said.

"I'm sorry," Jenn replied. "This whole thing's been tough on him. He's usually not quite so abrupt."

"That's quite all right," Sister Lingfelter said. "Well, we'd better be going. We have an appointment down the street with an investigator." She pointed with her thumb. "We just wanted to check on you. Monday is transfer day, and we might not be around much longer."

Jenn's forehead creased. "Just what is an investigator?" she asked.

Sister Lingfelter laughed lightly. "Someone who's investigating the Church. Someone we're teaching the gospel to," she said. "I guess we throw those kinds of words around all the time and don't realize people don't understand what we're saying."

"Oh," Jenn said. "And what's transfer day? I mean, why won't you be here?"

Sister Sandberg pushed herself to her feet and then offered her hand to Sister Lingfelter, "Well, we've been companions for nearly twelve weeks. I mean, we've been assigned here in your neighborhood, but Monday it's likely we'll be transferred to another area and probably with other companions."

"Why?" Jenn asked.

"I think it's to keep us from getting too comfortable," Sister Lingfelter laughed. "Anyway, it's probably my last transfer. I'll be released in another six weeks."

"Released?"

Sister Lingfelter took Jenn's hand in hers. "We serve for eighteen months. My time is nearly over and I'll go home."

"Where's home?" Jenn asked, still mildly confused.

"A little town in Utah," she replied.

"I've never been to Utah," Jenn said.

"Well, even if you had, you probably wouldn't have been in Providence."

Jenn nodded her head. "I suspect you're right." She turned to Sister Sandberg. "What about you?"

"Oh, I'm from Billings. I've only been out about six months."

"Been out?"

"On my mission," she replied with a smile.

"But the two of you seem like you've known each other forever," Jenn said softly.

The two missionaries looked at each other. "I suppose in a sense we have," Sister Lingfelter said. She shook Jenn's hand. "It has been wonderful getting to know you," she said. "I hope your brother continues to get better."

"Thank you," Jenn said. She was amazed by the sense of loss she felt in hearing that these two women wouldn't be part of her life any longer, even though their lives had barely intersected.

Sister Sandberg shook her hand and asked, "May we have a word of prayer before we leave?"

Jenn felt uncomfortable. She glanced around the room to make sure her mother and Damon were nowhere to be seen. "I guess," she said.

"Would it be all right with you if I said the prayer?" Sister Lingfelter asked.

"Sure," Jenn replied. She waited to see if the two women would kneel as they had done in the hospital, but they remained standing, folded their arms, closed their eyes, and bowed their heads. Sister Lingfelter offered a short prayer of thanksgiving and asked the Lord to bless Jenn and her family. Jenn felt as if she were standing on the shore of a vast ocean and waves of peace had washed over her.

"Jenn, would you accept a gift from me to you?" the blond missionary asked.

"I guess."

Sister Lingfelter took a copy of a book from her bag and handed it to Jenn. "I'd like you to have this book," she said.

Jenn turned the book over in her hands. "What's the Book of Mormon?" she asked.

"A second testament of Jesus Christ," she replied. "It was translated by a young man in New York over a hundred years ago. I'd like to have someone tell you his story when you feel ready."

Jenn stammered, "I told you before, we're not very religious people."

"I know you did. And I told you that you were a daughter of God." A tear trickled down Sister Lingfelter's cheek. She hugged Jenn briefly before the two missionaries left.

Jenn placed the small blue book on the kitchen table and finished preparing dinner.

FIFTEEN

"*Hello,*" *Jenn said* into the phone. "Oh, hi, Rolayne." She jerked the receiver away from her head as her friend began screaming at her. The shrieking was laced with profanity and insults, and Jenn could feel her blood beginning to boil.

"He said what?" she exclaimed when Rolayne stopped to take a breath. Her friend continued to scream accusations of what Jenn had done to Miles and Charlie. Realizing that she could neither reason nor win, Jenn finally hung up the phone. It rang again almost immediately. She lifted it off the cradle, dropped it back into place, removed it, and placed it on the kitchen counter. A few minutes later the phone squealed a hiccuped protest before stopping and lying mute next to an empty cookie jar. Jenn sank down on the kitchen chair.

"Who was that?" her mother called from her bedroom.

"Rolayne," Jenn called back flatly. She felt as gray as the Saturday morning mists that curled on the street outside her home. Without thinking, Jenn pulled the sleeves of her sweatshirt over her wrists. She was fuming inside at what her friend had suggested and felt a righteous anger directed at Miles and Charlie, two men who had claimed to be her friends, yet she felt a gnawing helplessness at what she could do to correct the situation. She sat immobilized for nearly ten minutes, gathered her strength, stood, and began to clean the kitchen. She picked up the small blue book and carried it to her room where she placed it on her bed.

"What's that?" Damon said from the door to her room. He pointed at the book.

"Just a book some friends gave me," she said.

Her brother nodded his head. "Sure," he replied quizzically. "I'm going out."

"Where?" Jenn asked.

"Just out," he replied sharply.

She felt a dagger of ice beginning to form in her stomach. "Be careful," she said.

"I'm always careful," he said with a slight sneer on his lips.

Jenn resisted the urge to argue with him. She watched him walk away from her room and into the kitchen. A moment later the back door opened and shut. Jenn looked out her bedroom window and watched him slip through the hedge. "Be careful," she said again under her breath. A whiff of cigarette smoke signaled her mother was up, and Jenn asked, "Want some breakfast, Mom?"

"I'm not real hungry, Jenn," she said through the bathroom door.

Jenn returned to the kitchen, poured a bowl of milk and cereal, and sat down at the table. A few minutes later her mother wandered into the room. "Sure you don't want breakfast?"

Her mother shook her head. "Nope. My check came yesterday, and I'm going downtown to pay some bills." She shrugged herself into a sweater. "Where's Damon?"

"He went out," Jenn said woodenly.

"Who'd he go with?"

Jenn shrugged her shoulders. "I don't know, Mom."

"I wish he'd stay home until he's a little stronger," she said. "Are you going to Rolayne's?"

"I don't think so." Jenn clenched her teeth.

"Well, if you go anywhere, leave me a note. I'll be back in a couple of hours." She grabbed her purse and trudged out the front door.

Jenn finished the bowl of cereal, washed her dishes, and tidied up the house. She looked at the phone lying dead on the counter and fought the urge to call Rolayne and tell her what had really happened. Finally, she returned to her room and lay down on her bed. She could not remember ever having felt so alone in her life. Idly, she picked up the Book of Mormon and opened the cover. A card fell out; Jenn picked it up and turned it over between her fingers. The same picture of a church was on one side and Sister Lingfelter's name and phone number on the other. A surge of emotion filled her breast, and tears sprang to her eyes. She sat up and wiped the tears with the sleeve of her sweatshirt before she walked to the kitchen, hung up the mute phone, lifted the receiver again, and called the number on the card. The phone rang four times, and then an answering machine said, "We're sorry we missed your call. You are important to us. Please leave your name and number, and we'll call as soon as we return. Have a heavenly day." A second later a chime sounded.

"Sister Lingfelter, this is Jenn Cooper. I just wanted to say good-bye before you leave. I'm sorry you weren't there." She hung up the phone and wiped her eyes again with her sleeve. She wandered back to her bedroom and looked out the window. The early morning fog had burned off, but the day was still overcast and gray. She checked in her backpack to see if she had homework and realized that she hadn't been in class the day before and that all her homework from the previous day was finished. With nothing else to do until her shift at the restaurant, she picked up the Book of Mormon, straggled down the hall to the front room, and sat in the rocking chair. She opened the book and began to read. "I, Nephi, having been born of goodly parents." Her mind began to drift. *Goodly parents.* She thought back to the earliest recollections she had of her parents. Her father had been a rough, unshaven man who often smelled of alcohol and tobacco. She could remember when he'd come home late at night expecting her to hug him, and she'd feel the wire brush scratchiness of his cheek. She rocked slowly as she remembered a mixture of longing and sadness.

As early as she could remember, her mother and father had argued, although she could not remember specifically what the arguments had been about. Jenn could remember lying in bed while her parents fought in the kitchen. It had been after one of those heated arguments her father had stormed out and gone drinking. She struggled to erase the memory—she didn't want to remember that night.

Her thoughts turned to her mother and what she knew about her early life. She had dropped out of school after the eighth grade and gone to work in the fields near their house. There was always work to be done: berries to be picked, weeds to be plucked, produce to be harvested. The pay was meager and the hours long, but the work helped put food on the table. After she had married she'd continued to work until Jenn was born. Jenn had never met any of her grandparents; all of them had died before she was a year old. *Goodly parents?* After the accident her mother stopped working altogether, and they subsisted on the welfare check.

Jenn looked critically at the front room of their home. The couch sagged as low as her spirits. The curtains on the windows were held together by spiderweb-thin strands of thread. She could feel the knobs of duct tape that held two spindles together on the back of the chair. It struck her that she was in a dungeon as surely as if there had been bars on the windows. She rocked slowly, feeling sorry for herself, until she drifted off to sleep and dreamed of being in a hole with silvery sides. No matter how hard she tried to climb out, she'd lose her grip and slide to the bottom. She was awakened by a knock on the front door. Shaking her head and blinking her eyes, she stood and crossed the front room. The two missionaries stood on the porch.

"I hope we didn't interrupt anything," Sister Sandberg said when Jenn opened the door.

"No. I was just kind of sitting there thinking," she replied. "I guess you got my message."

The two women looked at each other and shook their heads. "No, we just wanted to say good-bye in the event we're transferred. We figured you'd be in school on Monday, so we thought we'd drop by today," Sister Lingfelter said.

"So, what's your message?" Sister Sandberg interjected.

Jenn felt slightly embarrassed. "Nothing, really. I just wanted to tell you how much I appreciated what you did for my brother, you know."

Sister Lingfelter smiled. "We didn't do anything, Jenn." She pointed across the room at the couch. "May we come in?"

"Oh, sure. I'm sorry," Jenn said.

"Nothing to be sorry about." Sister Lingfelter led her companion to the couch, and the two sat down carefully. "How are things going?"

"Pretty good," she replied. "Damon seems to be almost back to normal. He's out with some of his friends. And I'm just plugging along." She tugged the cuffs on her sweatshirt down over her wrists.

"I see you've been reading the book we left you," Sister Sandberg said as she pointed to the Book of Mormon on the table next to the rocking chair.

"I just sorta started it," Jenn replied. "I mean, I haven't read much of it."

"Well, I'm sure you'll get to it eventually," Sister Lingfelter said with a trace of a smile. She looked into Jenn's eyes and continued, "Are you sure you're all right? I sense there's something wrong."

Jenn played with the cuffs of her sweatshirt while her eyes inspected the carpet in front of her. "I'm okay," she said softly.

"Are you sure?"

The tears started to dribble down Jenn's cheeks. "No, I'm not," she choked.

Sister Lingfelter pushed herself up from the couch, crossed to Jenn's side, and knelt down next to her. Comfortingly, she put her arm across her shoulders. "Want to talk about it?"

Jenn shook her head vigorously from side to side while she continued to cry. Sister Lingfelter hugged her quivering frame. "They tried to . . ." she faltered.

"Who?"

Jenn began to rock faster. "Miles and Charlie. They hauled me to a vacant lot, and they were going to . . . going to . . ." She began to sob violently. Sister Lingfelter pulled Jenn's face against her shoulder and held her while she cried. "Some friends they are!" she said emphatically.

The two missionaries nodded in agreement. "Jenn, burn the field."

"I can't. They're my friends—my only friends. If I don't have them, I don't have anybody." She continued to sob.

Sister Lingfelter hugged her and said, "Jenn, I'm serious. Those so-called friends of yours are leading you down a path you don't want to travel. Can you see that?"

Jenn nodded her head numbly. "I feel so alone. It's like everybody I've ever liked has deserted me."

Sister Sandberg arose from the couch and walked across the room until she was standing in front of the girl in the rocking chair. "Jenn, we'd like to introduce you to some new friends. Would you consider going to church with us in the morning?" The room grew completely still.

"I don't know. I mean, we're not real religious."

"I understand, but I promise it won't hurt you. We'd pick you up in the morning and stay with you through the whole service. Are you game?"

Jenn felt her body begin to relax. "I don't know."

"We're not trying to force you, but we'd really like to have you come. We'd like to share the most important gift we've ever received."

Jenn brushed the tears from her cheeks with the sleeve of her sweatshirt. It pulled back to expose her bruised wrist. A sudden resolve welled within her. "The two of you will stay with me?" The two women nodded. "I guess. What time? What do I have to wear?"

Sister Sandberg smiled. "We'll come by and pick you up about ten o'clock. You don't have to wear anything special, just Sunday-go-to-meeting clothes."

Jenn's forehead wrinkled. "I guess I'm not sure what that means."

"Just wear what you're comfortable in," Sister Lingfelter said. "I'm excited you're going with us." She grabbed the back of the rocking chair and pulled herself to her feet. "It will be a great going-away present for me." She and her companion gave Jenn a squeeze on her shoulders and made their way to the front door. "See you in the morning."

Jenn nodded. "Sure. See you then."

SI𝒳TEEN

"*You're going where?*" her mother said acidly. "What's gotten into you?" Jenn's cheeks burned. "I'm going to church," she said softly, "with those missionaries that helped me and Damon."

Her mother snorted, "Well, don't that beat all." She took another drag on her cigarette. "I quit believing in God after your father was killed." She blew a cloud of smoke over her shoulder and picked at a speck of tobacco on her tongue. "Just don't expect me to go with you." She walked into the kitchen and sat down at the table. "And don't forget to get dinner ready."

"I won't, Mom." She hurried down the hallway to her bedroom. She didn't have much choice of clothes hanging in her closet but finally settled on the navy blue skirt and white blouse that she often wore to work. There was a small speck of gravy on the tail of the blouse, so Jenn made sure it was tucked into the waistband of her skirt. She glanced at her wristwatch—it was ten minutes before ten o'clock. She felt both excited and nervous to be going. She brushed her hair and added a slight dab of lipstick before sitting down on the edge of her bed. She twisted a loose thread of the bedspread between her fingers. *What am I doing?* she wondered. *I don't belong in church.* Panicked, she searched for the Book of Mormon and looked for the card with Sister Lingfelter's phone number. *I'll call her and tell them I've changed my mind.*

At that moment there was a knock at the front door. Jenn struggled to her feet and walked to the front room. The two sister missionaries were waiting on the front porch. Jenn's mother glared at them from her chair in the kitchen. "I'll be back in a while, Mom," Jenn said as she let herself out the door.

"Don't be long," her mother said. "And don't forget you've got dinner to fix."

Jenn closed the door behind her. "Hi," she said nervously.

"Ready to go?" Sister Lingfelter said. "We're a little early, but we wanted to get to church in time to get a good seat." The three of them made their way carefully down the steps and onto the sidewalk. Sister Lingfelter took Jenn's elbow and walked beside her while Sister Sandberg walked a step behind them. Both missionaries carried small brocade cases.

"Maybe I ought to prepare you a little before we get to church. We're going to sacrament meeting. Today a new family in the ward is going to speak." She paused. "A ward is a unit of the Church, a congregation. Does that make sense?" Jenn nodded her head. "Well, a new family, the Fergussons, moved into the ward last month, and the bishop has asked them to speak today." Sister Lingfelter looked at Jenn to see if she understood.

"How long are we going to be? I have to fix dinner."

"Oh, sacrament meeting is just a little over an hour long. We'll be through long before noon, if that works for you."

Jenn nodded her head. They walked the few blocks to the church in silence, and then Sister Lingfelter led them up the front steps and pulled the door open. Jenn entered nervously and looked around warily. They were standing in the foyer of the church, and a bustle of people was moving toward the chapel. Jenn felt relieved that they looked like normal people. A number of the men and women greeted the two missionaries and shook their hands. Jenn hung back behind Sister Lingfelter.

"Bishop," Sister Lingfelter called out to a man dressed in a blue suit, white shirt, and red tie, "we'd like to introduce you to a friend of ours, Jenn Cooper. Jenn, this is Bishop Caldwell."

Bishop Caldwell was a short man with an almost bald head. A broad smile creased his face as he extended his hand to Jenn. "Welcome, Sister Cooper. I hope you have a pleasant experience. If you'll excuse me, I have to get up to the stand. It's nearly time for the meeting to start." He let go of her hand and made his way into the chapel. Sister Lingfelter fell into step behind him. The chapel was nearly filled with people who were all chatting with each other. Someone at the front of the chapel played the organ. Jenn was unfamiliar with the tune. Suddenly a young girl, perhaps four years of age, slipped from a bench and ran to Sister Sandberg. The missionary dropped to one knee and hugged the little girl.

"Mandy Parkin," Sister Lingfelter said. "Her family joined the Church last month. She's quite attached to Sister Sandberg." She smiled. "Is there room for the three of us?" she asked a family sitting on one side of the chapel. They nodded their heads and slid toward the wall, making room for Jenn and the two missionaries. The woman on the bench in front of them turned around and shook Sister Sandberg's hand.

"Are you two planning on dinner with us?" she asked.

"Absolutely, Sister Knight. Wouldn't miss it. We'll be there about five o'clock. Does that work for you?"

Sister Knight nodded her head. "Your friend would be welcome too," she said, indicating Jenn.

"Oh, I don't think so," Jenn said quickly. "I've got to fix dinner for my family." She felt slight panic.

"Well, you're welcome if you change your mind." Sister Knight turned back around as the prelude music concluded and Bishop Caldwell stepped to the podium.

"Welcome, brothers and sisters," he began. "Before we start the meeting proper, there are a couple of announcements." He shuffled a few sheets of paper. "Congratulations to Sam and Becky Grove on the birth of their new son. He was born Wednesday night. Both the baby and mother are doing well. He was seven pounds four ounces and twenty-one inches long. I don't think they've decided on a name for him yet." He paused for effect. "I think they were expecting a girl," he said with a smile. "We'd also like to remind you that the young men and young women are going to do baptisms for the dead next Saturday morning. They need to be here at the chapel, dressed and ready to go at six in the morning."

The bishop searched through the papers. "I'd like to welcome any visitors here. I hope you feel welcome." He cleared his throat. "We'll begin by singing hymn number 219, 'Because I Have Been Given Much,' after which Brother Lymon Christensen will offer the invocation." He turned and sat down. Immediately, the organ began to play, and a lady sitting on the front row stood and walked up to the stand next to the organ. Sister Lingfelter took the hymnbook from its bracket on the back of the bench and turned to number 219. She held the book open so Jenn could see the words while she and her companion sang vigorously with the rest of the congregation. When they had finished, a tall man with a shock of snow white hair walked to the pulpit and offered the opening prayer.

The bishop stood up again and said, "We have a little ward business to conduct. Releases have been extended to Sister Carma Campbell as a teacher in the Primary and to Brother John Saxon as a member of the activities committee. All of you who would like to join with the bishopric in extending a vote of thanks to them for jobs well done may do so by raising the right hand." All members of the congregation raised their hands.

Jenn looked at Sister Lingfelter. "What was that all about?" she whispered.

"I'll explain in a few minutes," she whispered back.

"Calls have been extended to the following members of the ward," the bishop continued. "Brother Brent and Sister Melissa Baxter as Primary teachers, and Brother Carl Clampton as a member of the activities committee. All of you who can sustain them in these callings would you please raise your right hand." Again the hands shot up. "Any opposed by the same sign," the bishop said. No one raised a hand. "Thank you. We'll take care of the setting apart immediately after the block, in my office."

Jenn turned quizzically to Sister Lingfelter again. "Later," the missionary whispered.

"We'll now prepare for the sacrament," the bishop said, "by singing hymn number 193, 'I Stand All Amazed,' after which the Aaronic Priesthood will administer the sacrament." Again the organ music began and the chorister led the congregation in singing the hymn.

84

Jenn watched as three young men stood and began breaking bread into sacrament trays. She realized that she recognized all three of them. Two of them were juniors, and one was a senior, Carl Hathaway, who was in her English class. The hymn concluded, and a number of younger boys stood up in front of the sacrament table. Carl knelt and began to offer a prayer.

Jenn sat immobile and nervous while the deacons passed the sacrament. She was unsure whether she should take a piece of the broken bread when it was offered to her. She declined and passed the tray on to Sister Lingfelter. When the sacrament service ended, Bishop Caldwell stood again. "Today we have the pleasure of hearing from a new family that has recently moved into our ward. We will hear first from Aaron Fergusson and his brother, Ammon; then we'll hear from Sister Heidi Fergusson. We will then sing an interlude hymn, number 134, 'I Believe in Christ.' Brother Bruce Fergusson will then speak to us. Following Brother Fergusson, we will sing the closing hymn, number 300, 'Families Can Be Together Forever,' and Sister Lois Webster will offer the closing prayer." He turned his head and smiled at the small boy who was sitting to one side of the pulpit. "Aaron," he invited.

Jenn watched as the little boy stood up and walked to the pulpit. Apparently, the bishop had placed a small platform behind it because the boy climbed up onto it. His head was barely visible above the pulpit. He reached up and pulled the microphone down toward his mouth.

"I'm going to tell you a story about Nephi and his brothers," he began.

Jenn listened in amazement as the four-year old boy spoke for a few minutes. Then his six-year old brother spoke. When he had finished, his mother took her place at the pulpit. She was a tall, frail-looking woman in a teal dress with a strand of pearls at her throat. She smiled at the congregation and then began her talk.

"The bishop asked me to tell you a little about our family. Bruce and I met when we were both going to school at Long Beach State. He likes to say it was a whirlwind romance, but it was more like a gentle breeze. We dated for nearly two years before he asked me to marry him. We were sealed in the San Diego Temple eight years ago. We have two wonderful little boys that you've heard from today." She stopped briefly and then continued, "As you probably have figured out from what Aaron

85

and Ammon have said, the topic for today is 'Families Can Be Together Forever.'" She spoke for nearly ten minutes about the strength she derived from knowing that they really would be together as a family throughout the eternities. When she finished the congregation sang a hymn, and then her husband stood to speak.

"Brothers and sisters," he began, "my wife has told you a little about our family. I want to express my love to her and to our two boys. My wife has supported me completely in everything I've tried to do since we were married. I love her with all my heart and the two boys are icing on the cake." His voice broke momentarily. "But now let me turn to the topic of the day." He spoke for fifteen minutes or so about the attack that was being made on the family by the world. Jenn's mind wandered a bit until he said, "If the family is destroyed, then Satan wins. He has tried to pull us apart by promoting the idea that our families are unimportant and that outside interests and groups are more important. That is why we see young men and women form cliques at school or join gangs. They feel acceptance with the other gang members that they don't feel in their own homes. But I testify to you that it is the family that will persist through the eternities, and those things that we see as being so important here will fade into unimportance. We have a loving Heavenly Father who knows each of us by name and who gave his Son, even Jesus Christ, to pay the ultimate eternal price so that we can repent and be washed clean in his blood that we may return to our Father." He spoke for a few more minutes before closing his talk.

Jenn sat stunned. She was trying to process the message that had been delivered while the congregation sang the closing hymn and a rather rotund woman climbed the steps to the podium and offered the closing prayer. As the postlude music began, the two sister missionaries stood and joined the flow of people moving from the chapel into the foyer.

"Well, what did you think?" Sister Sandberg said as they found a quieter corner.

"I said I'd answer your questions," Sister Lingfelter said. "What did you want to know?" Jenn shook her head slowly. "I can't remember."

Sister Lingfelter said, "I think you were wondering about the people who were released and sustained, if I remember correctly." Jenn nodded. "Those who were released had served in those positions for some time and were being released so that others could have the blessings of serving in those callings."

Jenn's forehead wrinkled. "You mean they're just regular people? I mean, don't you have to go to school or something?"

"No. They are just regular people."

At that moment Carl Hathaway pushed his way through the throng in the foyer. "Hey, Jenn, I didn't know you were a Mormon," he said with a smile.

"I'm not," she replied slightly flustered. "I just came with Sister Lingfelter," she said, gesturing toward the two missionaries. "I guess I didn't know that you were," she said. "I mean, I saw you up there with the sacrament." Her voice trailed off.

"Yeah," he said. "I'm a priest. We get to bless the sacrament." He stuck his hand out and took hers. "Well, good to have you here. See you tomorrow at school." He released her hand and made his way down the hallway.

Sister Lingfelter led them out the door of the chapel and onto the sidewalk. "I suspect this is probably enough for one day," she said with a smile. "Although Sunday School is just starting and Young Women will be after that." She looked hopefully at Jenn.

"I think this was enough for today," she said. "I appreciate you bringing me to church." She felt more peaceful than she had felt in months.

"Another thing I suspect is that you have a lot of questions. We'd like the opportunity to . . . " She stopped. "That is, we'd like to have someone come and teach you."

Jenn felt as if a stone had settled in her stomach as she realized these two young women would probably leave her tomorrow and she'd never see them again. "Isn't there any way you can stay here or come and teach me wherever you go?"

Sister Lingfelter shook her head. "It doesn't work that way, but let us walk you home. Maybe we can answer a few of your questions and then, if you agree, we'll have the new missionaries contact you and continue to teach you." She looked hopefully at Jenn, who finally nodded her head.

The three of them walked slowly to Jenn's home. When they arrived the two missionaries gave her a brief hug. "We'll have someone contact you," Sister Lingfelter said as she and Sister Sandberg turned and walked back toward the church. Jenn felt that her heart would break as she watched them go.

SEVENTEEN

Jenn fixed dinner and set the table. Her mother was sleeping in her bedroom, and Damon had disappeared. She thought of the experience she had had that morning at church. There were many things that puzzled her, but she could not deny that she had felt at home and that she had felt accepted by the people there. She had known Carl Hathaway for years. They had shared several elementary teachers and junior high and high school classes, and yet she had never known he was a Mormon. She had thought there was something different about him but hadn't attached it to religion. Tears formed in her eyes as she thought about Sister Lingfelter and Sister Sandberg leaving tomorrow.

While the meat loaf was cooking, she retrieved the Book of Mormon from her bedroom, sat in the rocking chair in the living room, and began to read. She read for nearly half an hour before the timer on the stove rang. She closed the book, went to her mother's room and awakened her, and then returned to the kitchen to set food on the table.

"Where's your brother," her mother asked.

"I don't know," Jenn replied. "He was gone when I got home from church." She was amazed at how easily she formed the words. It seemed completely right.

Her mother snorted, "And how was church?" She took a final drag on her cigarette and ground it out in the sink before sitting down at the table.

"It was okay," Jenn answered noncommittally.

"I wish you'd keep better track of your brother."

Jenn bit her tongue and just nodded her head.

Her mother cut a healthy slice of meat loaf and forked it onto her plate. They ate in silence. When they had finished, Jenn removed their plates and rinsed them in the sink. "I hope you ain't gonna get involved with them church people too much," her mother said.

"Why? They seem like nice people to me."

"Just listen to me. Don't get too attached to 'em." She lit a cigarette and blew a cloud of smoke toward the ceiling. "Get me a beer, will ya?"

"Sure, Mom." Jenn followed her mother into the front room and handed her the can from the refrigerator. She perched on the edge of the couch while her mother sank into the rocking chair. "Mom, I kind of invited them to come and teach me more about their church." Jenn fidgeted.

"You did what?" Her mother choked. "Not in this house," she said emphatically before taking a drink.

Jenn sat silently on the couch. She rubbed her hand over the well-worn fabric on the sofa arm while she stared at the dirty shag carpet between her feet. She felt her mother's eyes staring at her. "Okay, Mom, I guess I'll have to go to the church to have them teach me, if that's what you want," she said softly. She stood quickly, spun on her heel, and marched down the hallway toward her room, leaving her mother sitting in the haze of smoke that rose from the cigarette in her right hand. Jenn sat on her bed and stared out the window. She could hear the creaking of the rocking chair from the front room. Damon slipped through the hedge into their backyard. The evening mist was beginning to form, and she could see half a dozen shadowy forms retreating on the other side of the hedge. Damon pulled a comb from his hip pocket and carefully combed and patted his hair into place before walking across the sparse lawn toward the back door. He glanced around furtively before opening the door and walking into the kitchen.

"Where've you been?" his mother called out from the rocking chair.

"Out," he replied curtly. Jenn waited for her mother's retort, but none came. She forced herself to her feet and walked to the kitchen. "There's some meat loaf in the fridge, if you want it," she said.

"I'm not hungry," he said with a sneer. He swaggered down the hallway.

"No need to be rude," she said after him. He ignored her and went into the bathroom.

"Jenn," her mother said sharply from the shadows of the living room. "Leave your brother alone." She rocked for another moment or two. "If you want them missionaries to teach you, you might as well do it here. Just don't expect me to get involved."

"Thanks, Mom," Jenn said with a smile. "I appreciate that." She picked up the Book of Mormon from where she had laid it next to the rocking chair and returned to her room. A few minutes later she looked up and saw Damon standing in the doorway. "Where've you been?" she whispered.

"Just out," he replied. "None of your business anyway."

"I suppose." She returned to her reading while he continued to lean against the door frame. She found it disconcerting to have him standing there staring at her while she tried to read. "You need something?" she finally asked.

He shrugged. "A million bucks, I guess."

"Fat chance of that."

"Just wondering what you're reading."

"A book some friends gave me," she said somewhat embarrassed.

"Looks kinda like a Bible."

"Sort of," she said as she closed the cover and slid it behind her on the bed.

"Buncha crap," he said with a sneer.

Jenn felt suddenly protective, "I don't think so, Damon."

"If you say so," he said as he pushed himself away from the door post and headed back toward the kitchen. "Where's the meat loaf?"

"In the fridge," she said as she retrieved the book, sank back on her bed, and continued to read. Nearly half an hour passed before she looked up to see her mother standing in the doorway.

"Jenn, be careful. Those Mormons are bad people. They're p'lygamists, and they take all of your money from you. I don't know much 'bout them, but I know all they want is to get young girls married to one of their old elders." She took a puff on her cigarette. "Just be careful, toad."

EIGHTeeN

Jenn hefted the tray to her shoulder, pushed through the double swinging doors from the kitchen into the restaurant, and made her way to the corner table. A family with six children was seated in the circular booth. With her free hand she grabbed a tray rack from its resting place, flipped it open, and rested the laden tray on it. She then deftly placed the plates on the tabletop.

"Anything else I can get you?" she asked.

"It looks wonderful," the father of the family said.

With a nod of her head, she snapped the rack shut, replaced it against the wall, and carried the empty tray back into the kitchen. Steam rose from the warming table and swirled toward the vent hood. She slid the tray on top of the stack of empty trays, brushed the stray strands of hair from her forehead, and pushed the swinging doors open. The family in the corner were the only customers. Jenn glanced at her watch—it was nearly ten o'clock. She spotted Lorna beginning to count out the money from the tip jar and walked over to where she stood behind the cash register.

"Jenn," the older woman acknowledged. "Looks like a pretty good night. You've been busy." She continued to count the money. "Feet hurt?"

"A little. I can't believe how busy it's been for a Wednesday night. Mind if I take off? I've some homework to finish before I go to bed."

Lorna glanced at the family in the corner. "You go ahead. I can clean up after them. Don't you wonder why they don't have them kids home in bed instead of out wandering around in the middle of the night?"

Jenn shrugged her shoulders. "I'll see you tomorrow, then."

Lorna put her hand on her arm, while she finished counting silently. "Here's your share," she said handing Jenn a handful of bills. She nodded her head toward the family. "If they leave a tip, I'll add it in with tomorrow's, okay?"

"Thanks, Lorna. See you." She stuffed the bills into her pants pocket, went back into the kitchen, and hung her apron on its hook. Manuel, the dishwasher who'd replaced Louis, looked shyly at her and waved a soapy hand as she walked out the back door of the kitchen. A full October moon hung in the sky like a bright silver coin. There was a bit of chill in the air, and she wrapped her arms around herself as she walked quickly down the streets toward her home. Sparse traffic passed her as she swam through the pools of light cast by the streetlights. It had been more than three weeks since Sister Lingfelter and Sister Sandberg had taken her to church. She had waited expectantly for the new missionaries to contact her, but no one had. She had felt uncomfortable returning to church without someone to guide her. Between school and the restaurant she had little time to read the Book of Mormon except on weekends. Still, she was making her way through it. She had read King Benjamin's address the past Sunday afternoon and felt moved to tears.

She stopped at a street corner and waited for the light to change. A dark Chevrolet stopped across the intersection from her, and she found herself holding her breath until the light changed and it drove on past without stopping. Almost afraid to look, she glanced at the driver and saw an elderly gentleman. Jenn exhaled a puff of breath. Rolayne had been waiting after school two weeks ago and had created a scene by screaming obscenities. Gathering all of the control she could muster, Jenn had simply walked past her and continued on home while Rolayne bellowed after her.

Thankfully, she had seen neither Miles nor Charlie since their last terrifying meeting. The morning after their assault, she found the Chevrolet had been reclaimed from the strip mall. She was finding a certain freedom in having severed ties with her former friends, but along with it came a feeling of loneliness. She longed to have one more conversation with Sister Lingfelter or Sister Sandberg. Carl Hathaway had spoken to her at school a few times since he'd seen her at church, but even he seemed to be retreating.

The moon seemed to hang suspended from the top of the pepper tree in her yard as she climbed the steps and opened the sagging screen door. Quietly, she let herself into the front room. The kitchen light was throwing beams into the living room, and Jenn could see her mother sitting in the rocking chair. She was unsure whether she was asleep or not, but Jenn could see the glowing tip of a cigarette between the fingers of her hand.

"Somebody called for you," her mother said huskily. "Number's by the phone." She coughed against the back of her hand.

"Thanks, Mom."

"Busy night?"

Jenn nodded her head. "Real busy. I'm pooped, but I still have some English homework to do."

Her mother heaved herself out of the chair and staggered unsteadily down the hall. "Don't stay up too late." She burped and wandered into the bathroom.

Jenn walked into the kitchen. Her backpack hung over the back of one of the chairs, and she searched in it for her English textbook. She opened it to the bookmark and sat down on the chair at the kitchen table. Almost as an afterthought she stood, walked to the phone, and looked for the message. On a small scrap of blue paper her mother had written, "555–6193—ball." *I suppose it's too late to call tonight,* she thought and returned to her homework. An hour later she closed the book, yawned, stretched, and headed to bed.

The next morning she fought to keep her eyes open in her English class. They were taking a short vocabulary quiz when the intercom buzzed to life. "Mrs. Parker."

"Yes," Jenn's teacher answered, clearly annoyed that her class had been interrupted.

"Would you send Steve Sokalowski down to the counseling center, please?"

"He's taking a quiz," Mrs. Parker replied sharply.

"When he's finished, then," the disembodied voice said.

"Of course," she replied in a clipped tone.

A few minutes later they handed in their quizzes, and Steve left for the office. "I suppose this will be happening rather regularly over the next week or so," Mrs. Parker said. "It's time for your annual conference with your counselor. Since this is your senior year, I suppose you'd better go. I'm sure they're checking your records to make sure you have everything you need to graduate next June." She turned to the white board. "But enough of that. I'm sure you all read your assignment, so let's begin a discussion of the *Heart of Darkness*." She began to write on the board. "You'll have your choice of one of the following books," she continued to make the list, "and you'll contrast one of the themes from *Heart of Darkness* with a similar theme in one of these books."

Jenn struggled to keep her eyes open as Mrs. Parker completed the list. She had heard of several of the books and was trying to decide which one she'd read when the intercom sputtered to life again.

"Mrs. Parker?"

"Yes," she said through clenched teeth.

"May we see Jennica Cooper in the counseling center?"

"I suppose," she hissed. Mrs. Parker looked at Jenn and thrust her chin toward the door. "Send Steve back if you see him," she said.

"Sure," Jenn said. She gathered her books and headed down the hallway to the counselors. She stopped by her locker and deposited her English books and then walked up to the counter where the secretary sat. "You called for me?"

"Let's see, you're Jennica Cooper, right?" Jenn nodded. "Have a seat. Miss Hardy will be with you in a minute."

Jenn sat down on the bright red vinyl chair. There was a pile of pamphlets on the end table next to the chair. She sorted through them, trying to find something that looked interesting, but finally gave up and rested her head against the wall behind the chair. She closed her eyes.

"Jenn." Miss Hardy was shaking her shoulder gently. Jenn's eyes flew open.

"Oh, Miss Hardy." She stifled a yawn. "Ready for me?" Jenn glanced at her watch. Nearly fifteen minutes had passed since she'd closed her eyes for a minute.

"You look tired, dear," Miss Hardy said as she led her into her office.

"I guess I am. It was really busy at the place I work, and then I had English homework to do when I got home last night." She unsuccessfully tried to hide another yawn.

Miss Hardy opened a manila folder on her desk. "Well, I won't keep you long." She shuffled through the papers in the folder. "What are you planning to do after high school, Jenn?"

"I don't know. Get a better job, I guess. I really hadn't thought much about it." She shifted in her chair. "Why?"

"Well, your grades are certainly good enough that you can probably get a scholarship if you want to go to college," Miss Hardy said. "Actually, your grades are pretty impressive."

"I've never thought about college," Jenn said, amazed. "I mean, nobody in my family has ever gone to college. My mom didn't even graduate from high school."

"What about your father," Miss Hardy said as she looked over the top of her half-moon glasses.

Jenn felt the familiar feeling in her stomach as if spiders were crawling out of it and up her spine. "He . . . he died when I was real young. But he didn't go to college."

"Well, you could start a new trend. I'd be happy to help you fill out the paperwork and see what we could do. I think you'll have several scholarships to choose from."

"You really think so?" Jenn was amazed and fully awake.

Miss Hardy studied the grades in front of her. "It says here that at one time you wanted to be a teacher. Is that what you'd still like to do?"

Jenn shrugged her shoulders. "I guess. I mean, I don't really know what I want to do. But being a teacher would be as good as any, I guess."

Miss Hardy studied several of the pages. "According to some of the aptitude tests you've taken, you seem to have quite a flair for the sciences. Have you ever considered medicine as a career?"

"You mean, be a nurse?"

"Or a doctor. You have A's in all of your math and science classes, and your tests show a high probability of success in the medical field."

Jenn shook her head. "I don't think so. When my brother was in the hospital, I had a real hard time with the needles and blood and all. You know what I mean?"

Miss Hardy nodded her head. "What about engineering? Many of the universities are looking specifically for women to go into engineering. I'm sure we could get you a scholarship in that field."

"I'm not even sure I know what an engineer does, except drive a train," she said with a smile.

"Well, there are several fields—chemical, electrical, civil—in engineering. I have some pamphlets that describe what is expected of a student in engineering, what the demand is for engineers, and how much you can expect to earn. Would you be interested in one of those?"

"Sure," Jenn said. "I'm still not sure I'm college material, though."

"Don't sell yourself short," Miss Hardy replied as she stood and opened one of the many file cabinets in her office. A moment later she handed Jenn a yellow and brown pamphlet. "Why don't you take this home and talk it over with your mother? Then, if you'd like me to help, we could fill out a scholarship application and maybe send off some letters to a few colleges to see if they'd be interested in you. Okay?"

"I guess," Jenn said. She turned the pamphlet over in her hands. On the back were listed average salaries for engineers. She couldn't believe that anyone made that kind of money. "Thanks. I'll talk to my mom tonight." She stood and walked out of the office. Through the rest of the school day she periodically looked at the pamphlet. When the day ended she hurried home, dropped off her backpack, changed clothes, and prepared to go to the restaurant.

"See you later, Mom," she said as she headed out the door. "I hope I'm not so late tonight. I talked with my counselor this morning, and I need to talk something over with you when I get home."

"Are you in trouble?"

"No, Mom. I'll talk to you later."

"Don't be too late," her mother admonished as Jenn closed the door behind her. Jenn's mother crossed the kitchen and opened the refrigerator door. She took out a can of beer, popped it open, and started back into the living room. The phone message she had taken the previous day was sitting on the countertop near the phone. She wadded it up and threw it toward the wastebasket.

NI*n*ETEEN

"College! What kind of tomfoolery is that?" Jenn's mother stubbed out her cigarette on the top of the beer can and then dropped the butt into it. "Nobody in our family has ever gone to college, and we've done all right. 'Sides, how would you pay for it?"

Jenn looked at the threadbare curtains and the chipped surface of the table. "Mom, Miss Hardy thinks she can get me a scholarship that will pay for most of the expenses. I'd keep working to pay for the rest." She looked at her mother, still dressed in the housecoat she had put on that morning. "Please, Mom. It can't do any harm to try, can it?"

Her mother crushed the beer can in her hand. "Jenn, I don't know what's come over you lately. First you're hangin' out with them Mormon girls, and now you want to go away to college." She finished crushing the can and threw it into the trash can. "You'll drive me nuts, but I suppose there's nothing I can do to stop you." She stood up unsteadily and leaned on the counter. "I hope you know what you're doin'."

Jenn smiled broadly. "Thanks, Mom. I hope I do too."

"Don't forget to take out the trash," her mother said as she made her way out of the kitchen.

"I won't, Mom." She stood up from the table and picked up the trash can. A number of scraps of paper on the floor had not reached the mark. Jenn picked them up, dropped them in the can, and carried it out the back door to the garbage can. She tipped it upside down and poured the contents into the larger can. Just as she was about to head back into the house she spotted the scrap of blue paper. She lifted it out of the garbage can, smoothed it open, and saw the message from the previous night. She carried the kitchen trash can back into the house and glanced at her watch. Unlike the previous day, on this night the restaurant had been slow. She had left just after eight-thirty. It was just a few minutes after nine. Jenn picked up the phone and dialed the number. The phone rang four times, and then an answering machine picked up.

"Hello, we're sorry to have missed your call. Please leave your name and number after the chime, and we'll get back to you as soon as we can. Have a heavenly day."

Jenn's heart skipped a beat on the last phrase. "This is Jenn Cooper. I'm just returning your call," she said. "I work until at least nine o'clock tomorrow night, but you could reach me after that, or on Saturday." She left her number and hung up the phone. Quickly, she read through the assignment for her English class and climbed into bed. Her spirit was lighter than it had been in weeks with two wonderful events that had happened in one day.

Next morning she left for school early and went directly to the counseling department where she made an appointment to meet with Miss Hardy before hurrying to her first period math class. The day flew by until her appointment with the counselor. At the appointed hour she practically jogged to the office.

"Miss Hardy will be with you shortly," the secretary said.

Jenn sat down in the same red vinyl chair she'd occupied the previous day, but now everything seemed brighter. She was excited about the prospect of going to college and frightened at the same time. *Maybe I can't get a scholarship,* she thought, *and maybe I can't get into college.* She clutched the brochure on engineering in her hand and noticed that her palms were so sweaty that the pamphlet was limp with moisture. The door to Miss Hardy's office opened, and a boy walked out with his shoulders slumped. The counselor stuck her head out and beckoned to Jenn.

"Come in, dear," she said as she took the glasses that hung around her neck on a slim gold chain and placed them on her nose. "Well, how can I help you?"

Jenn twisted nervously on her chair, "Yesterday you said maybe you could help me get a scholarship." There was a note of anxiety in her voice.

"Oh, yes. Engineering, if I remember correctly." She pivoted in her chair and retrieved Jenn's folder from a credenza behind her desk. "Let's see." She leafed through the papers for a moment before looking directly at Jenn. "Do you have a preference whether you stay in state or go out of state?"

"What?" Jenn looked at her with a confused look on her face.

"Do you care where you go to school? Does it matter whether you go out of state if they have a good engineering program? Or do you want to live at home and go to school locally?"

"I don't know," Jenn said honestly. "I hadn't even thought about that." She felt her palms sweating even more and a trickle of sweat ran down her back. "What do you think?"

"Honey, I think we ought to look for a good engineering program and go for it." Jenn nodded her head in agreement. "Well, here are some possibilities then." She reached for a paperback book on the bookshelf at the side of her desk. "If you're willing to go far away, we could go for MIT, Cornell, or Carnegie-Mellon." She looked at Jenn's bewildered face. "MIT is in Massachusetts, Cornell in New York, and Carnegie-Mellon in Pennsylvania. Do any of those appeal to you?"

Jenn shook her head slowly. "I guess I didn't realize you were talking about going clear across the country."

"I can see why that would make you nervous," Miss Hardy said. "How about something closer to home?" She checked the book again, "Stanford is a possibility, but I'm not sure they are offering as many scholarships as they used to. How about Utah State? That's closer to home, and they have an excellent engineering department."

Jenn nodded her head. "I guess that would be okay."

"Still nervous? Have you traveled much, Jenn?"

Jenn shook her head. "I've never been outside of Fresno, let alone outside of California."

Miss Hardy smiled. "Well, I'm well acquainted with the Utah State campus and the people there. It's located in Logan and is surrounded by mountains that have snow on them much of the year. The people are friendly, and they have an excellent program." She turned several pages in the catalog. "Hmm. It appears that they are still looking for female students. They have several excellent scholarships that would probably meet your needs." She looked over the top of her glasses. "Does that interest you at all?"

"I guess," Jenn said almost in a whisper. She was feeling extremely nervous. *What if I get that scholarship? How much money will it cost? Will Mom really let me go out of state, especially to Utah?* "It's kind of a big step," she croaked.

"Why don't you let me do a little sniffing around and see if that's a possibility?" She continued to stare at Jenn. "Something's bothering you, dear. What is it?"

"I guess I'm just worried about how much it will cost and about being away from home. I mean, I've never even been away from Mom for a night, except when Damon was in the hospital. We've never been on a vacation or anything. This is kind of new to me, you know?"

Miss Hardy leaned back in her chair, "I remember when I left for college, I had some of the same issues. But you know what? It all worked out." She placed her hands flat on her desk. "You'll be fine, Jenn. Is it all right with you if I start making some inquiries and putting some paperwork together?" Jenn nodded her head. "As to the cost, I really can't tell you what it will take until I've explored a little bit. But I do know that Utah State employs a lot of students to help them work for part of their tuition, and I'm sure you'd qualify for a Pell Grant. I wouldn't worry too much about the money." She stood up and walked around the desk. "I'll get back to you in a few days, dear."

Jenn left the office with a hundred questions zipping around in her head. She was amazed that Miss Hardy thought she'd be able to succeed in college. Her self-esteem swelled, but it quickly deflated when she questioned her own abilities and her ability to earn enough money for living expenses. The rest of the day crawled by until she finally made her way to work at the restaurant.

Friday nights were either very busy or very slow. This night was one of the busy ones. Jenn barely had time to sit down and rest. At closing, she wrapped up a hamburger to eat on the way home. The twenty-minute walk gave her time to consider the events of the day. She had brought a sweater to work with her and pulled it around herself as she walked through the chilly evening. By the time she was three blocks from the restaurant she had finished the hamburger. She wondered how her mother would accept the possibility that she might leave home to go to school. *Not well, I suspect,* she thought. She shivered as a cold breeze caught up with her and caressed her with frigid fingers.

Jenn turned the final corner and walked briskly to her home. The house was completely dark. Jenn glanced at her watch. The luminous dial indicated it was twenty minutes after ten. She let herself in the front door as quietly as possible and was assaulted with warm, stale air that smelled of cigarette smoke. She tiptoed into the kitchen and opened the refrigerator. There was nothing inside but a nearly empty bottle of milk and two cans of beer. *I need to do some grocery shopping tomorrow.* As she poured herself a glass of milk by the light of the open fridge, she noticed another scrap of paper near the phone. Her mother had written, "Jenn call 555–6193." *Tomorrow morning,* she thought and then slipped as quietly as a ghost to her bedroom and prepared for bed.

TWENTY

Jenn had walked to the corner market and brought back two bags of groceries. She was just walking through the front door when the phone rang. She walked quickly to the kitchen, set down the plastic bags, and reached for the phone. "'Lo," she said.

"Is this Jenn Cooper?"

"Yes, it is."

"Jenn, this is Sister Ball. I just found a note from Sister Lingfelter. She indicated you might be interested in having someone teach you the gospel. Is that right?"

"I guess so," Jenn replied. "I went to church with them about a month ago, and they were going to get someone to contact me. I mean, I guess that would be all right."

"Wonderful. Sister Snow and I would like to make an appointment at your convenience. It sounds as if you're pretty busy with school and work, but we're very flexible. When would be a good time for you?"

Jenn was off guard. "I . . . well, I mean . . . well, I'm home today until three o'clock, and I'm home on Sunday, if that works out."

Sister Ball replied, "Would it be all right with you if we came tomorrow at four o'clock?"

Jenn felt momentary panic but finally said, "I guess that would be all right."

"We'd be delighted if you'd like to come to church with us in the morning." She left the invitation hanging.

"I don't think so," Jenn said timidly. "Maybe next week."

"Well, we'll see you tomorrow then. Have a wonderful day."

Jenn hung up the phone. Her heart was fluttering as she pulled out a chair and sat down. *What have I done?* she thought. She could hear her mother stirring in her bedroom, and a moment later she heard her coughing as she made her way to the bathroom. Jenn placed a pan on the stove and began heating it. She scrambled half a dozen eggs in a bowl, added a little milk, and mixed it thoroughly. When the skillet had heated, she dumped the egg mixture into the pan and began stirring it with a fork. Her mother stretched and yawned as she walked into the kitchen.

"Have a seat, Mom. I'll have breakfast ready in a minute." She put a couple of slices of bread into the toaster with one hand while she continued to stir the eggs with other.

"Pour me a cup a coffee, will ya?" her mother said from the table.

"Just a minute, Mom." Jenn finished scrambling the eggs and scooped them onto two plates. She poured a cup of coffee from the percolator and then buttered the toast when it popped from the toaster.

Her mother began to eat the eggs. "You were late last night," she said with a mouth half full of food.

"It was busy at work," Jenn said with a shrug. She watched her mother eat her breakfast, trying to get up courage to tell her what Miss Hardy had said the previous day. Finally, when her mother had finished her eggs and was drinking her coffee she said, "Miss Hardy thinks she might be able to get me a scholarship to Utah State," she said quietly.

Her mother choked on her coffee. "Utah State! You gotta be kiddin'. Why would you want to go there? Ain't California good enough for you?"

Jenn shrank back. "I don't know, Mom. Miss Hardy thought it was a good school. I mean, she thought it would be a good place to go. But if you don't want me to, I guess I can always say no."

Her mother looked at her over the rim of her coffee cup and sighed, "Just don't get uppity, girl. You hear?"

"I won't, Mom." She swallowed hard. "I'm kind of nervous about it, and I'm not sure I can even get a scholarship. You know what I mean?"

"Just don't get yer hopes up too high. This family ain't been blessed with real good luck." She drained the rest of the coffee and then paused for a moment before putting the cup down. "Jenn, I don't want to rain on your parade. I really am proud of you, toad."

"Thanks, Mom." She cleared the plates from the table. "Oh, by the way, that phone number you left for me was the missionaries. They're coming over tomorrow to teach me about their church. Okay?" She held her breath while her mother ruminated over the news.

"Just don't expect me to listen to 'em," she said. "And keep the visit short." She stood up and walked out of the kitchen, leaving Jenn to wash the dishes. A few minutes later, Damon walked barefoot into the kitchen.

"Morning," Jenn said.

Damon ran his hand over his head and grunted in reply. He opened the cupboard, took out a bowl and poured some cereal into it. "Any eggs left?" he said.

"Nope," Jenn replied, "but I can whip some up for you, if you'd like."

"Nah, this is okay," he said as he opened the refrigerator door and grabbed the milk bottle. "You were late last night."

"It was busy at the restaurant last night. Shelly was sick and didn't come in, so I had to cover a couple of extra tables." Damon grunted again and shoveled a spoonful of cereal into his mouth. "I didn't know you were here when I came home. I just tried to be quiet so I didn't disturb Mom."

"I was here," he mumbled through his mouthful of food. "The fuzz are doin' a crackdown, and I'm kinda layin' low."

Jenn finished wiping off the counter. "Are you being careful, Damon?"

"Always," he replied. "Don't worry about me, sister. I'm always careful." He lifted the bowl to his lips and drained the milk from the bowl. "Gotta go." He set the bowl in the sink and slunk out the back door.

Saturday at the restaurant was as slow as Friday had been frenzied. Jenn left for home before nine o'clock and walked briskly through the moonlight to her home. Although a small slice was missing, the moon still shown brightly through scudding clouds that drifted above. She was home well before nine-thirty. Her mother was sitting in her usual spot in the rocking chair with a can of beer in her hand. The television set cast flickering blue light across the room. Jenn greeted her mother, who nodded in reply, and then walked briskly to the bathroom. A few minutes later she draped her clothing over the back of a chair, climbed into bed, and took the Book of Mormon from the side of her bed before remembering she had not put her tip money away. She opened the book on the bedspread and then reached into her pants pocket and removed the small wad of bills. She knelt at the side of her bed and smoothed out the crumpled bills. Even for a slow night she had earned over thirty dollars in tips. Still on her knees she crawled to her dresser, pulled out the drawer, added the bills to her cache, and then returned to her bed. The book had shut, and as she opened it to find her place, her eyes fell on the book of Enos. Although she had read it previously, she read the three pages again. Two thoughts entered her mind. *He prayed all day, and I don't even know how to pray. He was so lucky—his sins were forgiven him.* She turned off the light and fell asleep.

Jenn spent most of Sunday morning doing homework. She was contrasting the role of women in *Heart of Darkness* with Frank Herbert's *Dune*. She was amazed at how both authors had elevated women in the eyes of the people. As four o'clock approached, she felt increased excitement and anxiety. She straightened up the sparse living room and waited for the missionaries. *I wonder what they'll be like. No one could replace Sister Lingfelter in my life.* There was a knock on the screen door.

Jenn opened the door and saw the two women standing there. One was tall and thin, the other short and rotund. The tall one extended her hand. "Hi, I'm Sister Ball, and this is Sister Snow. You must be Jenn?"

Jenn nodded her head. "Won't you come in?"

"Thank you." They followed Jenn into the living room.

"Please have a seat," she said, gesturing toward the couch. The two women sat down on the sofa. Jenn perched on the edge of the rocking chair and waited expectantly. After a slightly uncomfortable moment of silence, Sister Ball spoke up.

"I'm sorry we've been so slow contacting you," she began. "Sister Lingfelter and Sister Sandberg left us quite a few people to contact and we've been working our way through them."

"Have you seen Sister Lingfelter?" Jenn asked.

"We saw her on transfer day for a few minutes. I think we'll see her at zone conference if she hasn't gone home." Sister Ball looked at Sister Snow for confirmation and received a little nod from her companion.

"I really liked her and Sister Sandberg," Jenn said as she began to rock in the chair.

"Good," Sister Ball said. "Apparently they liked you too." She glanced at her companion again. "We're a little unsure how much they taught you. Maybe you could let us know where you are?"

Jenn looked confused. "I don't think they taught me much. I went to church with them one Sunday, and they answered a few questions about what went on there, but that's about all." She looked expectantly at the two women. "So, I guess you could start right at the first."

Sister Snow smiled. "Wonderful. But before we do, maybe we could find out a little about you, if that's all right?"

Jenn shrugged her shoulders, "Sure. There's not much to tell, but shoot."

"Well, we know you're Jenn Cooper, but we don't know much else about you. Why don't you tell us a little about yourself."

Jenn rocked a little faster. "I'm eighteen, I just had a birthday, and I'm a senior in high school. I work at Dipsy's—that's a restaurant—after school. That's about it."

"How about your family?"

"I have a brother, Damon—he's sixteen—and my mom."

"I see," said Sister Ball.

"How about you?" Jenn asked. "Where are you from?"

Sister Ball said, "I'm from New Jersey, a little town near Newark."

"I'm from Oregon," replied Sister Snow.

"Why are you here?" Jenn asked puzzled.

"We decided to go on a mission, and we go where the prophet sends us."

"Prophet?" Jenn's eyes widened as she envisioned a picture she had seen in one of her art books of an old, white-haired man standing amidst a flock of sheep.

"Yes." Sister Ball smiled. "But perhaps we're getting a little bit ahead of ourselves. We'd like to start with the story of a young man named Joseph Smith in New York nearly two hundred years ago."

Jenn settled back in her chair and listened as the two missionaries taught her. After half an hour Sister Snow said, "Well, we've taken quite a bit of your time, Jenn. Do you have any questions?"

Jenn shook her head. "I'm sure I will, but right now I'm just trying to understand what you've told me."

"Could we set up another appointment?" Sister Ball inquired.

Jenn nodded. "Yes, I'd like that."

"How about next Sunday at the same time?" She removed a small book from the brocade case she carried. When Jenn nodded, the missionary penciled the appointment into her book. "Now before we leave, could we have a word of prayer?" Again Jenn nodded her head. The two missionaries slipped to their knees beside the couch and beckoned for Jenn to join them. "Would you like to offer the prayer?"

Jenn felt panic grip her heart. "I don't think so," she squeaked. "I don't know how."

"I'll help you, if you'd like," Sister Ball said softly.

Jenn shook her head. "Maybe next time."

"I understand. Is it all right with you if I pray?" Jenn nodded her agreement. When the missionary had finished, the three of them stood up. "Jenn, thank you for letting us come. We'll see you next week."

Tears filled Jenn's eyes as she said, "I'll look forward to that." She led them to the door, let them out, and returned to the rocking chair. Damon stepped out of the gloom of the kitchen into the living room.

"Buncha crap," he said with a sneer. Jenn felt as if cold water had been thrown over the warmth she felt in her heart.

TWENTY~ONE

Jenn finished the last problem on her math exam, checked her answers, and then walked to the front of the room. She handed Mr. Balderson her test and said under her breath, "Is it okay if I go to the office now?"

He nodded. "If you're sure you finished. I wish they wouldn't interrupt us in the middle of a test."

Jenn nodded her head, returned to her seat, picked up her book, and walked to the office. Her heart was swirling with emotions as she approached Miss Hardy's office. She dared hope she'd be offered a scholarship, but another part of her felt unworthy and felt it unlikely to happen. And what if it did happen? Was she prepared to move away from home? What would her mother do without her support? And then there was Damon. Jenn felt protective of her younger brother, unwilling though he was to accept her help. She squirmed in the red vinyl chair, felt her shoulders tensing, and took a deep breath. She leaned her head back against the wall and shut her eyes.

"Miss Hardy will see you now," the secretary said.

"What?" Jenn's eyes flew open. "Oh, okay." She walked into the counselor's office. Miss Hardy sat behind her desk with the phone cradled against her shoulder. She pointed at the chair across from her and waved Jenn into it.

"I understand," she said into the phone. "But what you have to realize is that unless your son makes up that quarter credit of English, he won't be eligible to graduate." She rolled her eyes. "Yes, I do understand, but he still needs to make up that quarter credit of freshman English. There are a number of ways he could do it." She paused for a few moments. "Mrs. Jenkins, I do understand. I realize he was under a great deal of pressure at that time in his life, but he still needs to make up a quarter of a credit of ninth-grade English." She paused again. "There are a number of ways he can do that. Would you like me to send home information on night school and correspondence courses? Wonderful. I'll call your son down this afternoon and give him the information." Miss Hardy was writing herself a note on a bright violet sticky pad. "Thank you, Mrs. Jenkins, and good-bye." She hung up the phone.

"Well, Jenn. I have some good news."

"You do?"

"I've talked with Mark Decolate at Utah State. I faxed him your transcript, and he called this morning. They're willing to offer you an academic scholarship at USU. Isn't that great?"

Jenn twisted her fingers together. "What does that mean, Miss Hardy?"

"Well, it means that they'll pay your tuition, fees, and books. And as long as you keep a three point GPA they'll renew the scholarship." She could see Jenn was puzzled. "In other words, as long as you keep your grades up, you won't have to pay anything for schooling."

Jenn's heart leapt in her breast. "You mean I can go to school for free?"

Miss Hardy nodded her head. "What's more, Mark says they're willing to offer you a job on campus that should pretty well take care of your living expenses. You can stay in campus housing, so I don't think you have much to worry about." Jenn sat quietly fidgeting with her hands. "What's wrong, dear?" the counselor asked.

"It's just kind of overwhelming. I mean, nobody in my family has ever gone to college. I'm not sure I'll fit in." She lowered her eyes to the floor.

"You'll be just fine," Miss Hardy reassured. "I'll bet your family is going to be excited."

"Maybe," Jenn said quietly.

"There are some forms and applications that you'll have to fill out. I'd be happy to help you do that after you've talked this over with your mother." She stood up and helped Jenn out of her chair. "This is a wonderful opportunity," she said with a smile. "Let me know what your mother says." She patted the girl on her shoulder. "Now, let me give you a note so you can get into your second period class." She dashed off her signature on a preprinted note pad, ripped off the top sheet, and handed it to Jenn. "I'm thrilled for you, dear," she said as Jenn walked numbly out of her office.

The rest of the school day passed in a blur. Jenn could not keep her mind on what was going on in any of her classes as her imagination carried her off to college. When the last class ended, she hurried home. Her mother was sitting in the rocking chair in the living room when Jenn burst through the front door. On the way home she'd decided to take a positive approach with her mother. "Mom, I've got great news," she said excitedly.

"Oh?" Her mother stubbed her cigarette out in an old ash tray at the side of the rocker. "What?"

"I've been offered a college scholarship. It will pay for everything— well, nearly everything." She waited for a response from her mother.

"Hmm. What good will that do ya? Just means four more years of sittin' in classes. Don't see why ya have to do that. I never went to college, and I'm doin' all right." She rocked for a few moments. "But I suppose you've already made up your mind, haven't ya?"

Jenn looked dejectedly at her mother. "No, Mom, I wanted to talk to you about it." She sank onto the edge of the couch. "I won't go if you don't want me to," she said almost in a whisper.

"Don't see much need, but I don't suppose it'll hurt none. Go if you want." She lurched out of the chair and started for the bathroom. "You'd better hurry, or you're gonna be late at the diner."

Fighting back tears, Jenn changed clothes and headed to the

restaurant. She was still feeling whipped when she walked through the back door, grabbed her apron, and tied it around her waist. She wiped her eyes and walked through the swinging doors. Lorna was seating a couple in a corner booth. She winked at Jenn and said to the couple, "Your waitress will be here in a moment." Quickly, she walked to where Jenn stood. "Shelly just called in sick again. Can you cover her tables?"

"Sure," Jenn replied flatly.

"What's the matter, hon?"

"Oh, nothing."

"Doesn't sound like nothing to me. Get their order and let's talk."

A few minutes later Jenn had placed glasses of water on the table, taken the order, and turned it into the cook. Lorna was sitting by the cash register when Jenn approached. "What's up?" the older woman said.

"I got a scholarship to college," she said with just a wisp of a smile.

Lorna leapt to her feet. "That's wonderful!" She hugged Jenn. "Where to? Fresno State?"

Jenn shook her head. "Utah State," she replied.

Lorna sat back down on her stool. "That's great. I hate to lose you though. You're a real trooper." She looked in Jenn's eyes. "What's the matter, kid? You ought to be excited about this."

"Oh, Lorna, my mom's not real excited. I'm not sure she wants me to go." Tears threatened to flow again. "And I'm kind of scared. I mean I've never been away from home. You know?"

"Kid, you'll do fine." A bell rang from the kitchen. "Now go get them people's dinners before they get cold." She gave Jenn an affectionate pat on the behind and sent her toward the kitchen. The restaurant began to fill up with early diners, and with one waitress missing, Jenn was hopping from one table to another until closing time. When the last diners had left, she went to the kitchen and took off her apron before returning to the cash register.

"I'll see you tomorrow," she said.

Lorna nodded her head. "Here's your share of the tip money," she said handing her a handful of bills. "You made a bundle tonight, coverin' both your tables and Shelly's. Don't spend it all in one place." She winked at the girl. "Jenn, I'm excited for you. But I expect nine more months of work out of you before you head up to Utah. Ya hear?"

Jenn nodded. "I guess that's my next question. How do I get there?"

113

She stuffed the bills into her pocket and waved good night to her boss. A few minutes later she climbed the swayback steps and pushed the creaking front door open. Her mother had fallen asleep watching television. Damon was nowhere to be seen. Jenn prepared for bed and then pulled out the dresser drawer. She withdrew all of the bills that had been carefully stacked there for the past two years. Occasionally she had taken some of them to the bank and changed them for larger denominations so that the bills would fit in her secret hiding place. Carefully she counted her money. There was nearly three thousand dollars. "I wonder how long that will last at college?" she whispered under her breath. Carefully, she replaced the money, shut the drawer, and crawled into bed. A few minutes later Damon knocked on her window.

TWENTY~TWO

The rest of the week flew by. Miss Hardy helped Jenn fill out the necessary forms and mail them to Utah State. Shelly was still sick, and Jenn pulled double duty until Friday night. Saturday morning she fixed breakfast, inventoried the food, and prepared to walk to the grocery store. As she was making a list, the telephone rang. "'Lo," she said absently.

"Jenn? This is Sister Snow."

"Oh, hi."

"We're wondering if you'd like to go to church with Sister Ball and me in the morning?"

The week had been so busy that Jenn had taken little time to read the Book of Mormon, and she felt a sudden pang of guilt. "I don't know," she replied.

"Well, we'd like to invite you to go with us, if you'd like to go." Sister Snow waited expectantly.

Jenn pondered for a moment. "Sure. I guess so. Still eleven o'clock?"

"Yes. We'll be by about ten-thirty. Okay?"

"Okay," Jenn said. "See you in the morning." She hung up the phone and turned to see her mother standing in the doorway. "I'm headed to the store," she said, "to get a few groceries."

"Who was that?" her mother asked.

"Sister Snow," Jenn replied. "One of the missionaries."

"And what are they trying to do?"

"They invited me to go to church with them in the morning." Jenn said as she tried to escape.

"And?"

"And nothing, Mom. I'm going to go with them."

Her mother shook her head as Jenn walked past her and out of the front door. An hour later she was back with the groceries and was putting them away when Damon wandered into the kitchen. He was wearing a pair of baggy shorts with the crotch nearly at his knees and was struggling into a T-shirt.

"What's for breakfast?" he growled.

"Cereal," Jenn replied as she put a gallon of milk in the refrigerator.

"No bacon and eggs?" he groused.

"Not unless you've got them hidden somewhere," she said. He shrugged his shoulders. "Where were you last night?" she asked.

"Just out," he replied. He leaned closer to her. "Did you hafta buy the food?" he whispered.

She nodded her head, "Mom's check doesn't come until next Monday."

"I'm sure glad you're around," he said, pulling a box of cereal from the shelf, "or I'd prob'ly go hungry."

Jenn sat down at the table across from her brother. The morning light coming through the tattered curtains accentuated the planes of his face. When he began eating, Jenn said, "Damon, I have something to tell you." He raised the spoon to his mouth and raised an eyebrow. "I've gotten a scholarship to go to college. I won't be here with you and Mom next fall."

Damon chewed on the mouthful of raisin bran. "Good for you," he said thickly. "Where ya goin'?"

"Utah State University," she replied. "I'm going into engineering."

Damon choked on his cereal and finally sputtered, "Engineering? Why go to college to learn how to drive a train?"

"Not that kind of engineering," she said, not sure whether Damon was teasing. "Civil engineering. You know, learning how to build bridges and highways."

Damon grunted. "Just gonna be me and the ol' lady. That'll be different." He scooped the rest of his breakfast into his mouth, stood up, and belched loudly before sauntering down the hall toward his bedroom. "Just me and Mom," he chuckled.

Jenn washed Damon's bowl and put it in the dish drainer before sitting down with her homework at the kitchen table. Although she had done well in school, it had never been a priority in her life, but now that she was preparing for college, it seemed as if there were an urgency to her studies. She wished she could go back to the times she had paid little attention to what was being taught and absorb it. The essay she was writing on *Heart of Darkness* and *Dune* lay nearly finished. She picked it up and read it for perhaps the tenth time. She added a note here and there, deleted a word or two, and then set it down on the table. *I've got to get to school early on Monday so I can use the computer in the library to word process this essay,* she thought. Suddenly another thought popped into her head. *How will I ever be able to afford a computer to go to college?* She gathered her homework, stuck it in her backpack, and hauled it to her bedroom. The clock on her bedside table told her she had nearly two hours until she had to go to work.

Jenn lay down on her bed, folded the pillow behind her head, and picked up the Book of Mormon. The bookmark was stuck in the seventeenth chapter of Mosiah. She began to read the final words Abinadi spoke before King Noah burned him at the stake. Jenn recalled the pain she had suffered when hot grease spattered on the back of her hand as she was preparing some french fries at the diner. She could not imagine what it would be like to be burned alive. She shuddered and closed the book on her stomach. *How could he endure that?* She wondered. She stared at the ceiling and noticed a cobweb hanging from the light fixture. Air currents swirled upward and sent the strand swinging back and forth as Jenn watched, almost hypnotized. She opened the book again and read, "Having been put to death because he would not deny the commandments of God, having sealed the truth of his words by

117

his death." A tear ran down her cheek and formed a dark spot on her pillowcase. Then, strangely, a feeling of peace washed over her.

She began reading the next chapter when suddenly a verse sprang out at her: "Now I say unto you, if this be the desire of your hearts, what have you against being baptized in the name of the Lord, as a witness before him that ye have entered into a covenant with him, that ye will serve him and keep his commandments, that he may pour out his Spirit more abundantly upon you?"

Jenn reread the words. *Is that what's expected of me?* She felt as if her stomach was turning flip-flops. She sat up on the edge of her bed and sank to her knees. She had never prayed before in her life, and she struggled at first but finally poured out the questions in her heart. She rose, changed clothes, and headed to the diner with new energy in her step.

TWENTY~THREE

Sister Ball was walking in front of Jenn and Sister Snow when suddenly she stopped. "Do you remember what happened the last time you came to church?" she asked.

Jenn's forehead wrinkled. "You mean, who spoke?" Sister Ball nodded her head. "It was some couple and their two little boys; I don't remember their names."

"Well, today is going to be a little different. It's fast Sunday." Sister Snow glanced at her companion. "What that means is that people in the congregation will get up and bear their testimonies. So there won't just be one or two people speaking with some assigned topic. Anybody can get up."

"Sounds interesting," Jenn said with a smile.

"Sometimes it's really interesting," Sister Ball interjected. "You might hear travelogues or about somebody's operation. You just never know."

She looked faintly worried. "But you know, Jenn, people will say what they feel is important to them, and I suppose that's all right."

They reached the door of the church, opened it, and joined the people who were milling around in the foyer. Bishop Caldwell spotted the two missionaries and smiled his way through the congregation. When he saw Jenn, a flicker of recognition crossed his face. "Well, it's good to see you again," he said, giving her hand a vigorous pumping. "And always good to have the full-time missionaries with us."

"It's our pleasure to be here," Sister Ball said. They walked into the chapel and selected an empty row on the right side of the room. At that moment the organist began playing the prelude music, and people filtered into their seats. Bishop Caldwell and two other men sat on the stand. After about five minutes of music, the man on Bishop Caldwell's right stood up and moved to the pulpit. He introduced himself as Brother Sorenson, first counselor in the bishopric. Sacrament meeting progressed much as it had the previous month when Jenn attended. But after the sacrament had been passed, Brother Sorenson stood again.

"My dear brothers and sisters," he began. "A week ago I realized that I'd be conducting this week, and my mind has wandered all week as I've contemplated what I might say. With the holidays nearly upon us, especially Thanksgiving, I thought I might tell you some of the things I'm thankful for." He paused momentarily and then continued, "I'm so thankful for you good people. We've served in the bishopric for just over a year and have felt your support in all we've tried to do. I need to express thanks for my wife and our four wonderful children. Isn't that what this is all about? Families?"

Jenn craned her neck to see if she could spot Brother Sorenson's family, but no one seemed to be moving any more than usual. She focused on what Brother Sorenson was saying.

"Most of all I'm thankful for a loving Heavenly Father who recognizes you and me and has provided a way through his Son, Jesus Christ, to have our sins remitted so that we can return to him. I express my love and thankfulness to our brother, Jesus Christ, who gave his all in the Garden of Gethsemane and on the cross on Golgotha and was resurrected on that first Easter morning." He then bore testimony of the reality of the resurrection and closed his short talk.

Jenn sat stunned. There was little formal experience in her life as far as religion was concerned, but what little she had absorbed as a child was much different from what she had just heard. The Father and the Son were two different individuals. Of course! Sister Ball had talked about two personages when she'd told her the story of Joseph Smith and his experience in the grove. How could she have missed that? It made sense, but it was all so new.

A small child had made her way to the stand, and the other counselor apparently pulled out a little platform that the girl stood on. "I want to bear my testimony," the little girl began in a singsong voice. "I know the Church is true. I love my mom and dad. In the name of Jesus Christ, amen." She bounced down from the stand.

How can you know the Church is true? Jenn wondered, just as a tall, wrinkled man made his way to the pulpit. He had a coal-black fringe of hair that circled the back of his head. His shirt collar seemed several sizes too large for his neck and its protruding Adam's apple. The man's hands seemed extremely large, and his fingers wrapped completely around the edge of the pulpit. He reached up with one skeletal hand and adjusted the microphone.

"My brothers and sisters," he began. Jenn watched in fascination as his Adam's apple bobbed up and down. "It has been some time since I've taken your time to bear my testimony." He reached for a Kleenex from a box at the side of the podium. "My dear Anna passed away just over six months ago. It was a very trying time for all of us. Although we sorrowed to see her suffering, we still hated to say good-bye. Our daughter, Jean, whom many of you older members of the ward might remember, was especially distraught. She and her mother had some fairly heated disagreements and had grown apart over the years. I suspect that when we realize how fragile our lives are, we begin to see things in a new light. Anyway, Jean did not want to see her mother go until the two of them had smoothed over their differences. I called upon the Lord and asked him what he would have us do and received the answer that all would be well and that it was time for Anna to go home." He paused and wiped his eyes with the Kleenex.

Jenn felt a strange empathy with the man who was speaking. She noticed how quiet the room had become. The only noise was a baby who was sniffling a little. The man continued, "I can't thank the people of this ward enough. You brought comfort to me and my family at this time of need. I especially want to thank Bishop Caldwell for all he did in helping us arrange the funeral and the myriad other things that accompany such an event. But now I must turn to the reason I came to the pulpit today. Anna and I were so close that having her depart was almost like losing one of my arms or legs. I kept asking the Lord, 'Why?' or more specifically, 'Why me?' Unfortunately, I was so soaked in grief I didn't take time to listen to the answer." He wiped his cheeks again. "When I finally quit feeling sorry for myself and listened, really listened, for an answer, it came, and with it came peace in my life. I suppose most of you have experienced that feeling of complete and infinite peace. If you have not, I suspect I cannot describe it adequately."

Jenn felt a shiver go through her body. *I've experienced that peace,* she thought. Inexplicably, she began to cry silently. The man who was speaking continued for a few more minutes before he sat down. Jenn's thoughts were drawn inward as the rest of the meeting progressed. When the meeting ended, she continued to sit in the pew with her head bent slightly until Sister Ball said softly, "Would you like to stay for Sunday School?"

Jenn wiped her eyes and nodded her head at the same time. "I think I would," she whispered.

The two missionaries walked with her out of the chapel and down the hallway. "They have a Gospel Essentials class in the Relief Society room," Sister Snow said. Jenn nodded and followed the two women into the class. When church ended she walked home with the two missionaries. They left her at her door and promised to return later that afternoon. Jenn climbed the creaking stairs, pulled on the sagging screen door, and opened the front door. The odor of stale tobacco swirled around her. Although she had lived with it her entire life and had become so accustomed to it that it barely registered, today it seemed offensive in contrast to the fresh fall day outside. Her mother was in the kitchen fixing dinner.

"So, how was church?" her mother asked.

"Nice," Jenn replied. "Real nice."

"Them missionary girls coming over again?"

"Yes," Jenn said, "after dinner."

Her mother sighed. "Jenn, I warned you 'bout them Mormons. Next thing you know they're gonna want to marry you to some old guy with a dozen wives. I don't want you gettin' mixed up with them, ya hear?"

"Mom, a man spoke in church today about when his wife died. He didn't talk about any other wives." She realized she was sounding defensive.

"You mark my words, he's got 'em hidden somewhere."

"If you say so, Mom." She walked down the hallway to her bedroom, amazed at how quickly the good feelings of the morning could dissipate. *Faster than fog on a sunny morning,* she thought. She curled up on her bed and read from the Book of Mormon until her mother called her to dinner.

"Where's Damon?" Jenn asked as she sat down across the table from her mother.

"How should I know? He comes and goes without ever tellin' me anything," she said disgustedly. "You runnin' around with them Mormons and him runnin' with who knows who. You're gonna be the death of me yet."

They ate in silence, and just as dinner ended and Jenn was clearing the dishes from the table, Damon slipped through the back door. He looked furtively out the window before sitting down at the table. "Anything left?" he queried.

"Where you been?" his mother growled.

"Out," he replied as he stole another glance over his shoulder.

"Out," she mimicked. "Out, out, out." She shook her head and marched out of the kitchen. Jenn ladled some soup into a bowl and handed it to her brother. She put a couple of slices of bread on a plate and set it in front of him.

The phone rang, and Damon nearly jumped out of his skin. "Don't answer it," he hissed.

"Why not?" Jenn asked as she reached for the phone. "Hello," she said as she glanced at her brother. "Oh, hi, Rolayne." Damon exhaled and sank back into his chair. He watched as Jenn twirled the phone cord around her finger. "I don't think so," she finally said. "I'm busy this afternoon." Her face had become expressionless. "Ro, I just need some time."

She listened again for several minutes before saying, "I'd rather not get into that. Someday I might tell you what really happened." The voice on the other end of the line rose in pitch. Damon watched the color rise in his sister's face until she turned and hung the phone up without so much as a good-bye.

"What's goin' on?" he asked.

"Nothing," Jenn replied. "Rolayne invited me over to her house this afternoon, and I have other plans." Her voice was icy.

"Sis, what happened?"

Jenn stared at her brother. "Damon, sometimes your friends aren't who they say they are." She continued to clear away the dishes. "Sometimes you just have to move on."

TWENTY~FOUR

Sister Ball and Sister Snow arrived promptly for their appointment. Jenn's mother swiftly retreated to her room while Jenn met with the two women. Unlike the previous week, Jenn had a multitude of questions to ask them, and the lesson lasted for over an hour. Finally Sister Snow said, "I'm sorry we have to leave, Jenn, but we have another appointment."

"I'm sorry. I've kept you too long," she said.

"Not at all," Sister Snow replied. "Could we have a word of prayer before we leave?"

"Of course," Jenn replied.

"Would you like to lead us?" Sister Ball asked.

Jenn took a deep breath. "If you'll help me."

Sister Ball smiled, "Of course. It really is easy." She explained to Jenn the format for prayer and then said, "Would you like to kneel?" The three women knelt down next to the couch. Jenn felt mildly embarrassed by the shabbiness of the cushions and the unmistakable odor of tobacco and ammonia. The two sister missionaries waited patiently for Jenn to begin. Eventually, she said a short prayer, and after everyone said, "Amen," they rose to their feet.

"That was wonderful," Sister Ball said.

"I've never done that before," Jenn said. "I can't explain the feeling that came over me."

The two missionaries walked toward the front door. "Next week? Same time?" Sister Snow asked. Jenn nodded her head. "Would you like us to pick you up for church?" Sister Snow continued. Jenn nodded again.

"I'd like that," she said softly.

Sister Ball paused with her hand on the doorknob. "I'd like to challenge you to do something, Jenn. Pray every morning and every night. Can you do that?"

Jenn nodded her head again. "I think so," she replied.

"You know our Father in Heaven and his Son won't go where they're not invited," Sister Ball said with a smile. "Invite them into your life." She pulled the door open. "See you next Sunday."

Jenn watched them leave and then sank into the rocking chair. She pondered the feelings she had had that day. She was startled from her reverie by the sound of Damon clearing his throat in the kitchen. "Damon, is that you?"

He scraped the leg of the chair over the floor. "It's me."

"Have you been there the whole time?" she asked.

"So what if I have," he snarled. "Still a buncha crap." He walked into the living room. "But that Sister Snow is kinda cute. Too bad she's so old." He turned and stomped out the back door.

The next two weeks crawled by at school as Jenn waited for confirmation from Utah State University. Miss Hardy told her to be patient, that there was no rush, and that USU was processing lots of scholarship requests. Jenn had assumed that the notification would come to the school and was surprised when the Saturday after Thanksgiving a letter from USU appeared in her mailbox. She tore it open with trembling hands and found that she had been accepted and was being offered the scholarship Miss Hardy had outlined weeks before. She read the letter carefully and found that school began on August 18 and that she needed to be there the week before for orientation. *That's earlier than I'd thought.* A letter of acceptance was included, along with a self-addressed, stamped envelope. She carried the letter with her to the diner and showed it to Lorna.

"I'm proud of you," Lorna said. "This is a great opportunity for you, dear. Although it's going to be hard to replace you here." She gave Jenn a hug and said, "Incidentally, Shelly's sick again. Can you cover her tables tonight?"

"Sure," Jenn said with a smile. "What's wrong with Shelly?"

Lorna rubbed her chin with her hand. "I'm not sure, but I think she's pregnant."

"Oh," Jenn said. "She's only sixteen."

"Yes, she is," Lorna answered. "Unfortunately, that doesn't keep you from getting pregnant."

"I guess it doesn't," Jenn replied as she pushed through the double doors to get her apron. The shift went quickly because she was covering twice as many tables as she usually did. They were amazingly busy for the beginning of the holiday season. It was obvious that many of their customers had been Christmas shopping and were stopping to get something to eat before heading home. Their normal closing hour approached, and still the restaurant was filled with customers. Half a dozen people were waiting to be seated. It was nearly eleven o'clock before Lorna turned out the lights and locked the doors.

"Here's your cut," she said, handing a fistful of bills to Jenn. "It was a busy night, but this might make it worth it to you."

"Thanks," Jenn said, as she pulled on her jacket. "I've been thinking about Shelly all night. What's she going to do?"

"Beats me. I guess she'll work here as long as she can, and then she'll have the baby." Although Lorna tried to sound nonchalant, it was clear she was worried about the girl.

"Who's the father?" Jenn asked. "I mean, she isn't married or anything, is she?"

"I don't know," Lorna said as she wiped off the counter in front of her, "You know I don't pry into your lives very much." She wiped more vigorously. "I don't know, Jenn. It's funny how one single action can determine the path you take for the rest of your life. Here you are going away to college next summer with a future that looks awfully bright to a poor old woman like me; and here's Shelly, who'll probably struggle all of her life. And all because of a decision she made." She smiled bravely at Jenn. "I'm proud of you, dear. You'll do great things with your life." She rolled up the towel in her hands and swatted Jenn's behind. "Now get out of here and go home before it gets any later."

Jenn stuffed the scholarship letter and cash into her pocket, along with her hands and began walking home. "Choices," she said out loud. "It would be wonderful if we could look into the future and see what our choices will do to our lives." The night had grown cold, and she tugged her jacket around her. Most of the homes along her route were completely dark; only the street lights gave some relief. When she was two blocks from home, a black Chevrolet drew up alongside her and the passenger window rolled down.

"Want a ride? It's pretty cold," Charlie said.

A spark of panic flickered in Jenn's stomach. "No, thank you," she said as coldly as the weather.

"It's warm in here," Charlie said with a curled lip.

The light changed, and Jenn began to walk across the street. The Chevrolet flanked her as she sped up her pace. Vainly, she searched for a house that was still lighted. She was practically running, thankful she was wearing tennis shoes. The car kept pace with her, and Charlie kept inviting her to get into the car. She ignored him as best she could. They were one block from home. Her breath was ragged, and she was tiring. *Please, Lord, I need help,* she screamed in her mind.

Just as the Chevrolet pulled to the curb and the door opened, a Ford swerved around the corner on squealing tires. Charlie looked back quickly over his shoulder, slammed the door, and gunned the car away from the curb. The Ford pulled alongside the Chevrolet, and a gun barrel extended from the back window as both cars raced down the street and out of sight. Jenn's legs felt as if they were made of rubber, and she practically sank to the ground. But summoning all of her strength, she made it to her house and into her bedroom. She sank numbly onto her bed and began to sob. She was still there the next morning when feeble sunlight crept across her blanket and into her face. She awoke with a start and relived the terror of the night before. She forced herself out of bed. She bathed and dressed for church before preparing breakfast. Neither her mother nor brother stirred before she let herself out the front door and met the two missionaries for the walk to church.

"Did you have a rough night?" Sister Snow asked.

"Why?" Jenn replied.

"You look sort of . . . " Sister Snow struggled for the right word.

"Sort of tired," her companion suggested.

Jenn lowered her head. "It was a long, hard night," was all she said. Then, trying to change the subject, she asked, "Did you have a good Thanksgiving?"

"Too good," Sister Ball replied. "We were invited to three homes for dinner, and we had to eat at every one of them." She chuckled. "Sister Snow and I won't have to eat for a week." She rubbed her stomach. "How was yours?"

Jenn thought of the meager dinner she and her family had eaten. There was little to suggest it was a holiday. "It was okay, I guess." *I'm glad you weren't eating at our house.*

When church ended, Jenn left the two missionaries and walked home by herself. She fixed dinner for her family and then waited for the missionaries to arrive. She looked forward to the discussion with the two young women more than she had ever imagined and practically ran to the door to let them in when they knocked.

The hour flew by, and Jenn noticed Sister Snow was glancing at her watch. "We hate to leave, Jenn. You'd think we'd get smarter and spread out our appointments a little further," she said. "Have you thought about our challenge to you to be baptized?"

"Yes, I have," she said timidly. "But I haven't talked it over with my mother. I'll do that before next Sunday, I promise."

Sister Snow nodded her head. "We'll be excited to hear your answer." They knelt in prayer, and as they arose Sister Ball said, "Jenn, I have the feeling something is troubling you. Is there anything we can do to help? Any questions we can answer?"

Jenn twisted her fingers together. "I'm all right," she said. "I just had a little problem last night, but there's nothing you can do to help."

"Oh?" she waited expectantly.

"Just a field I have to burn," she said.

The two missionaries were about to leave when Sister Ball said, "You know, God moves in a mysterious way, sometimes."

Jenn nodded her head. "Yes, He does."

They closed the front door behind them, and Jenn sank into her usual place in the rocking chair and thought about what she'd been taught. "God moves in a mysterious way," she said out loud.

From the kitchen Damon said, "Yeah, sometimes he drives a Ford."

"What?" Jenn said, alarmed. "What did you say?"

"Nothin'." Damon walked through the front room and toward the front door. "I don' think Charlie and Miles are gonna bother you anymore. I think they got the message." He pulled the door shut behind him.

TWENTY~FIVE

"*Mom, we need* to talk." Jenn was sitting at the kitchen table with her schoolbooks scattered on top of it. All the time she had been doing her homework she had been mustering up courage to talk with her mother about joining the Mormon Church.

Her mother was sitting in the rocking chair watching television. "Is it too important to let me finish my show?" she asked acidly.

"No, Mom, finish watching TV." She packed her books and papers into her backpack, walked into the living room, and sat on the couch. Absently she worked her hand back and forth over its arm. She stared at the screen, but her mind wasn't registering the program as she rehearsed again in her mind how she was going to broach the subject with her mother. She could feel her shoulders tightening, so she took a deep breath, held it for a few seconds, and then exhaled.

The television program ended. "Now, what do we need to talk about?"

her mother asked as she blew a cloud of smoke from her lips and then rocked in the chair.

Jenn cleared her throat and said, "Mom, you know I've been going to church for a few weeks with the missionaries, and they've been teaching me. "

"Waste of time," her mother interrupted.

"Yes . . . well, no, really. I mean, Mom, I've decided I want to be baptized and join their church." Silence hung palpably in the room until her mother got up without a word and started to leave.

"Jenn," she said coldly, "I've warned you 'bout them Mormons. But you never listen to me anyhow. Just don't 'spect me to have anything to do with your church, you hear?"

"Does that mean I can get baptized?" Jenn called after her as she shuffled down the hallway.

"Don't you always do what you want, anyway?" her mother asked.

Tears of joy mixed with tears of frustration coursed down her cheeks as she sat on the well-worn couch. *Why does it have to be so hard?* She wondered. She waited until her mother had finished in the bathroom and gone to bed before making her way down the hallway. Once she was in her room, she knelt and offered a prayer of thanks and asked what would happen to her family if she took this momentous step. Again a feeling of peace began at her toes and moved upward as if she were being enveloped in a warm blanket. She climbed into bed and fell into an untroubled sleep.

The week sped by, and Jenn could hardly wait until Sunday morning. She and her mother had spoken little during the week, and she had not spoken at all to Damon about her decision. As she ran down the steps to meet the missionaries, she bubbled over. "Yes, sisters, I can get baptized," she said in greeting. They both hugged her.

"I knew you'd make the right decision," Sister Ball said. "We're overjoyed."

"When?" Jenn asked.

"I'm sure we can finish the discussions in the next couple of weeks so you're ready."

"Before Christmas, then?"

"I'm sure that can be worked out," Sister Snow said. "I'm excited for you."

"So am I," Jenn said with a smile. "This is the best present I've ever received."

That afternoon the missionaries taught Jenn the principle of tithing and talked about the atonement and repentance. "Mom said you'd want all my money," she teased.

"Nope," Sister Ball responded, "just 10 percent. And it really isn't yours to begin with, you know. You're just the Lord's steward."

"I'm not serious, Sister Ball. Tell me who I pay my tithing to."

"Well, you'll pay it to the bishop," she said. "Next Sunday I'll show you where the tithing envelopes are."

Jenn nodded her head. "That seems pretty simple." She paused. "Now repentance doesn't seem as simple, or maybe it seems too simple."

Sister Snow opened her scriptures. "It says here in the Doctrine and Covenants, 'By this ye may know if a man repenteth of his sins—behold, he will confess them and forsake them.'"

"That seems too easy," Jenn said. "Just confess them—to whom?"

"Ah, that may be the difficult part. Many people feel you just have to confess them to the Lord or to the bishop, but I've always felt you had to confess them to the person you've offended as well."

Jenn sank back in the rocking chair deep in thought. "I suppose that makes sense."

"You seem troubled," Sister Ball said with concern. "Is there some major problem we haven't discussed?"

Jenn shook her head, "No, not really. I was just thinking of the things I've done in my life that I need to take care of." She rocked silently for a moment or two. "What else do you have to do beside confess?"

Sister Snow glanced at Sister Ball, "Well, true repentance means you truly want to stop doing whatever you're doing that's wrong; that, as much as possible, you restore whatever you've done; and that you cast off the burden of the sin in your own mind."

"Is there something you've done, Jenn, that is troubling you?" Sister Ball asked again.

Jenn wrung her hands together. "Nothing really terrible," she whispered. "It's just that I've never really thought about the sins in my life. I really haven't thought I was sinning at all, and now I realize I was." Tears sprang to her eyes. "I have a lot of repenting to do, I'm afraid."

Sister Ball pushed herself up from the couch and knelt at the side of the rocking chair. "Jenn, that is what the Savior did for us. He allows us to repent and be washed clean from our sins through his sacrifice."

Jenn nodded her head. "I guess I just have to do what I can do to repair what I've done before I can feel worthy."

Sister Ball put her arm around Jenn's shoulders and hugged her. "That's what will prepare you for baptism." She stood, extended her hand to Sister Snow and pulled her to her feet. "With you working on Saturdays, we've scheduled the baptism after church on the twenty-first. Is that all right with you?"

"My birthday," Jenn sniffled.

"Really? That will make it doubly special." She and Sister Snow knelt by the couch, and Jenn joined them. "Would you mind if I said the prayer?" Sister Ball asked. Jenn nodded in agreement.

Sister Ball offered a prayer in which she asked Heavenly Father to bless Jenn that she might know what she had to do to feel worthy for baptism, and she expressed how much she and Sister Snow had learned to love Jenn. When she had finished, the three women knelt together for a moment before getting to their feet.

"You'll be fine, Jenn," Sister Ball said as she and her companion prepared to leave.

Jenn watched them walk down the sidewalk in the gathering dusk and then sat back down in the rocking chair. She did not turn on a lamp but preferred to rock in the darkness with her thoughts.

"It's a good thing I don' believe all that crap," Damon said from the kitchen, "or I'd have a whole dump truck of stuff I'd have to repent of." Before Jenn could respond, she heard the back door close.

The night surrounded her before she made her way to her bedroom. She knelt down by her bed and poured out her soul to her Father in Heaven. Then she pulled open her dresser drawer and removed the contents from their hiding place.

Buried deep was a small laminated picture of a woman and a driver's license. Jenn placed them on the bedspread and added a hundred-dollar bill. She replaced the rest of her money and then, just before replacing the drawer, removed another twenty-dollar bill. She returned to the kitchen and found an envelope and sheet of paper in a drawer. She sat down at the table and began to write.

Mr. Randall Grant
543 Pine Street
Ten Sleep, Wyoming

Dear Mr. Grant,
About two years ago you ate dinner in a cafe in California. When you left, you dropped your wallet. I found it and have been trying to return it to you . . .

Jenn suddenly realized she was trying to cover up what she had done. She crumpled the paper in her hand and started to throw it in the trash can but realized her mother might find it. She stuffed it into her backpack, took out another sheet of paper, and began again.

Mr. Randall Grant
543 Pine Street
Ten Sleep, Wyoming

Dear Mr. Grant,
A few years ago you stopped at a diner in California. When you left, your wallet fell out of your pocket. I was working in the diner that day and found your wallet. I am ashamed to say that I did not return it to you immediately. Instead, I kept the contents. There was forty-two dollars in the wallet, along with your driver's license and a picture. Afraid of being caught, I discarded the wallet but kept the contents. I am now trying to make amends for my action.
Enclosed are your driver's license, the picture, and a hundred dollars that I hope will replace the missing money and provide enough to purchase a new wallet. I am very sorry for my action and any problems it may have caused you.
Please accept my apology.

The pen wavered over the paper for a moment as Jenn decided whether to sign the letter. Then, with a sigh, she wrote her name and address. She folded the letter around the driver's license, picture, and money, and then inserted it into the envelope. Just as she was about to seal it, a thought crossed her mind: *What if they don't live there anymore? Maybe they were*

135

moving when they stopped here. She wavered for a moment and then went to the telephone and dialed information.

"Which city," the disembodied voice requested.

"Ten Sleep, Wyoming," Jenn whispered into the phone.

"One moment." There was a buzz followed by a couple of clicks and then the voice said, "And the name?"

"Grant, Randall Grant," Jenn said.

An electronic voice began to recite a phone number. Jenn hung up and sealed the envelope. The next morning on the way to school she dropped it into a mailbox. That afternoon on her way home from school she walked into the little corner grocery store. It had changed little over the years. Jenn could still see the cooler in the back corner, and a teenager was still behind the counter. He looked vaguely familiar, and Jenn realized he often was at work when she purchased groceries.

She approached him and said, "When I was a little girl . . . " The boy seemed totally uninterested in what she was saying. "I used to come here to shop. Well, I still do sometimes." The boy behind the counter stifled a yawn.

Jenn looked at her shoes. This was turning out to be harder than writing a letter to someone she'd never see again. "What I'm trying to say is that sometimes I shoplifted a candy bar." The boy's eyes flew open. "And I want to make up for it." She pulled the twenty-dollar bill from her pocket and placed it on the counter. "I don't really know how many candy bars I stole, but I'm sure this will pay for them."

"You're kidding, right?" The boy was looking at her with a look of befuddlement on his face.

"No, I'm serious. Please take the money." She felt completely at a loss as to what to say next. Finally, she squeaked out, "And please forgive me." She threw the backpack on her shoulder and hurried toward the door. Just as she pushed it open, she glanced back and saw the boy pocket the twenty-dollar bill. Jenn's heart sank and she began to turn around when a thought popped into her head. *That's his problem now, not yours.* She smiled and hurried home to change her clothes and get to the diner.

The following day she left the high school as quickly as possible and walked briskly to the elementary school she'd attended. She'd forgotten that high school got out nearly an hour before Sierra Vista Elementary, and she worried she'd be late to work. She wandered down the hallway to where Miss Crawford's room had been and looked at the name plate at the side of the door. Amazingly, Miss Crawford still taught there. Jenn opened the door timidly and looked into the room. The children were sitting on the floor while Miss Crawford read to them. She looked up as Jenn peered into the room and then beckoned to her to come in. All of the children's faces turned to see who had interrupted their teacher.

"May I help you?" Miss Crawford said.

"I . . . I just wanted to talk to you for a minute," Jenn stammered. "You probably don't remember me. Jennica Cooper."

A flash of recognition sparked in Miss Crawford's eyes. She said to her students, "This young lady used to be a student of mine." She beamed at Jenn. "She was one of my favorites." She struggled to her feet from the undersized chair. "You children keep reading while I talk to Jennica." She led Jenn to her desk and asked her to sit down. "What brings you here?" she asked.

Jenn swallowed. "It's kind of hard, Miss Crawford." She looked over her shoulder at the children, who were busy reading. "When I was in your class I cheated on some of my work," she began. Miss Crawford's eyes opened in astonishment. "I think you knew that, but I just had to come and tell you I'm sorry."

Miss Crawford pushed a strand of hair from her forehead and then patted the back of Jenn's hand. "I think I'd forgotten that," she said. "But this was a very brave thing for you to do." She patted her hand again. "Where are you now?"

"I'm a senior in high school," Jenn said.

"And then what lies ahead for you?" her former teacher asked.

Jenn smiled broadly. "I have a scholarship. I'm going to college."

Miss Crawford clapped her hands. "I always knew you were a bright one, Jennica. Where are you going?"

"Utah State University," Jenn replied. "I'm going to be an engineer."

Miss Crawford smiled. "Good for you, Jennica. I'm excited for you." She turned suddenly to her students. One boy was trying to pull a book away from one of the girls. "Michael," the teacher said sharply, "that is quite enough of that behavior." The boy hung his head.

"I've interrupted you," Jenn said. "I'm sorry, but I just needed to get that off my chest."

"Nonsense," Miss Crawford said. "You've made my day." She led

Jenn to the circle of students on the floor and said, "I told you this was one of my former students. She's graduating from high school this year and going to Utah to college. Isn't that exciting?" The children looked at Jenn, and a few of them clapped their hands.

"I'd better go," she said. "I have to get to work."

Miss Crawford led her to the door. "I'm proud of you. Keep in touch." She opened the door and led Jenn into the hallway. Then she closed the door behind her.

TWENTY~SIX

"I don't know if you've met Elder Johnson before," Sister Snow said. "He's going to interview you about baptism. He'll be coming right after church tomorrow; I hope that's okay?"

"Sure, I guess." Jenn said into the phone.

"You sound a little unsure."

"No, no," Jenn replied, "I guess I just didn't realize anybody else would be involved. I always thought you or Sister Ball would baptize me."

Sister Snow chuckled. "Actually, Jenn, it has to be someone who holds the priesthood. Do you remember when we taught you about Joseph Smith and Oliver Cowdery baptizing each other?"

"Sort of," Jenn said. "I mean, you've taught me so much that sometimes I have a hard time remembering it all."

"You're not alone. Anyway, the person baptizing you has to be at least a priest in the Aaronic Priesthood and the person confirming you a member of the Church has to hold the Melchizedek Priesthood."

"Oh."

"But Elder Johnson will clear all of that up when he interviews you. Are you sure you're okay with meeting with him after church?"

"Sure, I guess. How long will it take?"

"Not very long," Sister Snow replied. "We'll see you tomorrow morning."

After she hung up, Jenn sat on a kitchen chair and finished her Saturday morning breakfast. She felt totally at peace with the decision she had made, and yet she was nervous about the unknown. She held a spoonful of cereal halfway to her lips while she thought about all that had happened in the last couple of months. She was awakened from her reverie by her brother's voice.

"So you're really gonna do it?" He stood in the doorway, leaning against the jamb. He was wearing his usual low-slung shorts and a black T-shirt emblazoned in yellow letters: "Question Authority."

Jenn nearly dropped her spoon. "Yes, I am," she said with a touch of defiance in her voice.

"Hey, don't get yer back up with me," he said, holding both hands with his palms toward her. "I guess you know what you're doin'." He backed through the door and headed to his room.

Jenn watched him go and then began to clean up her breakfast dishes. She inventoried the refrigerator, made a list, and walked to the store. At first she thought she'd walk the several blocks to Albertson's rather than face the embarrassment she felt at the corner market, but then she lifted her chin and walked in. She pushed a cart through the narrow aisles, and when she had found all the items on her list, she went to the checkout stand. The same teenaged clerk who had been there last Monday was standing at the cash register. Jenn removed the items from her cart and placed them on the counter. Without meeting her eyes, the clerk rang up her purchases, bagged them, and told her the total. She gave him the money and he handed back her change, still without looking at her. She thanked him, grabbed her bags, and left the store. *The burden has shifted from my shoulders to his,* she thought as she walked quickly through the chilly December air to her house.

The following morning the two missionaries were practically

bubbling with excitement as they walked with Jenn to church. Jenn had become quite familiar with many of the people who regularly attended, and several greeted her with a handshake and a smile. Bishop Caldwell was conducting.

"Just a reminder, brothers and sisters, that next week will be our annual Christmas program. You might want to be here a little early if you want a good seat. Also, next Sunday will be the last regularly scheduled tithing settlement. The sign-up sheets are on the office door."

Jenn settled into what had become the regular pattern of sacrament meeting for her. Following the block of meetings, Sister Ball and Sister Snow stood with her in the foyer waiting for Elder Johnson. Most of the people had left, except for those who were waiting to meet with the bishop, when two young men entered the building. They spotted Sister Ball and Sister Snow and walked briskly across the foyer.

"Elder Johnson," Sister Ball said as she shook his hand, "this is Jenn Cooper."

He took Jenn's hand in his. "Glad to meet you, Jenn. This is my companion, Elder Mahaloni."

She shook Elder Mahaloni's hand. "I'm glad to meet you."

"Well, let's get started. Is there a room we can use?" Elder Johnson said as his eyes searched for a spot.

"Down here," Sister Ball said as she led them to an empty classroom. "The other ward is in sacrament meeting, and they won't be using this room for another half hour."

While the other missionaries waited outside the room, Elder Johnson entered the room with Jenn and pulled two chairs to the small table at the front of the room. "Please, have a seat," he said.

As Elder Johnson interviewed her for baptism, Jenn answered his questions honestly. When he had finished he said, "Now, is there someone you'd like to have perform the ordinance?" Jenn shrugged her shoulders and shook her head. "My companion and I would be honored if you'd permit us to baptize and confirm you," Elder Johnson said.

"That would be fine," Jenn answered softly. "Could you explain to me a little bit about what will happen? I've never attended a baptism before."

"Oh, sure," Elder Johnson said with a smile as he stood up. "Maybe Sister Ball would like to do that. Elder Mahaloni and I have another appointment we need to get to. Would that be all right?" Jenn nodded her head.

After the two elders had left, Jenn asked, "Where are they from? Do you know?"

"Elder Johnson is from Grand Junction, Colorado, and Elder Mahaloni is from the big island of Hawaii. He's only been out a little while." They could hear people coming down the hallway of the church. "Oops, I think the other ward is coming to use this room. We'll be over to your house in an hour or so. Maybe we could explain what will happen next week when we're there. Would that be all right?"

Jenn nodded her head as the three of them left the room. She hurried home to fix dinner. She had put potatoes in the oven on low heat before she left for church, and she was worried they might have overcooked. They seemed to be all right. She opened a can of corn and warmed it in a saucepan while she braised pork chops in the frying pan.

"What's the celebration?" her mother asked as she was drawn to the kitchen by the aroma of cooking food. "You don't usually go to this much trouble."

"Nothing, Mom. I just thought this sounded good when I was shopping yesterday."

"I'll pay you back when my check gets here," her mother mumbled.

"It's okay, Mom. I live here too. I ought to be contributing."

"Hmph," her mother grumbled. "I s'pose."

Jenn set places for three of them for dinner and then asked her mother, "Is Damon here?"

"I dunno," her mother said. "All he contributes is grief."

Jenn walked down the hallway to his room and found it empty. She sighed and shook her head before returning to the kitchen. Once the chops were cooked, she placed one on her mother's plate and one on hers, forked potatoes out of the oven, and added a spoonful of corn before setting the plate in front of her mother.

"Looks good," her mother said.

Jenn set her own plate on the table and sat down across from her mother. They ate in silence for several minutes, and then her mother said, "You still goin' through with this church thing next week?"

"Yes, Mom."

Her mother picked up the bone from the pork chop and sucked on it while she stared out the window. "Ya know, I ain't had much to do with religion since God took yer dad. I guess I just didn't think it was fair. But I guess if you've found religion, I ain't gonna stand in yer way."

"Thanks, Mom," Jenn said. She was strangely touched by her mother's concession. "Mom, I know you haven't wanted to get involved, but I want you to know you're invited to the baptism next Sunday." She took a deep breath, exhaled, and then said, "In fact, I really hope you'll be there. It's a pretty big step in my life."

Her mother put down the bone and wiped her hand on the side of her house dress. "I'll think about it, toad." She continued to stare wistfully out the window.

Suddenly the back door swung open, and Damon strode into the room. "Smells good," he said jauntily. "What's for dinner?"

Jenn smiled at him. "Have a seat, little brother, and I'll get you some food." She quickly filled a plate and placed it in front of him.

Without a word he began to shove the food into his mouth. "This is real good," he managed to say. "Real good." Not a word was spoken until Damon had finished the meal.

"Damon, yer sister's gettin' baptized next Sunday," his mother said. "She's invited me to come. What about you?"

Damon twirled the fork between his fingers. "Sure, why not?" he said. "Don't suppose it can hurt none." He set the fork down. "'Sides, it's Jenn's birthday. Maybe we can have a party after." A wicked gleam sparkled in his eyes. "I'll bring the booze," he laughed.

"No thanks," Jenn said with a chuckle.

"What's so funny?" their mother asked.

"Nothin'," Damon said. "Just an inside joke."

Jenn was finishing the dishes when there was a knock at the front door. "Damon, would you let the missionaries in?" Jenn called over her shoulder.

"Sure," he said while their mother scurried down the hallway to her room. He opened the door, and Sister Ball stuck out her hand.

"Damon, isn't it?" she said. He nodded his head. "I'm Sister Ball, and this is my companion, Sister Snow."

"Pleased to meet ya,'" Damon mumbled. "Jenn's washin' the dishes."

"Thank you," said Sister Ball. The two missionaries moved to their accustomed seats on the couch while Damon retreated to the kitchen. Jenn appeared a moment later, wiping her hands on a dish towel. Both missionaries started to get to their feet when Jenn waved them back onto the couch.

An hour later they rose to leave, having answered Jenn's questions about the baptism. Both of them seemed pleased and surprised that both her mother and Damon would probably attend the service. Sister Snow reached for the doorknob as Sister Ball said, "The timing on this couldn't be better, Jenn."

"You mean, my birthday?" she said.

"That too," replied Sister Snow. "But a week from tomorrow is transfer day and Sister Ball and I might get moved. We're just glad to be here for your baptism."

Jenn felt as if she'd been punched in the stomach. "You mean, you both are leaving?"

"Maybe," Sister Ball said with a smile. "Who knows, we might be around for another six weeks."

Jenn remembered the loss she had felt when Sister Lingfelter had been transferred, but it was nothing like the despair she was feeling over the loss of these two good women. Tears began to stream down her cheeks. "I don't want you to go," she sniffled.

"Well, maybe we won't," Sister Ball said fighting back tears of her own. "The important thing is, we'll be here next Sunday."

TWENTY~SEVEN

The letter arrived the following Thursday, one week before Christmas. Jenn pulled the mail from the mailbox and hurried into the house to change before going to work. Usually all they received were bills and junk mail, so the white envelope stood out. Jenn glanced at is as she tossed the mail onto the kitchen table. The return address stopped her in midstride: *Lingfelter.* Jenn plucked the envelope from the pile of mail and ripped it open. Inside was a letter from Sister Lingfelter.

Dear Jenn,

As you probably know, I've finished my mission and I'm home in Providence. I always felt as if we dropped the ball with you. You seemed so genuine, and yet Sister Sandberg and I were a little nervous about pushing you too hard. Now that I think about it, I think we were just afraid we might scare you away, but we could see such potential in you. I hope you will

give the missionaries a chance to explain the gospel to you.
All my love,
Alicia Lingfelter

Jenn folded the single sheet of paper and replaced it in the envelope. Then she carried it to her bedroom and placed it next to the Book of Mormon. She glanced at the clock and realized she needed to hurry or she'd be late for work. *I'll write her a letter tonight,* she thought with a smile on her face. *Will she ever be surprised!*

Shelly was sick again, however, and Jenn was late getting home from work. She quickly completed a homework assignment before falling asleep. The next morning she struggled to stay awake in her math class, and the rest of the day seemed to drag on slowly. Ten minutes before the end of school, she was summoned to Miss Hardy's office. She sat on the red vinyl chair with her backpack at her feet, leaned her head against the wall, and closed her eyes just as Miss Hardy opened her office door and called her name. "Jenn, please come in."

Jenn hoisted her backpack to her hip and followed Miss Hardy into her office. She set the backpack on one chair and sank into the other one.

"You seem tired, dear," the counselor said. "Is everything going all right for you?"

Jenn forced a smile to her face. "Yes, yes it is, Miss Hardy. I was just up late last night. We were busy at the restaurant, and one of the other girls didn't come in." She yawned behind her hand. "But I'm fine."

Miss Hardy swiveled on her chair and selected a manila envelope from the credenza behind her desk. "I thought you might want to start thinking about housing," she said as she swiveled back and handed Jenn the envelope. "This is the information about on-campus living. I thought you and your mother might want to go over it during the holidays. If you decide you're going to live on campus, you'll need to get an application sent in right after the first of the year; it fills up fast."

"How much is it going to cost?" Jenn said, slightly alarmed.

Miss Hardy opened the envelope and withdrew the papers from inside. She skimmed through a couple of them before her finger stopped partway down the page. "The prices vary depending upon how many of you share an apartment. But it looks like it will cost around three hundred dollars a month."

"That's a lot of money," Jenn swallowed.

Miss Hardy replaced the papers in the envelope. "Jenn, there are a number of solutions. As I said last month, there are jobs on campus that help defray the costs of going to school, and I'm sure you are eligible for a Pell Grant or other student loans." She saw the look of confusion on the girl's face. "What I'm trying to say is, don't worry about it. We'll find a way to handle your expenses. Okay?"

Jenn shook her head numbly, took the envelope, and stuffed it in her backpack. She could feel mild panic building within her. *I'm not sure I can do this,* she thought. When she shouldered her backpack, she saw Miss Hardy studying her face. "I'll take a look at this," she said meekly.

"Why don't we plan on spending some time together after the holidays? Then if you have questions, perhaps I can answer them," she said with a smile. "You're going to be fine, Jenn."

"I hope so," she said as she headed out of the office.

The next day Jenn was cleaning up the breakfast dishes when there was a knock on the door. Jenn answered it and saw two missionaries standing in the cool grayness of the morning. Sister Ball had a garment bag lying over her arm.

"We brought a baptism dress for you to try on," she said. "To make sure it's the right size." They stepped into the living room, and Sister Snow helped her companion remove the dress from its protective bag. "Would you go try this on?" Sister Ball asked.

Jenn took the gleaming white dress from her outstretched arms and hurried to her room. A few minutes later she walked back into the living room wearing the spotless garment.

"It looks just right," Sister Snow said. "Would you like to bring it to the church, or would you like Sister Ball and me to bring it?"

"Maybe it would be easier if the two of you brought it—if that's okay?"

"No problem. We'll have it hanging in the dressing room by the baptismal font right after church. We'll have towels as well, but you might want to bring dry underwear," she said with a smile. "We're so happy for you," she concluded.

Jenn retreated to her bedroom and emerged a few minutes later with the white dress. The two missionaries carefully placed it inside the garment bag.

"We'll see you tomorrow," Sister Ball said brightly.

"Okay," Jenn said with a beaming smile. She let the two women out the door and then turned back toward the kitchen.

"You look good in white," her brother said.

"You startled me! I didn't see you," she said catching her breath.

"Sorry." Damon inspected his hands for some time before continuing, "I'm proud of you. You seem different—real happy."

"I am," she replied. "This is the best thing that's ever happened to me."

Damon absently rubbed his right eyebrow. "Yeah, well, I gotta go." He grabbed his jacket from the back of the kitchen chair, pulled it around his shoulders, and headed out the back door. Jenn watched him slip through the hedge at the back of their property. Most of the leaves had fallen, and she could see him continue around the neighbor's house and onto the street. Without warning, tears sprang to her eyes. *Be careful, little brother.*

A few minutes later she found herself walking briskly toward the corner market. *Tomorrow's my birthday. I'm going to celebrate.* She pushed open the door of the little store, took hold of one of the wobbly-wheeled carts, and began filling it with items from her shopping list. She included a cake mix and a can of frosting and, in a moment of whimsy, grabbed a box of birthday candles. When she approached the checkout counter, she noticed the same familiar clerk. "Good morning," she said cheerfully.

"Good morning," he mumbled. He glanced at her over the top of his glasses but would not meet her eyes.

At least my slate is clean, she thought. *I wonder if I showed my guilt the way he does?* When she had paid for her groceries, she hung the half-dozen plastic bags from her fingers and started home. By the time she reached the front door her fingers were numb from the weight of her purchases. She went quickly to the kitchen and put away the groceries. Then she opened the cake mix and prepared to mix and bake it. She hummed softly as she went about her task. Before she left for work she iced the cake and stuck eighteen candles in it. *Tomorrow we'll celebrate!*

Wind was whipping around her legs as she walked to the diner. Drops of rain began spattering against the sidewalk as she walked inside. Throughout her shift the clouds thickened and the rain increased in intensity. There were few customers, and at nine o'clock Lorna said, "I think we might as well close early."

Jenn went to the back room, hung up her apron, and put on her coat. The rain was pounding on the roof of the restaurant, and a steady stream was shooting out of the downspout near the back door. She walked back through the swinging doors and peered through the front window at the torrential rain. The street lamp on the corner was barely visible, and the gutters were beginning to overflow. "I think I'm going to wait a minute and see if this lets up," she said as she slid into a corner booth where she could watch the rain.

"If it don't, I'll give you two a ride home," Lorna said.

"Thanks," Jenn said. Shelly, the waitress for whom Jenn had often covered, slid into the booth across from her. "How are you feeling, Shelly?" Jenn asked.

"You know," she said with a toss of her head. "Good as can be expected."

"When are you due?"

"February 3," she said. She traced the pattern in the Formica tabletop with her finger. Suddenly, her shoulders heaved, and she began to sob. "Then what do I do? My mom and dad won't even talk to me. I don't know how I'm going to take care of a baby."

"Won't the father help?" Jenn asked.

Shelly shook her head vigorously. "No," she wailed. "He don't want to have nothing to do with the baby—or me," she cried. "This is what hell must be like," she said as she laid her head on her arms.

Tell her about adoption. The thought popped into Jenn's mind but she shook it off. The thought came again, more forcefully. *Tell her about adoption!* Jenn shook her head. *I don't know anything about adoption,* she thought. *Lord, I need help so I can help this girl,* she prayed. *Please help me.*

Lorna began to turn off the lights when there was a knocking on the door. "Tell him we're closed," she nodded to Jenn.

"Okay," Jenn said. She walked across the diner to the front door and saw Bishop Caldwell and his wife standing there in the rain. Quickly she unlocked the door and let them into the diner. "Hello, Bishop," she said. She glanced over her shoulder at Lorna, who was shaking her head. "We closed early," she apologized.

"Oh, we didn't come to eat," he said. "We just saw you through the window and thought you might need a ride home. It ain't a fit night out for man nor beast," he said dramatically. "Big day tomorrow."

"Yes, it is," she said with a smile. Just then she heard Shelly sobbing in the corner.

"Is something wrong with your friend?" Sister Caldwell asked.

Jenn nodded her head, "Yeah. But nothing I can help her with," she said.

"Would she like a ride home, too?" Bishop Caldwell asked. "We have our van and there's plenty of room."

"I'll see." Jenn walked back to the booth where Shelly sat crying. "Want a ride home?" Shelly seemed oblivious to what was going on around her and sat red-eyed at the table. "Come on," Jenn said, helping Shelly to her feet. "At least you won't get soaked in the rain."

"You sure this is all right?" Lorna called from behind the cash register.

"It's fine," Jenn said. "These people are friends of mine." She pulled Shelly's light coat around her and followed the Caldwells to their van. Lorna relocked the door behind them.

Once they were safely out of the rain the bishop asked, "Where to?" and Shelly choked out her address.

The windshield wipers could barely keep up with the rain that beat like a snare drum against the van. The wind rocked it with bursts of breath that made Bishop Caldwell hang on to the steering wheel so hard his knuckles showed white against the blue-green light of the dashboard. Jenn put her arm around Shelly's shoulders and tried to console her as they splashed through the night.

Sister Caldwell turned in her seat as much as the seat belt permitted, "What is wrong, dear? Is there something we can help with?"

Shelly continued to sob noisily. "She's expecting a baby in a couple of months and she's afraid," Jenn said, fearful that she might alienate Shelly if she said more.

"I see," Sister Caldwell said softly. They drove on without speaking while the rain and wind whipped the van. "Is the father around?" Sister Caldwell inquired.

Shelly shook her head. "No," she wailed.

They drove on silently until the van slowed up in front of a house. "Is this your place?" the bishop asked.

Shelly nodded her head and managed to croak out, "Thank you." Jenn was about to open the door when Sister Caldwell unsnapped her seat belt and turned completely in her seat.

"Shelly, I don't want to seem presumptuous, but have you considered adoption?"

Jenn's heart leapt into her throat.

Shelly continued to shudder. "Not really." She spoke in little puffs of air.

Sister Caldwell snapped open her purse and took out a small white card. "If you do decide you'd like to investigate that possibility, here's a card with my name and phone number and the number for LDS Social Services. I'm a volunteer helper with them in their adoption program." She handed the card to Shelly and snapped her purse shut. "It's all done very privately and quietly, and we can guarantee your child would have loving parents." She patted Shelly on her hand. "Please think about it."

"I will," Shelly said. She had quit crying and held onto the card as if it were a lifeline. "I really will." There was a low roll of thunder as the sound of the rain softened. Jenn slid the door open, and Shelly walked across the lawn as quickly as she could.

"Well, we'd better get you home," the bishop said. "Tomorrow's a big day for you." He shifted into gear and pulled away from the curb. "You're the answer to our prayers," he said, smiling at her in the rearview mirror.

Oh, no, Bishop, you're the answer to mine.

TWENT𝒴~EI𝑔HT

"*Mom, the baptism* will be at two o'clock," Jenn said as she turned the doorknob. "You know where the church is, don't you?" Her mother mumbled a reply from her bedroom. Sister Ball and Sister Snow stood on the splintered front porch waiting for her. The clouds from the night before hung over the town, but the rain had stopped. Jenn's spirits were high as the three walked briskly toward the church.

"Do you have your Christmas shopping finished?" Sister Snow asked.

Jenn's steps slowed. "No, I don't," she admitted. Christmas at the Cooper house had barely been celebrated for as long as she could remember. Often they didn't even decorate a tree, let alone purchase gifts for one another. "I've been pretty busy," she said apologetically. "I need to get on that tomorrow."

The air around Jenn practically crackled with excitement as she sat through sacrament meeting. Finally, the block of meetings ended, and she walked with the two missionaries to the dressing room behind the font. While the two sisters waited outside the dressing room, she changed into the white dress that had been provided. Nervously, she peeked her head out of the dressing room. Sister Snow took her arm and led her into the Relief Society room. The chairs had been turned to face an accordion-folded metal curtain, and many of them were filled with ward members. She searched for her mother's face in vain. The front row of seats had been kept vacant except for Elder Johnson, who was dressed in white, and Elder Mahaloni in his dark suit. After Jenn and the two sister missionaries were seated, Bishop Caldwell stood up in front of the accordion door.

"Brothers and sisters," he began, "we are so delighted to be here today to witness the baptism of Sister Jennica Cooper. Many of you have become acquainted with this young lady over the past several weeks. Sister Ball and Sister Snow, the full-time missionaries who have been assigned to our ward, have taught her, and she's now ready to enter the waters of baptism." He glanced at a half-sheet of paper he held in his hands. "We'll begin by singing 'Baptism.' The words have been printed on the program. After that we'll then ask Sister Snow to offer the invocation. We will then have a short talk by Elder Mahaloni. We'll go to that point." He sat down on the end of the front row.

Someone began playing the piano, and the sister who usually led the music in sacrament meeting stood up to lead the music. After the opening hymn had been sung, Sister Snow stood and offered a prayer in which she thanked Heavenly Father for leading them to Jenn. She asked that He bless her as she took this step in her life. When she finished she sat down next to Jenn and patted her on the knee. Just as Elder Mahaloni stood up to speak, Jenn heard the back door of the Relief Society room open and close. She looked over her shoulder and saw her mother and Damon standing in the doorway. Both of them looked worried and confused. Sister Ball spotted them at the same moment, stood, and walked to where they were standing and led them to the front row. They sat down and looked at Jenn in her white dress. Damon nervously winked at Jenn.

Elder Mahaloni waited until they were seated and then began his talk. He talked about the importance of baptism, saying that it was one of the few ordinances done in the Church in the name of the Father, the

Son, and the Holy Ghost. He had a slight island lilt to his voice, but he spoke with assurance and power. Jenn was enthralled by what he had to say. After a few minutes he concluded his talk, and the bishop stood again. "We'll now proceed with the baptism. Sister Ball, would you help Sister Cooper?"

Sister Ball led Jenn to the side of the folding door. The bishop and Elder Mahaloni pushed the door open and revealed the baptismal font. A wave of moist air with the slight scent of chlorine engulfed Jenn. A large mirror hung at an angle over the top of the font so that everyone could watch the baptism. Sister Ball pushed open a door and led Jenn to the top of the steps that led into the water. Elder Johnson walked quickly down the steps opposite her and extended his hand to help her into the font. The bishop looked down at the two of them. "If it's all right with you, Sister Cooper, Elder Mahaloni and I will serve as witnesses?"

Jenn nodded her head as Elder Johnson took hold of her wrist with his left hand and placed her hand on his wrist. Elder Johnson raised his right arm to the square and said the baptismal prayer. Then he placed his hand behind her back and gently lowered her into the water. Immediately, he raised her to her feet and smiled before he led her to the bottom of the stairs that led to the dressing room. Sister Ball stood at the top of the stairs waiting for her.

Jenn could hear the sound of hymns being sung while she dried off and changed clothes. It was hard to explain what she was feeling, but it felt as if her sins had literally been washed away. She toweled her hair and hung the wet baptismal dress on a hanger in the shower stall in the dressing room before returning to the Relief Society room. Bishop Caldwell had positioned a chair so that it faced the people who had come to witness the baptism. He indicated that Jenn should sit there. The accordion doors had been pulled shut again. Once she was seated, the bishop put his hands on her shoulders. "I understand Elder Mahaloni will be confirming you a member of the Church," he said. Jenn nodded. "Then, following the confirmation, we have asked Sister Ball to give the closing prayer." He began to sit down and then he smiled and said, "This is a special day in many respects. Today is Sister Cooper's birthday. The Relief Society presidency thought we ought to celebrate that. So, Sister Ball, while you're saying the benediction, will you ask a blessing on the food?"

154

Elder Mahaloni stood behind Jenn with Elder Johnson, now dressed in a dark suit, on his left and Bishop Caldwell on the right. They placed their hands on her head, and Elder Mahaloni confirmed her a member of the Church and gave her the gift of the Holy Ghost. He then pronounced a blessing on her before closing the prayer. Jenn felt tears coursing down her cheeks during the blessing and was surprised to see tears in her mother's eyes when she opened hers. The three men shook her hand, and then the bishop nodded at Sister Ball. She stood and offered a benediction on the meeting. As soon as she finished, people swarmed around Jenn and congratulated her. Someone at the opposite end of the room raised a tambour door and passed plates of cake and ice cream to the throng. Spontaneously, several others began singing, "Happy Birthday."

Jenn felt an arm around her shoulder and turned to see her brother standing next to her. "I'm proud of you," he said with a smile before he disappeared back into the crowd. She looked for her mother but couldn't find her in the sea of faces. Eventually, the food drew everyone away from Jenn, and she caught her breath. Bishop Caldwell shook her hand.

"Welcome, Sister Cooper," he said with a smile.

Jenn did feel welcome in a way she could not express. "Thank you, Bishop," she replied. Someone handed her a plate of cake and ice cream, and she sat down. The bishop sat next to her, and his wife joined them a moment later.

"What lies ahead for you, young lady?" Bishop Caldwell asked.

"Finish high school. Then I'm off to college," she said.

"Which one?" Sister Caldwell asked. "Or haven't you decided yet?"

"Utah State offered me a scholarship," she said, slightly embarrassed. "So, I'm off to Utah next summer." She took a bite of cake. "Although I'm not sure how I'm going to get there."

"Aren't the Hathaways going there?" Sister Caldwell mused.

"I think you're right," the bishop replied. "I suppose Carl's going to drive that hot little red car of his." He thought for a moment. "And I think he and his sister would be excited to have someone share the cost of gas."

"He's in my English class," Jenn said. "I suppose I could ask him."

"Nothing ventured, nothing gained," the bishop replied.

Sister Ball and Sister Snow were waiting for her in the foyer when Jenn finally separated herself from the well-wishers. "All right if we walk

155

home with you?"

"Sure." Jenn remembered that tomorrow was transfer day, and a dart of panic struck her heart. "Are you two really going to be transferred?" she asked.

"I don't know," Sister Ball said. "I only have six weeks to go, and then my mission is finished, so they might leave me here. But Sister Snow has nearly a year left, and they'll probably send her to inspire another companion," she said with a smile. Although the words were lighthearted, the mood was not.

"What will I ever do without you?" Jenn said dejectedly.

"You'll do just fine," Sister Snow said. "You have a whole lot of new friends waiting for you in this ward. It won't take long before you've forgotten us completely."

"Not on your life," Jenn said emphatically. "I'll never forget you."

They hugged at the front porch, and the missionaries watched as Jenn entered the house. "She's a special one, isn't she?" Sister Snow said. Sister Ball merely nodded her head.

TWENTY~NINE

Jenn's mother was standing at the kitchen counter when she entered the house. Jenn went to her and hugged her, "Thanks, Mom," she said. "It meant a lot to me to have you there."

Her mother grunted. "That was nice, Jenn. Not what I expected at all. The Mormons here must be different from the p'lygamists in Utah. That's why I'm worried about you goin' off ta school." She continued to peel potatoes into the sink. "I'll put these taters, on and we'll have dinner pretty soon."

Jenn went to her bedroom and changed clothes. Her hair was still damp, and she brushed it for a few minutes before sinking down on the edge of her bed. She still felt an overwhelming sense of peace and knew that it would not take much to cause tears to flow again. The letter from Sister Lingfelter was sitting next to the Book of Mormon on her side table. She reached for it, withdrew it from the envelope, and read it again.

I need to write her and tell her what has happened. Another thought entered her mind. *I wonder where Sister Sandberg is? She ought to know I was baptized too.* Her thoughts returned to Sister Ball and Sister Snow, and she wondered if they would be transferred. She was still sitting quietly on her bed immersed in thought when her mother called, "Dinner's ready."

Jenn walked quickly to the kitchen and noticed that uncharacteristically her mother had set the table. They sat down to eat dinner. The kitchen was quiet except for an occasional creak or groan from the old house. Jenn's mind replayed the events of the day, and she smiled warmly at her mother as she looked around the kitchen.

"Mom," she asked, "what would you like for Christmas?"

Her mother put down her cup of coffee. "I don't need nothin'," she replied. "I'm fine."

Jenn blushed and then said, "Mom, if you had any wish at all, what would it be?"

Her mother stood abruptly and put her coffee cup in the sink. "I tol' ya, I don't need nothin'." She walked stiffly into the front room and sat in the rocking chair. Jenn finished her dinner, cleared the table, washed the dishes, and placed them in the drainer before joining her mother in the front room. She sat down on the edge of the couch and faced her mother.

"Mom, what's wrong?"

Her mother rocked silently while she puffed slowly on her cigarette. "Nothin'," she said abruptly.

Jenn sank back on the couch and watched her mother rock. "Mom, I'm not trying to pry, but I would like to get you something for Christmas."

"No, Jenn!" her mother growled. "You don't have to get me nothin' for Christmas."

"Mom, I know I don't have to get you anything, but I want to. And I'd rather get you something you'd like . . ."

Her mother ground out her cigarette. "Jenn, listen to me. The stuff I want for Christmas you can't get me. I want your father to've had more sense than to go gettin' hisself killed. I want your brother to have more sense than to go gettin' shot in the head."

She rocked more violently before saying, "Jenn, you just don' realize nothin'. We've never had much of a Christmas 'round here, but it ain't 'cause I haven't wanted to. I stretch that welfare check every which way but loose, but there ain't no extra for Christmas."

"Mom, I'm not asking you to get me anything. I just want to get you a present."

"Why?" her mother asked as she lit another cigarette.

Jenn shrugged her shoulders, "I don't know . . . because you're my mother . . . because I love you," she said softly. It was the first time she had voiced that love since she was a tiny child. She could feel the tears welling up again.

Jenn's mother rocked silently while she stared over Jenn's head and out the window. "I don't know why," she mumbled. "I haven't been much of a mother to you." She swiped at her eyes with the back of her hand.

"Mom," Jenn said, "that's not true." She rose from the couch and knelt down next to the rocking chair. "I know you've tried to raise me and Damon the best way you knew how." Dusk crept into the room silently and stealthily. "I know I didn't always do what you wanted, Mom, but I'm trying, really trying, to do better."

Her mother patted her on her shoulder, "Oh, Jenn, I've always wanted the best for you. I'm proud that you're going to college. I never dreamed anyone in my family would do that. And I'm proud of what you did today."

The room grew darker until Jenn stood and turned on the lamp. "You still haven't answered me. What would you like for Christmas?"

"I told you, I don't need nothin'." She pulled herself up from the rocking chair and wandered down the hallway toward her bedroom.

THIRT*y*

On Monday night the diner served a steady flow of people until nearly nine o'clock and then, just as if a door had closed, no more customers came in. Ten minutes later Lorna decided to close early. She handed Jenn and Shelly their share of tips. "Must be the Christmas season," Lorna said. "Everybody seems to be pretty generous."

The two girls hung up their aprons and walked out the back door together. Shelly suddenly stopped and winced. "Are you all right?" Jenn asked.

"I get these pains every once in a while. I think the little guy sticks his elbows into my backbone," she said, trying to smile.

"Do you want me to call a cab?"

"I'll be all right," Shelly said, shaking her head. "Besides, cabs cost money." Jenn put her hand under Shelly's elbow and helped her down the street to the corner, where she sank onto a bench at the bus stop. "I'll be okay. You go on home." She winced again and placed her hands on the small of her back. "I don't have far to go."

Jenn sat down next to her. "I'll pay for the cab, Shel. You wait here, and I'll run back to the diner and call for one."

Shelly winced again, "I can't let you do that. I'll be okay."

"Consider it my Christmas present to you." She walked quickly the half block back to the diner. Lorna was just locking the back door when Jenn approached her out of the darkness. "Lorna," she said. "I need to use the phone."

"My gracious, child," she gasped, "You scared me to death. What's wrong?"

"I just want to call a taxi. I don't think Shelly's in any condition to walk home."

"I'll drive her," Lorna said. She finished locking the door, shook the knob to make sure it was secure, and walked briskly to her car. "Climb in," she said to Jenn. "Where's Shelly?"

"Just down on the corner," Jenn said, pointing toward the bus stop.

A few seconds later, they helped Shelly into the front seat of the car, and Jenn climbed into the back. Five minutes later they were in front of Shelly's house. Even though it was not yet nine-thirty, the house was completely dark. Jenn climbed out of the backseat and helped Shelly to the front door. "Is anyone home?" she asked. "I mean, are you going to be all right?"

"I'm fine. Mom and Dad go to bed early." She fumbled a key from the pocket of her maternity pants and unlocked the door. "Thanks," she said as she closed the door. Jenn hurried back to the car and slid into the front seat.

"I hope she's going to be all right," Lorna said as they pulled away from the curb. "The baby's not due for another six weeks." They drove in silence toward Jenn's home. "I wonder what she's going to do when the baby comes."

"I don't know," Jenn said as they stopped in front of her house. "Thanks for the ride."

"No problem. Incidentally, I don't think we'll have much business on Christmas Eve, so I'm thinking we might close after lunch on Wednesday. What do you think?"

"You're probably right. Tomorrow's the last day of school before the holidays, so I can work Wednesday lunch if you need me."

"I'll think about it, Jenn. See you tomorrow afternoon." Lorna drove away.

Most of the next day at school was consumed with a Christmas assembly and homeroom parties. School let out early, and Jenn had nearly three hours until she had to be at the restaurant. She caught a bus and rode to the mall where she joined the swarm of last-minute shoppers. An hour later she had purchased a skirt and blouse for her mother and a pair of jeans for Damon. She was amazed that the stores would gift wrap her purchases, and her heart was light as she carried them to the bus stop and rode home. She climbed the splintered stairs, placed the gifts out of sight on the front porch, and walked into the house. She could hear her mother in the bathroom and quickly checked to see if Damon was in his room. Jenn found it empty so she retrieved the presents, carried them to her room, and slid them under her bed. She changed clothes and prepared to go to work just as her mother emerged from the bathroom.

"See you later, Mom," Jenn said as she nearly skipped out of the house. When she arrived at the diner, only two customers were there. A few minutes later Shelly came in, out of breath. "Looks like it might be a slow night," Jenn said.

"I hope so. I'm pooped. I couldn't sleep all last night what with the little gymnast inside of me."

The two girls retrieved their aprons from the back room and busied themselves straightening salt and pepper shakers and menus on the tables. A few customers came in as the night progressed, but by nine o'clock Lorna flipped the front door sign from "open" to "closed." "I think we might as well call it a night," she said. Jenn and Shelly finished wiping down the last tables, took off their aprons, and hung them up. "Jenn," Lorna said, "I appreciate your offer to work tomorrow, but I don't think we're going to be busy enough that I'll need you. Besides, you deserve a day off." She handed each of the girls an envelope. "Here's your Christmas bonus."

Eagerly, Shelly ripped open the envelope and looked at the check. "I don't deserve this," she said to her boss. "I mean, I've missed so many days because of . . ." She rubbed her stomach. Tears flowed down her cheeks. "Thank you," she managed to squeak. Lorna put her arm around Shelly's shoulders and gave her a hug.

"You've been a good worker, kiddo. After the baby comes, you have a job waiting for you."

Jenn folded the unopened envelope and slid it into her pants pocket. "Thanks," she said quietly. "I didn't expect this."

"Just my little Christmas gift to you two girls," Lorna said. "Now, Shelly, let me lock up and I'll give you a ride home." She turned to Jenn, "You want one, too?"

"Thanks, but I think I'll walk," she said. "I'll see you on Friday. Merry Christmas." She let herself out the back door and walked slowly toward home. The evening was cool, but much of the haze of the past few days had blown out, and the stars twinkled overhead. A nearly new moon hung in the sky, showing a tiny sliver of light. Jenn wrapped her sweater around her and shivered as a light breeze picked up a discarded candy wrapper and skipped it down the street like a stone on a flat pond. *I am so blessed,* she thought. She turned the corner of her street and saw one house with a few Christmas lights burning in the window. She thought of the gifts beneath her bed, and a smile formed on her lips. "It will be a merry Christmas," she whispered to herself.

The house was quiet, with only the living room lamp left on. Jenn went to her room, prepared for bed, and sank to her knees. She was amazed how easily the prayers came now, when just a few weeks ago she had offered the first prayer of her life. When she finished she slipped between the sheets and fell into a peaceful sleep.

Christmas Eve dawned clear and cool. Jenn fixed breakfast and then prepared to do some additional shopping. "I need to get Lorna and Shelly a Christmas gift," she said under her breath. When she pulled on her pants she felt the folded envelope in the pocket, removed it, and ripped off the end. Inside was a check for a thousand dollars and a small handwritten card that said, "My contribution to your college fund."

Jenn sat down on the edge of her bed and stared at the check, dumbfounded. *I can't believe this.* Quickly, she slid out the dresser drawer and added the check to her cache. Ten minutes later she was on the bus, headed again to the mall. She was home by noon, carrying a large plastic bag that contained gifts for Lorna and Shelly, a small artificial tree, and some lights and ornaments. She pulled the tree from its box and set it up on top of the table at the end of the couch. It took but a few minutes more to string lights on the tree and hang the ornaments from its branches. "Merry Christmas," she said out loud. She scurried down the hallway to her room, pulled the gifts from under the bed, returned to the living room, and placed them under the tree. She had scarcely finished when her mother pushed open the front door. She was carrying two small plastic bags of groceries.

"Good heavens," her mother exclaimed, "where did that come from?"

"Merry Christmas, Mom," Jenn smiled.

"Oh, Jenn, you shouldn't have," her mother said. She examined the tree with a broad smile on her face. "It's beautiful." Suddenly she noticed the presents under the tree. She reached reverently for one of them and picked it up. Tears sprang to her eyes as she saw her name on the tag. "You really shouldn't have," she said as she reached out and hugged her daughter. "Thank you, Jenn. You make me ashamed of myself."

"Merry Christmas," Jenn said again. "I need to go deliver a couple of other presents." She picked up Lorna and Shelly's presents, grabbed her sweater, and hurried out the door. Her mother was still standing in front of the tree, crying.

THi RTY~ONE

The restaurant was fairly busy when Jenn arrived. Lorna was helping the two lunch waitresses and seemed surprised to see Jenn walk through the door. Jenn walked quickly to her side. "Need some help?" she asked.

"Man, I didn't think it would be this busy," she replied. "But I think we can handle it. What brings you out this way? I thought you'd have better things to do on your day off."

Jenn extended her hand with the small wrapped gift. "Merry Christmas," she said.

"Oh, Jenn, you didn't have to do this," she said with a wag of her head. "But thank you. Now you scoot out of here and have a good holiday. I'll see you the day after Christmas."

"Sure you don't need some help?"

"We'll be fine, honey. Merry Christmas."

Lorna hurried back to the cash register. "Sorry to keep you waiting," she said to the couple who stood there ready to pay their tab.

Jenn waved good-bye and hurried out of the diner. The wind had picked up a bit, and she wrapped her sweater more tightly around her as she walked briskly the dozen blocks to Shelly's house. She climbed the steps to the front porch and pushed the doorbell. She thought she could hear sounds from within, but no one came to the door. Finally, she knocked on the wooden screen door frame. A few moments later the door was opened by a small, neatly dressed woman who wore black-framed glasses that magnified her eyes.

"Hi," Jenn said timidly, "I brought this . . . " she pulled the screen door open and thrust the present toward the woman, ". . . for Shelly."

"And who might you be?" the woman asked.

"I'm Jennica Cooper. I work with her at the diner," Jenn said, still holding the gift.

"Oh," the woman said somewhat relieved, "Please come in. I'll get Shelly." She held the door open for Jenn and said, "Please have a seat."

Jenn sat down on the white leather love seat. A matching couch formed an "L" and faced the living room window. In front of the window was a large Christmas tree covered with lights and ornaments. Beneath it were dozens of presents. Jenn felt suddenly smaller and less worthy to be there. Christmas carols were playing softly from some hidden source. Jenn perched on the edge of the couch, holding the small wrapped gift in her lap. After some time Shelly waddled into the room, wearing a pale pink bathrobe. Jenn sprang to her feet. "I brought this for you," she said. "Merry Christmas."

Shelly sat down heavily on the couch. "Thank you," she said meekly. "I'm sorry I didn't get you a present."

"I didn't expect one," Jenn said brightly. "How are you doing?"

Shelly bowed her head. "I'm okay." She beckoned for Jenn to move over next to her on the couch. "I called your friend," she whispered. "I have an appointment on Friday morning to talk about adoption."

"Wonderful," Jenn whispered in return. "How do your parents feel about that?"

"I haven't told them yet. I mean, I don't know if these people can help me, you know."

"Where's your appointment? How are you going to get there?" Jenn asked.

"I've got the address. It's not too far away, and I can take the bus."

"Do you want me to go with you? I don't have to be to work until three."

Shelly suddenly burst into tears. "Why would you do that?" She wiped her eyes and nose on the sleeve of her robe. "I mean, you don't really know me or anything."

"Shelly, what time's the appointment?"

"Ten o'clock."

"I'll be here at nine-thirty to pick you up. You just be ready, okay?" Jenn stood up and patted her friend on the shoulder. "Merry Christmas." She let herself out of the house and walked home. Her mother was sitting in the rocking chair admiring the tree when Jenn walked in. She couldn't help but notice the difference between the tree at Shelly's house and the tiny one in their living room. She greeted her mother and then walked into the kitchen. She opened the phone book, found the bishop's number, and dialed his phone. Someone answered after the second ring.

"Hello."

"Sister Caldwell?" Jenn was surprised how easily that rolled off her tongue. "This is Jenn Cooper."

"Oh, yes, Sister Cooper. Merry Christmas. What can I do for you? Or do you need to talk to my husband?"

"Oh, no, Sister Caldwell. You're the one I need to talk to. Do you remember the night you gave my friend Shelly a ride home?"

"Of course."

"Well, she's going to talk to someone at Family Services on Friday, and I kind of volunteered to go along with her. I'm just trying to find out what to expect."

"I see. It's very kind of you to accompany your friend. I wouldn't worry about anything, Sister Cooper. The people there are kind and competent, and they'll explain a lot of options to Shelly." She paused, "Are her parents coming with you?"

"Well, no, not really. Shelly hasn't told them she's going. Is that going to be a problem?"

"How old is your friend?"

"Sixteen," Jenn replied.

"Well, at some point we'll have to involve the parents since she's underage, but we'll cross that bridge when we come to it."

"I guess," Jenn said.

"How is she getting to the office? I suppose since she hasn't told her parents, they won't be bringing her."

"I'm going to hire a cab," Jenn said.

"Oh, you don't have to do that," Sister Caldwell said. "I'll come and pick both of you up. It may give us a few minutes to answer your friend's questions informally."

"Are you sure?" Jenn asked.

"Of course, Sister Cooper. What time do you need me to pick you up?"

"I told Shelly I'd be there at nine-thirty," she replied.

"All right, I'll be at your house about nine-twenty."

"Thank you, Sister Caldwell," Jenn said.

"Think nothing of it, dear. Merry Christmas to you and your family."

"Merry Christmas to you." Jenn hung up the phone.

"What's that all about," her mother said from the living room.

Jenn came in and sat on the couch. "There's a girl at work who's pregnant, and Sister Caldwell, my bishop's wife, has offered to get her some help. She might want to put the baby up for adoption."

"Be careful, Jenn. You don't want to get involved with all that stuff."

Jenn nodded her head. *That's the problem, isn't it. We never get involved in anything that might split our cocoon of comfort or pose any kind of challenge. We're not even very interested bystanders; we just drift aimlessly down the stream of life, leaving puffs of smoke that dissipate in misty memories.* Jenn blinked her eyes. *Where did that come from?* she wondered as she said, "I'll be careful, Mom."

Her mother nodded her head and lit a cigarette. "That's why I worry about you goin' away to college. Ya know what I mean?"

"Mom, I worry too, but I'll be all right."

Her mother continued as if she weren't even aware of Jenn's interruption. "Ya don't even have a driver's license. Ya don't have no bank account. Ya never been away from home before. How're ya gonna do it, child?"

"I'm not sure, Mom, but I know I have to do it." She stood up and walked to her bedroom. *Mom's right. I don't even have a checking account.*

Jenn slid open the dresser drawer and extracted the money and Lorna's check. She stuffed the cash into the pocket of her backpack, hefted it to her shoulder, and walked into the living room.

"Where're you off to?" her mother said, as she exhaled a cloud of smoke.

"Just finishing some last-minute things before Christmas," Jenn said with a smile. "I won't be gone long." She walked quickly out the front door and down the street toward the bank. She had been to the bank several times to exchange smaller bills for large ones, but she had no idea what was necessary to open an account. She walked quickly, afraid that the bank might close early on Christmas Eve, but found it still open as she walked through the front door of the branch. It was a small bank with only two teller's booths and two small offices on the opposite side of the lobby. Jenn took a deep breath and approached one of the tellers.

"May I help you?" the teller said. She was not much older than Jenn, and had dark brown hair and startling blue eyes.

Jenn mustered her courage. "I'd like to open a checking account."

"Oh, well, if you'll go see Mrs. Tolman, she can help you," the girl said pleasantly. "She's in that office," she said, pointing across the room.

Jenn thanked her and made her way to Mrs. Tolman's office. She paused at the doorway until the woman beckoned to her to come in. She was talking on the phone and pecking away at her computer when Jenn sat down on the opposite side of her desk. She slid the backpack to the floor and waited for Mrs. Tolman to finish her conversation. Finally she hung up.

"Yes, dear, how can I help you?" she asked.

Jenn felt sweat forming in the palms of her hands. "I'd like to open a checking account, I think."

Mrs. Tolman reached into a desk drawer and withdrew a cream-colored card. "Well, let's have you fill this out," she said with a smile. "Then we can take care of the rest of it." She removed a pen from a holder on her desk and extended it to Jenn while she slid the card across the desk.

Jenn filled out the card and handed it and the pen back to Mrs. Tolman. "I think I did that right," she said.

Mrs. Tolman scanned the card. "I think that's all we need." She withdrew another form. "Now, how much did you want to deposit?"

169

"I don't know," Jenn said hesitantly. "I mean, I haven't counted it."

Mrs. Tolman smiled. "Well, we require a minimum deposit of twenty-five dollars to open an account. I suppose you'll be depositing at least that much?"

"Oh, yes," Jenn said. She reached into the backpack and brought out the stack of bills and the check. "It's just that I'm not exactly sure how much there is here." She placed the money on the desk top.

Mrs. Tolman's eyes widened slightly before she said, "Would you like me to count it with you, dear?"

"I guess." Jenn began separating the hundred-dollar bills into stacks of ten and Mrs. Tolman verified the count. A few minutes later they determined that Jenn was depositing $4,650.

"Do you have some identification?" the woman asked. "I need to see some so we can cash the check." She stacked the bills neatly on her desk. "A driver's license, perhaps?"

"I'm sorry, I don't have one," Jenn fumbled. "I do have my student activity card from the high school." She fished the card from a pocket in her backpack.

"That will do nicely," Mrs. Tolman said as she stood up. "Now if you'll just endorse the back of the check, I'll deposit this for you, and then you can decide which style of checks you'd like."

Ten minutes later Jenn walked out of the bank with a temporary check book stuck in the side of her backpack. She had kept five twenty-dollar bills in case Shelly had some unexpected expenses. She walked home feeling as if she had opened a new doorway in her life. She climbed the stairs and walked into the living room of her house. The lights on the little tree shone brightly on the table.

Her mother had fixed dinner for the three of them, and Jenn was just washing the dishes when she heard car doors slam in front of the house. Puzzled, she walked to the front room and looked out the window into the darkness. In the front yard were about two dozen people arranging themselves into rows. Her mother joined her at the window just as the group began to sing Christmas carols.

Jenn opened the front door, walked out onto the porch, and tried to see the faces of the carolers. A smile lit up her face as she recognized people from her ward. She led her mother onto the porch, and they listened for a few minutes. When the singers had finished, they waved to

Jenn and her mother as they piled back into the cars.

"Merry Christmas, Sister Cooper," one of the women said.

"Merry Christmas to you," Jenn called back. An indescribable feeling of warmth engulfed her. "Merry Christmas."

THIRTY~TWO

Feeble sunlight wedged its way between the clouds and into Jenn's room. She awoke with a start, filled with the anticipation of giving Christmas gifts to her mother and brother. She dressed quickly, hurried to the kitchen, and began fixing breakfast when she noticed several more presents had been placed under the Christmas tree. She wiped her hands on a dish towel and knelt next to the tree. She picked up one of the packages and saw her name written on the card. Amazed, she picked up another of the presents and saw Damon's name on it. Her mother's name was on another box. Shaking her head, she returned to the kitchen and began scrambling some eggs. A few minutes later her brother walked into the kitchen wearing nothing but a pair of shorts. He yawned and scratched himself.

"Hey, Sis, what's for breakfast?" He pulled one of the chairs away from the table, turned it around, sat down on it backward, and rested his chin on the back of the chair.

"Bacon and eggs," Jenn said. "And pancakes."

"You must've helped Mom with the grocery money," he said.

"A little," Jenn admitted. "Merry Christmas."

"Oh, yeah," he mumbled. "I found a bunch of stuff on the porch last night when I came home." He jerked his thumb over his shoulder. "I stuck it under your tree."

Jenn could hear her mother approaching, and she quickly scooped the eggs and bacon onto three plates. "I'll get the pancakes going," she said. "Merry Christmas, Mom."

"Merry Christmas," her mother fumbled. "Where'd the food come from?"

"I picked up a few things yesterday," Jenn said with a smile. "I thought we ought to have a special Christmas breakfast." She poured pancake batter into the skillet. "Sit down, and I'll have these pancakes ready in a minute."

When breakfast was over they went into the living room, and Jenn began distributing gifts. She was still unsure who had left the gifts for them and waited to open her gifts until Damon and her mother had opened theirs. The mystery packages contained more clothes and a couple of games for the family. When Jenn finally opened her gifts, she found they contained clothing as well. The last package she opened had a beautiful, modest dress inside. *Something to wear to church,* she thought, and suddenly she suspected that her ward members had been their secret Santa. Mixed emotions swirled through her. She was grateful to them for the gifts but embarrassed that they had felt a need to help her family. *Erase that pride* suddenly sprang into her mind. She returned to her room, closed the door, and knelt beside her bed.

Later that afternoon there was a knock at the door, and when Jenn answered it she found Sister Ball and Sister Snow standing there. "Merry Christmas," the two missionaries said in unison. "May we come in?"

"Of course," Jenn said. "You're still here! You didn't get transferred."

Sister Ball shook her head. "Nope. We escaped by the skin of our teeth." She laughed. "I'm sorry we haven't been by sooner to follow up on your baptism. But the Christmas season is always a little hectic." She walked to the little Christmas tree. "Looks like the one in our apartment," she said with a smile. "We'll see you at church on Sunday, and maybe we can set up an appointment to do a little more teaching, if that would be all right?"

Jenn nodded her head. "I'd like that."

"Well, we'd better be on our way. Have the rest of a Merry Christmas." The two missionaries shook her hand and then walked out the door.

The next morning Sister Caldwell showed up at the appointed hour and drove both Jenn and Shelly to the appointment. When they left, Jenn couldn't help but feel that a great burden had been lifted from Shelly's shoulders. After Sister Caldwell dropped Shelly at her house, she drove Jenn home.

"Thank you, Sister Caldwell," Jenn said. "I didn't know how to help her, but you sure did."

"Thank you for thinking of me," Sister Caldwell said as Jenn opened the car door. "Well, we'll see you on Sunday."

"Yes, you will," Jenn replied. "Thanks again." She skipped up the stairs and into the front room. The clock on the kitchen wall told her she had two hours until she had to leave for the diner. It seemed strange to have free time on her hands. All of the holiday homework was finished, and there was nothing else she had to do. She wandered to her bedroom and sat down on the bed. The letter from Sister Lingfelter still stood on the nightstand. Jenn read it again, searched in her backpack for a notebook, returned to the kitchen, and sat down at the table. At first the words were hard to find, but the more she wrote, the easier the pencil seemed to move. Jenn thanked the missionary for introducing her to the Church and then recounted all that had happened since Sister Lingfelter and Sister Sandberg had left. Almost as an afterthought, she mentioned that she had been awarded a scholarship to Utah State and that she would be going to Utah in the summer. She asked if Sister Lingfelter knew Sister Sandberg's address, signed her name, folded the four pages, stuck them in an envelope, and sealed it.

Jenn looked at the clock. Time had flown, and she needed to hurry to get ready to go to work. She walked briskly out of the house and dropped the letter in the mailbox next to the grocery store as she passed it on the way to the diner. When she arrived, she barely had time to hang up her sweater and put on her apron before the rush began.

"Where did all these people come from?" she asked Lorna.

"They've been out returning presents, and they're hungry," she replied with a smile. "So let's feed them." She patted Jenn on the shoulder. "I've tried to find somebody to fill in for Shelly, but I haven't done it yet. Can you handle her tables along with yours?"

"Sure," Jenn said brightly, as she grabbed a tray with glasses of water and headed to where two tables had been pushed together to accommodate twelve people. By the time the diner closed, Jenn felt as if she couldn't take another step. She sat down at one of the tables and rubbed her ankles.

"Feet hurt?" Lorna asked, pulling up another chair.

Jenn nodded her head. "I don't think I've ever seen it this busy."

"Economy must be recovering," the manager said. "At least you don't have to split the tips with anyone." She handed Jenn a stack of bills.

Jenn took the stack of bills and said, "You ought to keep half of this. You worked right alongside me."

Lorna shook her head. "No, kid, you keep it. You'll need it for college."

Jenn swallowed. "I guess. I wish I knew more about what I'm getting into." She doodled her finger on the tabletop. "No one in my family has ever gone to college. Most of them didn't even finish high school."

"Worried?"

Jenn nodded her head. "A little—well, maybe a whole lot."

"Jenn, we always worry about the unknown. You've probably heard the old saying, 'I'm an old man with many worries, a few of which have really happened.' I just think you have to have a little faith in yourself. You're going to be fine." She placed her hands on the small of her back and twisted her body, trying to relieve the stiffness. "But I have to admit I'm going to miss you." She pushed herself to her feet. "Now, get out of here. It's late, and there's no need to hang around with an old woman."

When Jenn arrived home she took off her shoes and wiggled her toes. The Christmas tree was still lighted, and her mother was asleep in the rocking chair. Trying not to awaken her, Jenn crept down the hallway to her bedroom. Ten minutes later she was climbing into bed when she heard the back door open. A moment later Damon stuck his head into her room.

"You still awake?" he whispered.

Jenn sat up in bed and nodded her head. "Where have you been?"

"Out," he said abruptly. He scraped the toe of his shoe on the floor.

"Sis, can I ask you a question?"

"Sure."

"Well, it's kinda hard to say. I mean, I really don't know . . . "

"What's the matter?" Jenn said with growing alarm.

He dropped his head. "Well, I mean, have you checked your money lately?"

"What?" Jenn's jaw dropped open. "What do you mean?"

"Well, I think maybe somebody robbed you," he said furtively.

"What do you mean?" she stuttered.

"I told you this was kinda hard," he whispered. "But, like, there's no money there." He pointed his finger toward the dresser drawer.

"How would you know that?" she said accusingly.

Damon dragged his toe around on the floor for a minute before he said, "Well, I mean, I kinda looked there while you were at work, and there isn't anything there." He jabbed his thumb toward the dresser.

"Damon, have you been taking my money?" she questioned.

He backed up a step into the hallway as if he were going to run. "Just a couple a bucks. I mean, I borrowed it, and I'll pay it back."

Jenn's eyes narrowed. "How much, Damon? How much?"

He rolled his eyes toward the ceiling. "Like, maybe a couple hundred bucks?"

"You stole two hundred dollars from me?" she said, as she stared at her brother. "What for?"

He shrugged his shoulders, "Just stuff. I mean, I don't have a job, and Mom sure ain't gonna give me any money." He scuffed his toe. "I'm sorry, Jenn. I'll pay it back."

"Sure you will. How?"

Suddenly, he straightened. "I dunno. But you didn't need it. You never spend it on nothin'. Besides, I think somebody stole all of it."

"Oh? When did you discover that, you little thief?"

"Like I said, I looked while you was at work, and all the money's gone."

Jenn could feel the anger boiling within her. Before she said anything she'd regret, she said, "Go to bed! We'll talk about this tomorrow." She sank down into her bed and turned her back toward her brother. She lay for hours smoldering over her brother's thievery before she finally fell asleep. The next morning her head felt as if it were being crushed between two elephants and she could barely force her eyes open. When she reached the kitchen and poured herself a bowl of cereal she felt a little better, although the anger still smoldered within her like a glowing piece of charcoal. Damon had already fled.

She drew a bath and slid into the hot water. Before long she fell asleep, and when she awoke the water was tepid. She toweled herself dry, dressed, and wandered into the living room. Her mother was still asleep. Jenn sat in the rocking chair and planned revenge against her brother. She was still sitting and rocking when she heard someone climb the front steps. She walked to the front door in time to see the mailman walking to the next house. Jenn reached into the mailbox and pulled out two envelopes. The first was the electrical bill. The second was addressed to her. The return address indicated it was from Randy Grant in Ten Sleep, Wyoming. With trembling hands, Jenn opened the envelope and removed the single sheet of lined notebook paper. She unfolded it and read:

Dear Miss Cooper,

I am writing this note to thank you for your honesty. My husband and I often wondered what happened to his wallet. My sister in Hemet was ill, and we had made an emergency trip to visit her. We were on our way back to Wyoming when we stopped for dinner, and my husband lost his wallet. Thankfully, we had just filled our car with gas and were able to make it to one of my husband's old missionary companion's homes in Auburn before we ran out of gas.

You did not need to return the money, although the driver's license and picture were welcome. We had long ago forgiven whoever took the wallet, but it was wonderful to have you contact us. If you are ever in Ten Sleep, we'd be happy to have you visit us.

Yours truly,
Jan and Randy Grant

Jenn folded the sheet of paper and replaced it in the envelope. *How could they forgive me when they don't even know me?* she wondered. She sank back into the rocking chair and rocked until it was time for work.

THIRTY~THREE

The next day Jenn walked to church wearing her new dress. She carried the well-read copy of the Book of Mormon with her. She walked into the foyer and was surprised at how comfortable she felt. Bishop Caldwell shook her hand as she walked into the chapel. "Would you be able to meet with me for a few minutes after the block?" he asked.

Jenn felt a pinprick of concern stab her heart, "Sure, Bishop," she said, trying to calm her fears. The speakers in sacrament meeting talked about setting goals as the new year approached. Jenn tried to concentrate on what they were saying, but her mind kept wandering to the meeting with the bishop. She wondered if he had learned about something in her past and was going to kick her out of the Church. The letter from the Grants immediately surfaced in her mind, and she wondered if they'd sent a copy to the bishop. Finally, church ended, and she made her way to the bishop's office. The door was closed, and timidly she knocked. Brother

178

Fulmer, the ward clerk, opened the door and invited her in before he left. Bishop Caldwell stood up from behind his desk and shook her hand. He directed her to a chair and invited her to sit down.

"Sister Cooper, I know you have been a member of the Church for just one week, but I feel that we ought to call you to a position."

Jenn's mind raced. *Me? I don't know anything. I can't do anything!* She cleared her throat. "Me?" she voiced.

The bishop nodded his head. "We have ten little three-year-olds in the Primary, and they're driving Sister Newhouse crazy. We will be splitting the class into two groups of five, and I feel inspired to issue the call to you to serve as a Sunbeam teacher."

Jenn's eyes flew wide open. "Bishop, I don't think I know as much as those three-year-olds. I'm not sure I can do this." She could feel her whole body trembling.

"Sister Cooper, have a little more faith in yourself. Sister Broadbent, the Primary president, will be happy to help you, and I think you'll find you're up to the task." He smiled broadly at her. "Sister Cooper, this is a call from the Lord. We'll supply all the help you need, but if you will rely on Him, I'm sure you'll do just fine."

"Bishop, I just don't know."

"But the Lord does. Will you accept this call?"

Weren't you complaining about just drifting downstream, she thought. She swallowed and said, "If you think I can do it, then I guess I'll give it a try."

"You'll do fine," he said as he stood up from behind the desk. "I'll have Sister Broadbent get you the material you'll need. Thank you for accepting the call." He shook her hand and led her to the doorway.

Jenn walked home slowly. *What have I done?* She felt that she was no more ready to teach anybody about the Church than fly. She had gone about a block when she heard her name being called. Jenn turned around and saw Sister Ball and Sister Snow waving at her. She waited until they caught up to her. "Hi," she said. "I saw you in sacrament meeting, but you were sitting with another family."

Sister Snow nodded. "Investigators. But we didn't mean to ignore you." She saw Jenn's worried expression. "What's wrong?" she asked.

"Bishop Caldwell just asked me to teach the three-year-olds," she replied, "and I don't think I can."

"You're absolutely right," Sister Ball said. "You can't."

Jenn's eyes flew open.

"But you and the Lord can," she finished. Don't ever forget that." She gave Jenn a hug. "I was just trying to get a reaction. But, Jenn, you and the Lord are a powerful team."

The three women were standing on the sidewalk talking when they heard another voice calling to them. Carl Hathaway, the young man who was in Jenn's English class, was waving his hand. Sister Ball waved back, and the three of them waited until Carl jogged to where they were standing. "Hi," he said, slightly out of breath.

"Hi," Jenn replied.

Carl took a couple of deep breaths before continuing. "I hear you're going to Utah State next year," he said. Jenn nodded her head. "So am I," he said, "and so's my sister, Sophie. She's a senior there. Anyway, the bishop said you might want to ride to Logan with us. We're going to drive straight through. Sophie says it takes about eighteen hours, but we figure if we trade off driving we can catch a nap while the other one drives. You'd have to split the gas money with us." He paused to catch his breath. "And we'll only have room for two suitcases—two small suitcases each. What do you think?"

Jenn looked embarrassed for a moment and then said, "I'd love to Carl, but I probably won't be much help driving. I've don't have a driver's license. I've never driven."

He shrugged his shoulders. "That's okay. Sophie and I can drive, but you'd still have to pay your share of the gas."

"No problem," Jenn said. "I've been wondering how I was going to get to Utah."

"I guess this will solve it for this year. 'Course, next year I'll be going on a mission and Sophie will have graduated, so we won't be much help then. Well, got to get home. We'll plan on you, then." He turned around and jogged back down the sidewalk.

"Looks like the Lord's taking pretty good care of you," Sister Ball said. "Now, we were going to try to set up some time with you to do a little more teaching. Maybe we could go over what's expected of a Sunbeam teacher while we're at it. What do you think?"

"Sounds wonderful to me," Jenn said with a smile. "I'm still working at the diner from three o'clock on, but I'm home in the mornings during the holidays."

"Well, tomorrow's our preparation day, but how about Tuesday, around ten o'clock?"

Jenn nodded her head. "I'll be waiting." The two missionaries shook her hand, turned, and started toward the church. Jenn watched them go before continuing her walk home. She saw Damon sitting on the porch chair as she approached the house. He stood up as she climbed the steps.

"Sis," he said, "I'll pay you back, I really will."

We had long ago forgiven whoever took the wallet came into her mind. "What?" she said to herself. *We had long ago forgiven whoever took the wallet.*

"I said, I'll pay you back," he murmured.

"Sit down," Jenn said. "Damon, I'm going to try to explain something to you, and I want you to listen." He nodded his head, clearly uncomfortable with what was going on. "Damon, there's a difference between the sin and the sinner. I don't approve of what you did. It was wrong. You stole money from me." He nodded his head. "But you're my brother, and I love you. What I'm trying to say is, you don't need to pay me back unless you want to. I forgive you." Jenn felt as if a weight were being lifted from her shoulders.

"What?" Damon said, shocked. "But I will pay you back, I promise."

Jenn smiled at him. "That's up to you. All I want you to know is that I forgive you." She pulled open the screen door and walked into the house.

THIRT*y*~*FO*UR

The holidays ended, and Jenn found herself back in school. The end of the first semester was drawing near, and final exams were looming. Knowing that this was not the end of her education, Jenn found new reason to apply herself. She was sitting in her English class when a student came to the door. Mrs. Parker took the note from him, examined it, and then continued with her lecture. A few minutes before the end of the class she said, "Well, I think that's enough for today. Now, Jenn and Carl, Miss Hardy would like to see the two of you in her office. She waved them toward the door with the back of her hand.

"What do you think this is all about?" Carl Hathaway asked as the two of them navigated the labyrinth of the school to get to the counselor's office.

"Beats me," Jenn replied.

Miss Hardy was standing at the counter in the counselor's office when Carl and Jenn walked in. "Go in, take a seat," she said gesturing toward her office. "I'll be in in a minute."

Jenn and Carl seated themselves. "You do a really good job blessing the sacrament," Jenn said, trying to make small talk.

Carl blushed. "Thanks."

Miss Hardy bustled through the door. "Well, you two. In about six months you're going to be starting school at USU. I think it's time we talked about student housing." She sat down in her swivel chair. "I'm assuming you two know each other?"

Jenn nodded her head, "In fact, I'm riding to Utah with Carl."

"Oh?" Miss Hardy's eyebrows raised.

"And his sister, Sophie," Jenn continued.

Miss Hardy's eyebrows lowered. "I see. Well, it sounds as if you've worked that out." She thumbed through a manual on her desk. "It appears that there is some on-campus housing still available, and quite a few places near the campus that rent to students."

Carl said, "Sophie lived on campus her first year, but she's rented an off-campus apartment with five other girls since then. She thinks she can help me find a place."

Miss Hardy nodded her head. "What about you, Jenn?"

"I haven't even started looking, Miss Hardy."

"Well, on-campus housing is probably easier then, unless you're planning a trip to Utah to do some apartment hunting."

"No, ma'am," Jenn replied. "Any help you can give would be appreciated."

Miss Hardy pressed the book flat with the palms of her hands and turned it around so that it faced Jenn. "I'm assuming you'll be looking at shared housing? The least expensive I can find is $940 per semester. So you'll be looking at about $1,900 for the year." She looked over her glasses at Jenn. "As I indicated, I think I can get you a Pell grant that will cover all of that."

"If it's only $1,900 a year, I can handle that," Jenn said.

Miss Hardy smiled. "Oh, you've been saving up?"

Jenn nodded. "I'm guessing I'll have to buy food on top of that?"

"Yes," Miss Hardy said. "You'd be surprised how many kids live on soup and noodles. In other words, you can spend as much as you want on food."

"I suppose," she replied.

"Would you like me to get you an application? They'll begin accepting them next week."

"I'd appreciate that," Jenn said.

"What about you, Carl? Are you sure your sister can find something for you?"

He nodded. "I'm sure."

"Well, drop in next week and pick up the application," she said to Jenn. "It sounds as if you two are putting things together pretty well."

Jenn glanced at the clock on the wall of Miss Hardy's office. "I'd better hurry, or I'll be late for work."

"Need a ride?" Carl asked.

Jenn started to shake her head. Then she stopped and said, "I'd appreciate that, Carl." Five minutes later Carl dropped her off in front of her house.

"See you tomorrow," he said before speeding off.

Jenn changed clothes and hurried to work. When she arrived, Lorna beckoned to her.

"Jenn, this is Louise," Lorna said. "She's filling in for Shelly."

At the end of the evening, Lorna said to Jenn, "I hope Shelly has that baby soon and gets back here. I'm not sure how much of Louise I can take."

Jenn smiled. "She is a little different. I'll see you tomorrow."

She walked out the back door of the diner and started for home. It was cold enough she could almost see her breath. Jenn tugged her sweater tightly around her and continued down the sidewalk. Mentally, she began doing the math. *$1,900 for housing, so by the time I quit working at the diner, that will leave me nearly $3,000 for food. Even if I spend $100 dollars a month, that will be less than $1,000 dollars. That means I'll have $2,000 at the end of the year.*

Suddenly she realized that she had only enough money for the first year of school. *I'll just have to find a job,* she thought. "I can do this," she said out loud. "If I can teach Sunbeams, this ought to be easy."

When she arrived home from school the next day, a letter was waiting for her. The return address said Lingfelter. Eagerly, Jenn ripped open the envelope and removed the folded pages within.

Jenn, or should I say, Sister Cooper, what wonderful news! Sister Sandberg and I just knew you were one of the golden ones. I suppose before long you'll be given a calling, and you'll feel like an old hand at this church business. I was especially pleased that you'll be going to USU. "Go Big Blue." I'm finishing my junior year there right now .

I'm about to propose something to you that may seem strange. There are many things you don't know about me; one of them is that I am the youngest girl in a family of ten children. All of them are married except me and my younger brother, Matt, who is serving a mission in Bolivia. So we have a large house in Providence, which is about twenty minutes from USU. My folks and I have been thinking how wonderful it would be if you would like to come and stay with us while you're going to school in Logan. We have six empty bedrooms, and I drive to school every day. It would reduce your expenses considerably if you would consider this.

Please think about our offer and let me know. We'd be happy to have you as our guest.

Yours truly,
Alicia Lingfelter

Jenn's heart thumped in her chest. *I wonder what they'd charge me to stay with them? If it is less than $1,900. . . .* She sank on her bed, fell to her knees, and offered a prayer of thanks.

On Saturday morning she sat down at the table and wrote a response to Alicia Lingfelter. She dropped the letter in the mailbox on her way to work.

TH*i*RTY~FI*V*E

The final semester of school began, and Jenn found it harder to keep her mind on school. She had told Miss Hardy she had found some off-campus housing, much to the counselor's surprise. She still had not received an answer from the Lingfelters, but she felt confident that it would come. Jenn found she looked forward to Sundays and her class of five Sunbeams, although she often felt they were teaching her more than she was teaching them.

The people of the ward had embraced her as one of their own, and she felt comfortable each Sunday as she sat in sacrament meeting and learned more of the gospel. Valentine's Day was approaching, and Jenn wondered if there would ever be anyone who would want her as his valentine. Louise, Shelly's replacement at the diner, had managed to alienate everyone else who worked there, and Jenn herself found that she often avoided her. Late Friday night Lorna had just turned the sign over from "open" to "closed" when the phone rang. Jenn picked up the receiver. "Lorna's Fine Foods, how may I help you?"

"Is that you, Jenn?" the voice said.

"Shelly," Jenn exclaimed. "How are you?"

"I'm fine," she said. "I'm in the hospital."

"And?" Jenn said excitedly.

"A seven-pound, four-ounce little boy. Twenty inches long."

"Oh, Shelly," Jenn said, suddenly overcome with emotion. "Is everything all right?"

"He's beautiful," she said. "Jenn, his parents are coming in a few minutes to pick him up." There was a hint of sadness in her voice. "They're really nice people. They've been married nearly ten years and haven't been able to have any children."

"Oh, Shelly," Jenn said again.

"Tell Lorna, okay?"

"Sure."

"Thanks, Jenn. I don't know what I'd have done without you." There were a few more muffled sobs. "Tell Lorna I'll be ready to come back to work in a couple of weeks."

"You don't know how much we've missed you," Jenn said. "You take care." She hung up the phone and called to her boss. "Lorna, that was Shelly. She had a boy."

The next day Jenn bought a ceramic pot filled with tulips and walked to Shelly's house. She rang the bell, and Shelly's mother answered the door.

"Hi," Jenn said, "I don't know if you remember me? I'm Jennica Cooper. I work with your daughter at the diner."

"Oh, yes, please come in." She held the door open for Jenn. Shelly's in her bedroom." She led Jenn down a dark hallway to the end bedroom. Shelly was propped up with pillows as she lay in bed. A huge smile formed on her lips when Jenn entered the room.

"Jenn," she said. "You look great."

Jenn handed her the planter. "I thought you might want something to brighten your day," she said. "You look great yourself."

Shelly's mother slipped out of the door. Shelly patted the side of her bed. "Sit down," she said. She craned her neck to see if her mother had left. "I'll never be able to thank you enough for what you did for me."

"I didn't do anything," Jenn replied.

"It was really hard," Shelly said, "but I know it was the best thing for him. They're going to send me pictures, and they'll let me visit whenever I want."

"That's great. You're really brave, Shell."

Tears overflowed from her eyes and ran down her cheeks. "Not as brave as you think."

"Well," Jenn said trying to change the subject. "Lorna is hoping you'll be back soon. The girl who's been filling in for you is driving everybody nuts. You'll probably get a raise because Louise has been so bad." She laughed. "So, get your strength back and then come and save us." Jenn stood up. "Now, I know a good visit is a short visit, so I'm out of here."

"You don't have to go," Shelly said tearfully.

"Yup. I have to get to work and referee Lorna and Louise." She turned at the doorway. "But we'll see you soon."

Three weeks passed, and Shelly returned to work. Lorna and Jenn heaved a sigh of relief, as did the cooks and dishwasher. Jenn continued to save most of her wages and tip money, but she now deposited the money in the bank each week. Her new checks had come in the mail before she used any of the temporary ones. Jenn had not heard from Sister Lingfelter and was beginning to feel a bit nervous because the application deadline for on-campus housing had passed.

"I'll write her this weekend," she said under her breath. Saturday morning heralded a glorious day. The diner had been busy the night before, and Jenn had slept in until the sun awakened her. She was fixing her breakfast when the phone rang.

"Hello," she answered.

"To whom am I speaking?"

"Jennica Cooper," she replied.

"Miss Cooper, this is Sergeant Hill. I don't know if you remember me."

"Of course I do, Sergeant. You investigated my brother's shooting." Jenn's heart did a flip-flop. She had not checked to see if Damon was in his room, and she feared something had happened to him. "What can I do for you?"

"I just wanted to give you some news. We believe we've identified the man who shot your brother."

"Really?" Jenn said, shocked. "Who?"

"I'm afraid I can't give you that information just yet. We still need to notify his next of kin." He cleared his throat. "He was involved in a gang-related shooting last night and was killed." Jenn could hear him flipping through a few pages of his omnipresent notebook. "He was in the hospital for several hours before he passed away, and while we were interviewing him he indicated he was the one who shot your brother."

"Why?"

"A dispute over some territory. He wasn't very explicit, I'm afraid. But I wanted you to know. I'm sure this will close the case, unless other information comes forward."

"Thank you, Sergeant. I appreciate you letting us know. I'll tell Damon and my mother."

"Well, then, good-bye."

Jenn replaced the receiver and turned back to her breakfast. Damon was standing in the doorway. "Who was that?" he asked.

"The guy who shot you was killed himself last night. In a gang fight."

"Serves him right," Damon said, absently rubbing his right eyebrow.

"I suppose," Jenn replied. "Those who live by the sword, die by the sword."

"What?" Damon looked at her curiously. "What's that supposed to mean?"

"It means you need to be careful, little brother."

"I'm always careful," he replied as he walked out of the room. "Oh, by the way, this letter came for you yesterday." He tossed the envelope like a Frisbee in her direction.

Jenn slit open the envelope and removed the folded sheet:

Dear Jenn:

I'm sorry to be so slow in responding to your last letter. It has been hectic here at school with the new semester beginning. I forgot to give you Sister Sandberg's address, but it's probably a good thing. She was transferred the weekend I last wrote you. Probably the best thing to do is write to the mission home. The address is on the card that I've enclosed. They'll forward the letter to her. It's hard to believe, but she only has about six months left.

Mom and Dad are excited that you're going to come and stay with us.

189

The biggest argument has been which bedroom to put you in. Mom is pushing for my sister Char's room, which is decorated in sissy pink, while my dad thinks you ought to have Gayle's room, which is decorated in lime green. Personally, I think you ought to choose which room you want. They're all empty anyway, although I think we ought to leave Matt his room for when he gets home from Bolivia in November. Now, I need to warn you about my mom; she's a huggy-feely kind of person, so you'll probably feel kind of smothered for a little while until you get used to it. On the upside, she's a great cook. Of course that means you'll probably put on a few pounds, but, as I recall, you could use a few anyway.

Next question: how are you getting here? Dad says he'll drive down to California and pick you up if you need him to. He's retired and looking for things to occupy his time. So, if you need a ride, it's available. Just let us know.

As soon as you have your class schedule, let me know. We need to make sure ours mesh a little bit so we don't strand you at school, although Dad says you can drive Matt's car if you want to. It's a junker Honda, but it runs. So maybe that won't be a problem anyway.

We're excited you're going to be living with us and are just waiting to hear whether you need us to pick you up.

Yours truly,
Alicia Lingfelter

Jenn sat down at the table and reread the letter. *I'll write her tomorrow after church* she thought. *They're willing to do so much. The least I can do is let them know they won't have to come pick me up.*

The next day was Fast Sunday, and for the first time since her baptism Jenn took the opportunity to bear her testimony. She told the congregation how much she had learned to love them and thanked them for accepting her into the ward. Sister Ball and Sister Snow were not there, but Jenn realized that, as they had predicted, she had quit leaning on them and was now integrating herself into the ward. When the meetings were over she walked out the door into the bright spring sunshine. She spied Carl Hathaway and some of the other priests standing in the parking lot. She waved at Carl. *I need to let him know that I will need to be dropped off in Providence.*

Jenn walked briskly to where the young men were gathered. They were looking at a Lexus sedan that was parked next to the building. "Carl," she said.

The young men all turned and looked at her. "Hi, Jenn. We were just wondering whose car this is."

"I don't know," she said. "I don't remember seeing it before."

One of the young men was staring through the window on the driver's side. "Man, I think this is a hot car. Somebody hot-wired it."

The other young men immediately crowded around the window. Jenn's heart sank into the pit of her stomach, and her mind flashed back to last summer when she and her friends had dumped a Cadillac in this same parking lot.

"What did you want?" Carl asked her.

"Nothing," she said weakly. Her throat felt as if it had been squeezed shut. "I'll talk to you tomorrow."

"Okay," he shrugged. He turned to the other priests. "Guess I'd better go call the cops."

THI*R*TY~SI*X*

"*Sergeant Hill?*" *Jenn* said with a quavering voice.

"Hill here," he replied. "What can I do for you?"

"Sergeant, this is Jennica Cooper," she said. "I'm not sure if you remember me . . . "

"Damon Cooper's sister, right?"

"That's right," she said tightly.

"What can I do for you?" he asked. "We've closed the case on your brother."

"I understand," Jenn said. "I just needed to know some information, and I thought maybe you could help me."

"What kind of information?"

Jenn glanced around the kitchen. She'd waited to make the phone call until her mother had gone to the store and Damon was nowhere to be seen. Still, she glanced furtively into the front room. "Last fall there was a car stolen, and I wanted to see if I could get the victim's name."

"Well, you'd want Auto Theft, but I don't think they'll give you the information you want." She heard pages being turned. "I can transfer you, if you'd like to try."

"Thank you, I'd appreciate that," she said. The line went dead for a minute and then began to ring. It was picked up on the third ring.

"Auto Theft. Higgs speaking."

Jenn swallowed and then said, "Officer Higgs, I'm trying to find some information on an auto theft that occurred last September, actually the Saturday before Labor Day."

"Who was the victim?" the policeman asked.

"That's what I'm trying to find out," she said. "It was a Cadillac that was stolen from an Albertson's parking lot about midnight."

There was a pause on the other end of the phone. Then Officer Higgs said, "And why did you need this information?"

Jenn gnawed on her lower lip. "I witnessed the whole thing, and I just wondered if the owner of the car was all right."

"You witnessed it?" The interest in Officer Higgs's voice escalated. "Just a minute."

Jenn could hear the sound of fingers typing on a keyboard. In the background, she could hear the sound of several conversations being carried on, although she couldn't make out what was being said. Finally, after what seemed an eternity, Officer Higgs said, "Do you remember what color the vehicle was?"

"Light colored. The lights in the parking lot weren't all that bright." Fingers clicked on the keyboard again. Jenn could feel sweat beading up on her neck and running down her back. She heard the front door open and her mother's footsteps in the living room. Abruptly she hung up the phone. Her knees were shaking badly as she helped her mother put away the groceries.

On the following day, she walked into her English class. Carl Hathaway waved at her across the room. She waved back just as the tardy bell rang. Mrs. Parker closed the door, walked to the whiteboard in the front of the room, and waited for the class to grow quiet.

"I want to compliment you on your research papers. Some of you seemed to have really embraced the historical figure you studied. I'll hand back your papers at the end of class because I don't want you distracted while I introduce the new project." She picked up an erasable marker and wrote on the whiteboard: *Current problem!* She underlined it twice. "Your next project will be to research a contemporary issue. I have some suggestions if you can't come up with something of your own. When you wrote your last paper you went to the library and found a biography; with this project you will have to use current media. I'm sure you all remember how to use the *Reader's Guide to Periodical Literature,* but just in case you've grown a little rusty, I have a handout that explains how to use it." She walked to her desk and picked up a stack of papers from one corner. Quickly, she fanned them, counted out the number for each row and distributed the handout.

Jenn looked at the paper in her hand. She hadn't used the *Reader's Guide* since junior high school. A knot of panic formed in her stomach.

"I know many of you are computer literate," Mrs. Parker continued, "so you might want to use the internet to gather your information. Many of the national newspapers are available on the worldwide web, along with our local papers. You can generally search for key words quite easily. So, if you were going to do a paper on drunk driving, you'd enter "drunk driving" into the search engine, which would turn up a surprising number of articles." She returned to the whiteboard and wrote:

Length: 3–5 pages, single-spaced
Word processed or handwritten in ink.
Spelling and grammar will be considered in grading.
Possible topics: drunk driving, teenaged smoking, nuclear
weapons, the economy, the price of gasoline, balancing
business and the environment, shoplifting, gang violence.

"I hope that gives you some ideas. I'd like you to break up into groups of five or six and discuss possible topics. By the end of the hour I need each of you to fill out one of these cards." She fanned them above her head. "I need your name and the topic you've decided on. Any questions?" She glanced around the room. "Okay, break up into groups."

There was considerable noise as desks were rearranged to facilitate the small group discussions. Jenn found herself in a group of three other girls and two boys. Carl Hathaway was one of them. The discussion ranged from the silly to the significant. When the topic turned to theft, Carl told the group about the stolen car he and his friends had found the previous Sunday. Carl's account of the police investigation was quite vivid, and when the appointed hour came, Jenn took one of the cards, wrote her name on it, and put "car theft and joy-riding," as her topic.

On the following day, the class went to the library to begin their research. Jenn went to one of the computer terminals and launched a web browser. She did a Google search for the local paper and watched as the site popped into view. She searched the screen for some way to access earlier editions of the paper but could see none. Carl Hathaway walked up behind her.

"Having any success?" he asked.

Jenn jumped. "I didn't hear you, Carl," she said while her heart leapt in her chest. She took a deep breath and exhaled slowly. "No, I'm not having any success. I don't know how to find the older papers."

"Let me show you," he said. He took the mouse from Jenn's fingers and moved the cursor to the top of the screen. "They're right here, under Previous Editions. Which one are you looking for?"

Jenn felt panicky. "Oh, I don't know. Just show me how to use it," she said shakily.

Carl clicked on the icon and typed "December 25" in the search box. A few seconds later the front page of the Christmas edition appeared on the screen. "That's all there is to it," Carl said proudly.

"Thanks," Jenn said. "I think I can find the stuff myself. I appreciate your help, Carl."

"No problem," he replied as he sat down at the terminal next to hers and began typing on the keyboard.

As inconspicuously as she could, Jenn looked at the small calendar in her backpack and found the date of the day before Labor Day the previous fall. She entered it into the search engine and waited until the front page appeared on the screen. As casually as possible she scanned through the paper, page by page, looking for any mention of a stolen car. There was nothing she could see so she returned to the front page and entered the date for Labor Day. Again there was nothing she could find that related to the Cadillac she had helped steal the previous year. She was about to exit from the site when she noticed an index on the left side of the screen. Jenn scrolled down through it until she saw "police docket" among the choices. She moved the cursor onto the words and watched as the cursor turned into a small, white-gloved hand. She clicked.

A few seconds passed before a listing of all the cases reported to the police in the past week appeared on the screen. She scanned down until she found the listing for the stolen car. She clicked on the case number, and a brief paragraph appeared on the screen:

"Car theft: 1999 Cadillac Seville, Cotillion White, stolen 2425 N. Blackstone. Recovered undamaged. Owner, Felix Castelanas (76), assaulted by gang who stole car."

Jenn's mouth turned to cotton. *Assaulted!* Quickly, she wrote down the name of the owner of the car and stuck the paper in her backpack. Then she began searching for information for her report.

Traffic at the diner was slow, and during a lull Jenn opened the phone book and searched for a Felix Castelanas. She found two of them and jotted down both phone numbers and addresses. She was unsure what she was going to do next but knew that somehow she would have to make contact with them and try to make things right. As she walked home after work, she mulled over what she had to do. After she arrived home she lay awake in her bed, reliving the moment when she had knocked the old man to the ground and stolen his keys. *I wish life were like a tape recorder and I could rewind the past nine months and erase a few things I've done.* At last she fell into a troubled sleep.

When Saturday morning arrived she slipped out of bed before either her mother or Damon awoke and tiptoed to the kitchen. With trembling hands she dialed the first of the two numbers for Felix Castelanas. The phone rang five times before an answering machine picked up.

You've reached 555–3981. We're not able to come to the phone at the moment. Please leave your name, phone number and a brief message and we'll get back to you." The voice sounded too young to be the man Jenn was searching for. Her hands were shaking badly as she replaced the receiver on the cradle. She sat down at the table and waited for the trembling to stop. Then she dialed the second number. The phone rang four times and then someone answered.

"Hello," the accented elderly voice said.

Jenn took a deep breath and said, "Hello. Is this Mr. Castelanas?"

"*Sí.* Who is this?"

Jenn felt as if her shoulders were pushing up to her ears, and she could barely breathe. "This is Jennica Cooper, Mr. Castelanas."

"Do I know you?" he said brusquely.

"No, I don't think so," she said.

"What are you selling? I don' want any."

"I'm not selling anything, sir. I'm doing a report in school on auto theft, and I noticed that your car was stolen last September."

"*Esas muchachas del infierno,*" he spat. "What do you want?"

Jenn tried to calm herself before replying. "I wonder if I could arrange some time to interview you about the car theft?" she stammered.

There was a long pause before Mr. Castelanas answered, "I don' think so. How do I know you're not just trying to get in my house to rob me?"

"I . . . I . . . I don't know, Mr. Castelanas. If we could meet somewhere you'd feel comfortable, I'd like to have you tell me what happened to you. You could decide where."

Again there was a pause. "Do you know where the library is?"

"There are several of them, Mr. Castelanas. Which one do you mean?"

"The one on Fifth Street. Do you know where that is?"

Jenn thought for a minute, "Yes, I do, Mr. Castelanas. Would you meet me there?"

"*Sí*. When do you want to meet?" he asked.

"I work after school, so it would have to be on Saturday," she ventured. "I don't suppose you'd be able to meet with me today?" There was no answer for some time. "Mr. Castelanas?" Jenn asked.

"I suppose. Perhaps three o'clock? There are some small rooms we could use—behind the checkout counter."

"Three o'clock would be fine," she replied.

"How will I know you?" he asked.

"I will be wearing a white skirt and a blue blouse," she replied. "And I'll be carrying a notebook so I can write down what you tell me."

"Humpf."

"I'll see you at the library at three o'clock this afternoon," she said. Her heart was beating wildly.

"*Sí,*" he said before hanging up.

Jenn took the bus to the library and arrived nearly half an hour early. She entered the building and sat in one of the chairs near the front door. She carried a yellow legal pad in one hand and her purse in the other. While she waited she wrote down questions she wanted to ask Mr. Castelanas. Jenn was still unsure how she was going to approach this man, how she would confess her part in the car theft, and how she would try to make amends, but she had brought several twenty-dollar bills with her. She watched the hands on the clock above the checkout counter move as slowly as dandelion down on a still spring day. After fifteen minutes passed she stood and walked behind the counter to where a number of small conference rooms were located. None were occupied. She returned to her seat and reread the questions on the legal pad.

Promptly at three o'clock, a nearly bald elderly man walked through the door. He was dressed in gray trousers with a knife-edge crease, an open-collared white golf shirt, and a navy blue blazer. He carried a silver-topped cane in his left hand. He wore thick, rimless glasses and glanced around the room with ferretlike motions. Jenn's heart nearly stopped. Even though she had only seen Mr. Castelanas for a brief second or two the night of the crime, she had no doubt that that was the man who had just walked into the library. She rose to her feet and approached him.

"Mr. Castelanas? I'm Jennica Cooper." She extended her hand toward him.

He looked at her through thick lenses that magnified his burnt sienna eyes. His gaze focused on her face, and he finally took her hand in his. It was frail and birdlike, and his skin rustled like dry autumn leaves. "This way," he said as he stumped on with his cane toward one of the small rooms. When they were seated on opposite sides of the table in the room, he asked, "Why, after all this time, are you asking about my car?" He laid his cane on the tabletop between them.

Jenn gulped. "I'm doing a report for my high school English class on car thefts," she managed to say. Her throat felt as if every drop of water had been sucked out of it, and her tongue felt swollen and unwieldy.

Felix Castelanas inspected her face closely and then leaned his elbows on the table and pushed his face as close as the table permitted toward Jenn's face. "Do I know you?" he asked as he squinted and creased the bridge of his nose. "You look familiar."

Jenn's heart began to race and a sheen of sweat formed on her forehead. She struggled to speak. "I . . . we . . . I mean . . ." She fluttered her hands in front of her with the palms up.

The old man shrugged and settled back into his chair. "What do you want to ask me?" he said folding his hands on the tabletop.

"Could you tell me what happened?" The words were barely audible.

"What?" he said. "I can't hear too well." He tapped his finger on his ear.

Jenn struggled to swallow and then said a little more loudly, "Could you tell me what happened that night?"

The old man tented his fingers and placed his thumbs under his chin while he rested his elbows on the table. He gently tapped his fingers together in front of his lips while he sat silently for nearly a minute. Jenn was becoming increasingly uncomfortable. Finally, he spoke in a voice that seemed somewhat removed from where they sat.

"I had gone shopping for some groceries. It was late at night but I had not been sleeping well since my dear Maria passed away. God bless her soul." He crossed himself. "The parking lot was dark so I parked under one of the lights and bought my food. When I got to my car, I opened the trunk to put my purchases inside. Just as I closed it, this gang of girls knocked me to the ground and stole my car. They ripped my trousers and bruised my knee." Tears formed in his eyes. "I thought I was going to die." He blinked his eyes quickly. "Another customer, a lady, saw it happen and called the police before she came to help me. The policemen came and talked to me. Then they drove me home. A few hours later they called to tell me they had found the car." He removed his glasses and cleaned them with a large white handkerchief he pulled from his hip pocket. "That is all I know."

As Mr. Castelanas spoke, guilt began to grow in Jenn's breast until she could hardly breathe. When he finished his narrative they sat in silence for a few moments until she was able to choke out, "Was your car damaged?"

He shook his head slowly, "No. They ate some of my groceries, but that was all."

"How much did your trousers cost?" she asked softly.

"What?" He put his hand behind his ear. "My trousers?"

"The ones that were ruined."

He shrugged his shoulders. "I don' know. They were old. Maybe twenty-five dollars, maybe thirty. I don' know for sure." He drummed his fingers on the tabletop.

"And your knee. Is that why you use a cane?"

"No, no, no." He spread his hands expansively. "No, it was the other leg. I didn't even go to my doctor."

Jenn swallowed and tried to create some saliva in her mouth. "Will you ever be able to forgive these girls, sir?"

Felix leaned forward and shrugged again. "I think I had almost forgotten about it until you phoned me. No, that's not true. I'm afraid to go anywhere after dark. That's what bothers me the most." He shook his head. "I don' know what has happened to these kids today. I'm an old man, and my Maria and me, well, we didn't have no kids, so maybe I don' understand."

Jenn placed the legal pad flat on the table and reached for her purse. She took a deep breath and said, "Mr. Castelanas, I want you to know I didn't lie to you. I really am doing a report on car thefts, but I was one of the girls who stole your car, and I want to make it right." She zipped open her purse, removed three twenty-dollar bills, and slid them across the table toward him. "I hope this will cover the cost of your trousers and the food. And most of all I want to beg your forgiveness. It was a stupid, terrible thing to do to you."

He sat motionless and blinked his magnified eyes. "Your priest made you do this. You went to confession, and he made you do this?"

Jenn shook her head slightly. "No, Mr. Castelanas. I'm doing this because I need to. I'm trying to clean up my life."

He stared at her silently, while the corners of his mouth twitched. Then, with majesty, he grasped his cane, pushed it to the floor and rose. He pushed the money back to Jenn. "They were old pants," he said. He turned and stumped out of the room. Jenn gathered her purse and her notepad and hurried after him.

"Please," she said, offering him the bills.

He shook his head and continued to walk as quickly as his cane permitted toward the front door of the library. Jenn pushed the door open and held it for him. The white Cadillac was parked in a handicapped parking place, and the old man walked purposefully toward it. He fished in his trouser pocket for the keys, pushed the remote, and unlocked the door. Jenn stood on the sidewalk and watched as he pulled the door open and climbed painfully into the car.

"Please," she pleaded again.

He shook his head and closed the door. Jenn raised her hand and waved at him as the driver's window slid downward. "How did you get here?" he asked.

"The bus," Jenn replied.

"Want a ride home?" he said with a smile.

THIRT𝒚~SE𝑽EN

The final semester of school drew to a close, and Jenn began to feel the mixed emotions of excitement and fear as college approached. Her mother wore the clothing Jenn had given her as a Christmas present to the graduation ceremony, which was held outside the school in the football stadium. After returning her cap and gown and picking up her diploma, Jenn realized that this chapter of her life had come to a close.

She worked as many hours as Lorna permitted and squirreled the money into her checking account. Sister Ball had gone home, and Sister Snow had been transferred. Jenn's Primary class kept her occupied each Sunday, and she was putting together more and more names and faces of ward members.

Jenn and Alicia Lingfelter continued to correspond, and Carl Hathaway had agreed to detour the few miles to Providence and drop Jenn off at the Lingfelters' home. Finally, the day arrived when Jenn was to leave for college. She'd spent a nearly sleepless night wondering if she'd forgotten anything. As she lay in her bed she inventoried every item that was in her two small suitcases before finally drifting off to sleep for a couple of hours before the alarm clock rang.

Carl Hathaway and his sister, Sophie, arrived promptly at eight o'clock and helped Jenn squeeze one of her suitcases into the trunk and the other into the backseat of the car. Jenn's mother hugged her tightly before saying, "Now, you remember who you are, young lady." She brushed tears from her eyes, turned, and hurried back into the house. Damon gave her a little hug and vanished himself. Jenn crammed herself into the backseat of the car and leaned her head on her pillow on top of the suitcase that stood on end in the backseat. She felt so insecure that she wanted to curl up into a ball and cry. She hugged the pillow tightly as they made their way to the freeway. The little red car had barely left town when she fell asleep.

Sophie fell asleep too while Carl maneuvered the car up Highway 99 toward Sacramento. They had traveled for nearly four hours before Jenn woke up as Carl said, "How about stopping to get some lunch?" Without waiting for a reply, he pulled into a Perkin's parking lot. Less than an hour later they were back on the road, with Sophie driving toward Auburn and Donner Pass. Late in the afternoon, they dropped into Reno. "We can get a real good dinner for cheap at one of the casinos," Sophie said as she pulled into the parking lot across the street from a building that had more lights on it than Jenn had ever seen before. They skirted the slot machines and made their way to a dinner buffet. "It's cheap 'cause they think people will stay longer and spend more money gambling," Carl said as he forked a meatball into his mouth. "We'll probably cost them money," he laughed.

The three of them walked out of the casino and across the road to the parking lot. "I'll drive till I get tired, and then you can take over, okay?" Carl said. Sophie nodded her head, slipped into the passenger seat, promptly closed her eyes, and tried to sleep. Jenn watched as the car traveled across the barren desert of Nevada while the sun sank slowly behind them in the cloudless sky. It looked as if there was water on the road, she noticed, but the car never reached it—it always slid ahead of them as elusive as forgotten memories. By the time they reached Winnemucca, the sun was setting, and when they reached Battle Mountain, Carl pulled off the freeway and asked Sophie to take over. They changed seats, and he soon fell asleep. She drove until they reached Wendover and then pulled off the highway and into a Chevron station to get gas. Jenn could barely unkink her legs as she climbed out of the backseat. The three of them stretched and yawned before Sophie said, "I'm tired. Why don't we try to sleep for a little while before we cross the salt flats?"

After filling the car, they parked it in the back corner of the casino parking lot and made themselves as comfortable as possible. Jenn didn't think she was particularly tired and she was feeling guilty about not being able to help drive, but it took only a few minutes before she fell asleep in her little burrow in the backseat. She awakened when Carl started the car.

"'Bout five in the morning," he said. "I can't sleep anymore, so I thought we'd get moving. We'll stop for breakfast in Salt Lake, unless you're starving before then."

The rim of the mountains to the east was just being outlined with a pearlescent glow as they crossed the desert and headed for Salt Lake. Dawn had broken as they rounded the south shore of the Great Salt Lake and headed into the city. Carl pulled off the freeway on North Temple and into a Denny's parking lot. "Even stopping for a nap, we've made really good time," Sophie said as they sat down for breakfast.

"How much further to Providence?" Jenn asked timidly.

"About an hour and a half. We're real close," Sophie replied.

Jenn felt her heart thump in her chest. *I guess I'm not just drifting down the stream,* she thought. When breakfast was finished, they pulled into a gas station and filled up the car. "My turn to pay," Jenn volunteered. "I can't believe we're nearly there."

Sophie guided the car back onto Interstate 80 and then onto I-15 as they swung north toward Logan. Jenn looked with amazement at the mountains that vaulted into the sky to the east of the freeway. There seemed to be so little room between them and the lake to the west. She was tired of sitting but excited to be so close to Sister Lingfelter. Then panic began to grow in her heart. *What if this doesn't work out? What if they don't let me stay with them. Where will I go?* She sank down in the backseat even further as they exited the freeway and made their way past Brigham City and up the canyon toward Sardine Summit.

Jenn had never been in the mountains before, and she couldn't believe how clean the air was or how beautiful her surroundings were. She felt as if she were a butterfly just emerging from her cocoon. There was exhilaration in this newfound freedom, but there was comfort in the past when she had been a caterpillar.

"There's a turnoff just ahead," Sophie said as they drove out of the mountains and into Cache Valley. A few minutes later they turned east and followed a ribbon of road toward the foothills where the town of Providence was nestled. The three of them were searching for the Lingfelters' house when suddenly the door of a house flew open and Alicia Lingfelter came running down the walk toward the street waving her arms wildly above her head. "Must be the place," Sophie said with a smile as she pulled to the curb.

Jenn vaulted out of the backseat and ran toward the tall blonde woman who engulfed her in a hug. "I can't believe you're here," Alicia said.

"Neither can I," Jenn replied. Carl and Sophie had climbed out of the car and were stretching. "These are my friends Carl and Sophie Hathaway," Jenn said, pointing toward them. "This is . . . " and suddenly Jenn didn't know what to call Sister Lingfelter.

"Ali," Sister Lingfelter said as she extended her hand. "I remember when you used to bless the sacrament," she said to Carl. "Come on in, won't you." She led the three of them up the front steps of her home. A wide porch ran the full width of a house shaded by tall spruce trees. Jenn could smell their perfume as she trailed behind Sister . . . Ali . . . Lingfelter. A peaceful feeling flooded over her, and she began to relax. A car came around the street corner, and the driver honked the horn two quick beeps and waved. Ali waved back.

In contrast to Jenn's house, the Lingfelter home was a palace. Jenn stood in the living room and turned around slowly. On the east wall was a fireplace with bookcases on both sides. On the mantle was a statue of the Savior about two feet high with his arms outstretched. Mesmerized, Jenn walked toward it. She felt as if He were extending His love to her. She stood transfixed, looking at it.

"Mom and Dad are at the temple," Ali said as if an explanation was needed. "They go every Wednesday morning. They ought to be back soon. Please, have a seat."

As soon as they were seated on the floral-printed couches, Ali asked,

"So, how was the trip?"

"Long," Sophie replied. "We're just glad to be here."

"Any problems?"

Carl and his sister shook their heads. "Nothing to it," he said.

Ali turned to Jenn, "Well, catch me up on what's been happening in your life," she said expectantly.

Jenn shrugged her shoulders. "Not much, really. Of course I wrote you that I had been baptized." Ali nodded her head. "And then Bishop Caldwell called me to be a Primary teacher. It about scared me to death, but it has been such a blessing."

"That brings up a decision you're going to have to make, Jenn. A lot of the kids who are going to USU go to the student wards even though they don't live on campus."

"That's what I've done," Sophie said. "The golden toaster's a great place to go to church."

Jenn's eyebrows shot up. "The golden toaster?"

Ali laughed, "That's what the USU kids call it. The building does kind of look like a big toaster." She continued, "Your other option is to have your records moved to our ward. After all, you'll be living here, and you'd be welcome to go to church with the rest of us. But it's up to you."

"If you want to go to a college ward, we'll come and get you," Carl said shyly.

Jenn sat with her hand folded in her lap. "I don't know," she finally said. "I guess I'll just have to play it by ear."

"Well, it isn't a decision you have to make today. But a decision you do need to make is which room you'd like. And I'd suggest you do it before Mom and Dad get home and try to pressure you." Ali stood up and bade Jenn follow her across the front room and up the stairs. When they reached the second story, Ali pointed to four open doorways. "Those are all empty bedrooms. The bathroom is there." She pointed at a doorway at the end of the hall. "My room is this one," she said, pointing at the room nearest the bathroom. "That one with the closed door is my brother Matt's. But you can choose any of the other four."

Jenn looked in each of the rooms. It was clear that the former occupants had different tastes, and each room had its own flavor. It was hard to decide, but Jenn felt quite at home in a room that was decorated in peach tones and had a single canopy bed. Besides, it was across the hall from Ali's room. A few minutes later Carl had carried her two small suitcases up the stairs and placed them on her bed.

"Well, we'd better be on our way," he said. "We need to get our stuff moved in." Ali and Jenn followed the brother and sister out to the car. There was an awkward moment while Jenn thanked the two for the ride and hugged Carl good-bye.

"We'll see you on campus," he said as they drove away.

Ali took Jenn's elbow and guided her back into the house. "I'm so excited to see you," she bubbled. "I can't believe you're really here."

"I can't either," Jenn said soberly. "Can I ask you a question?" Her friend nodded her head. "Why are you doing this?"

"Doing what?"

"Inviting me into your home. Giving me a place to stay. I mean, you don't even know me, do you?"

Ali's eyes crinkled. "Oh, but I think I've known you for a long time. After all, we're both daughters of God."

THIRT𝒴~EI𝘨HT

Ali's parents arrived home a couple of hours later. Her mother was a short, substantial woman with piercing blue eyes and blond hair turning gray. As predicted, she enveloped Jenn in a bear hug that almost took Jenn's breath away. Ali's father was tall and thin with a full head of snow white hair. He wore rimless glasses that perched on his nose like a sparrow on a wire. A little more reserved than his wife, he gave Jenn a brief hug and welcomed her to their home. They ate a quick lunch, and then Ali offered to take Jenn to USU and familiarize her with the campus before she began orientation the next morning.

Jenn had been in a car for more than a day, but she jumped at the chance to see the college. She and Ali climbed into a ten-year-old Toyota that was a weather-faded blue but sported a red right front fender. "Not fancy but serviceable," Ali said as they drove through town and down to the highway. Less than half an hour passed before she parked the car in a student parking lot. Although school did not begin until the next Monday, crowds of students were walking around campus. Ali led Jenn through the maze of buildings and identified each one, including the "golden toaster." "Before we leave, we'll get some Aggie ice cream," she said, pointing toward a building on the northwest corner of campus.

A banner across the front of the student union building welcomed the freshman students to USU. The two women entered the building and approached a group of tables arranged in a square on the floor of the ballroom. "This is where you will need to come in the morning," Ali said. Jenn nodded her head. *I'm not sure I'm ready for this,* she thought. So much was happening so fast.

"Let's go get some ice cream," Ali said with a smile. They walked a couple of blocks to where the ice cream was sold, chose their flavors, and sat outside on a bench while they licked their cones.

"This is really good," Jenn said.

"None better."

"No argument from me," Jenn said with a grin.

"Well, we'd better head home for dinner. I hope the ice cream didn't ruin your appetite. Mom's been planning tonight's menu for a month."

They drove home on the upper road to Providence. Jenn could not believe how friendly everyone seemed to be. When they arrived home, Jenn unpacked her clothes and hung them in the closet or placed them in the white dresser that occupied the wall opposite the bed. Overcome with the reception she'd received, she sank to her knees beside the bed and offered a prayer of thanksgiving. Her head drooped onto the bedspread, and she fell asleep. She awoke when Ali gently shook her shoulder.

"Dinner's ready," she said. "Can't disappoint Mom."

"I didn't realize I was so tired," Jenn said as she followed Ali downstairs to the dining room. The table had been set with a white linen tablecloth and deep blue china. It was the first time Jenn had ever sat at a table with matching plates and silverware. A vase filled with red roses sat in the middle of the table.

"Come, sit here," Mrs. Lingfelter said as she patted the chair on her right. Her husband sat opposite her and Ali sat in the other chair across from Jenn. "Before we begin, Dad," Mrs. Lingfelter said, "I just want to tell Jennica how honored we are to have her staying with us." She beamed a smile in Jenn's direction. "It's just so wonderful to have more than one daughter rumbling around in this big old house. Thank you for agreeing to live here this year."

"I'm the one who should be thanking you," Jenn said with an embarrassed smile.

"Oh, think nothing of it. We have plenty of room, and it's so wonderful to have you here." She patted the back of Jenn's hand. "Now, Dad, you'd better say the blessing before the food gets cold."

Obediently, he offered a blessing. Another first for Jenn. As Ali had predicted, the meal was magnificent. When it was over, the four of them sat contentedly around the table. "That was delicious," Jenn said. "I'm stuffed."

"I'm glad you liked it, dear," Ali's mother said. "Now, I think we need to make a couple of decisions."

"Oh?" her husband replied. "Like what?"

"Like, what is this dear girl going to call you and me? I don't want to make her uncomfortable, but I'm so used to our kids calling us Mom and Dad, that nothing else seems quite right. Would that be all right with you, Jenn?"

Jenn played with the edge of the tablecloth with her fingers. "I guess."

"Is something wrong? If that isn't what you'd like, well, we can come up with something else," said Mom Lingfelter.

"It's just that I've never really had a dad," Jenn said slowly. "I mean, of course I had a dad, but he died when I was quite young."

"I'm sorry," she replied. "What happened?"

Jenn took a deep breath. The subject was one she had tried to avoid all her life. It was not something she wished to talk about, but she felt the question had been asked out of sincere concern. *It's funny,* she thought, *there aren't a whole lot of experiences from my life that I've run away from, but I feel almost as embarrassed for me as I am for my dad.* "He was killed," she said in a voice barely above a whisper.

"How awful," Mom Lingfelter said as her hand flew to her mouth.

Jenn's hands gripped the tablecloth even more tightly. *Here I go. Once they hear the truth about my father, they're not going to want me to stay.* "He was killed in a barroom brawl. He'd been drinking, and somehow he got into a fight." Her voice was as tight as a violin string. "I don't know a whole lot more except somebody hit him on the head with a pool cue.

By the time the police got there, he was nearly dead. They took him to the hospital, but he was gone by the time they arrived." Her hands were sweating, and she'd nearly tied the edge of the tablecloth into a knot.

Silence descended on the room like a down-filled comforter. Jenn could hear the ticking of the grandfather clock in one corner of the room. *I wonder if they'll ask me to leave tonight? Where can I go? How will I get there?*

"How terrible for you and your mother," Mom Lingfelter said with a shake of her head. "How old were you?"

"I'd just turned three," Jenn replied in a whisper as tears began to roll down her cheeks. "I've never had a dad," she repeated.

"Well, you've got one now," Ali's father said. He pushed himself away from the table, walked to her side, knelt on the floor, and put his arms around her. She sank into his shoulder and cried convulsively. When she gained a measure of control, he helped her to her feet and led her into the living room.

"Do you want me to go?" she asked timidly.

"Whatever for?"

"I don't know. I thought maybe after hearing about my dad you wouldn't want me to stay." She was still fighting to control her emotions, and she shook gently.

"My dear," Dad Lingfelter said, "you can't be held accountable for what your father did or didn't do. I'm just pleased you've done so well with your life. No, we don't want you to go. We're thrilled to have you with us." He tugged on his lower lip. "Although, I must say I'm a little disappointed you didn't choose Gayle's room. Green has always been my favorite color." His eyes sparkled with his little joke.

THIRT𝑦~NIN𝑒

The orientation the next day answered most of the questions that had been bothering Jenn since she'd made the decision to come to Utah State. She was given another copy of her class schedule, and as she walked around campus with the other new students, she found the locations of each of her classes. The group she was assigned to consisted of about two dozen young men and women, most of them from Utah but a handful from out of state. Ali had driven her to the campus and agreed to pick her up at four o'clock when the orientation ended.

"Kind of a lot to learn, isn't it?" said a young woman dressed in white tennis shorts and a blouse.

Jenn nodded her head. "I'm glad I had a chance to check out the campus yesterday. At least I kind of know where things are now." She offered her hand. "I'm Jenn Cooper."

"Lee Ann Robins," the girl replied. "I'm from Cedar."

"Cedar?" Jenn wrinkled her forehead.

"Cedar City," Lee Ann gestured with her head toward the south. "It's in southern Utah."

"Oh. I'm from California."

Lee Ann smiled at her. "Surfer girl, huh?"

"Not quite," Jenn replied. They'd reached the union building, where tables with sack lunches had been set outside. Jenn chose a turkey sandwich and sat at one of the tables arranged on an outside plaza. Lee Ann sat down across from her.

"Okay if I sit here?"

"Sure," Jenn replied.

Lee Ann's gaze flitted around the tables in the plaza. "That kid with the crew cut and the aviator shades is kind of cute," she said, pointing toward a nearby table with the tip of her nose.

Jenn looked quickly at the boy and said, "Yes, he is."

Lee Ann munched on her sandwich for a minute before saying, "What are you majoring in? Or have you decided?"

Jenn swallowed her bite of sandwich. "Civil engineering. I have a scholarship."

Lee Ann shot her hands in the air as if she were signaling a touchdown. "You've gotta be kidding. I barely passed algebra."

Jenn was slightly taken aback. "What are you majoring in?"

Lee Ann shrugged her shoulders. "I don't know yet. Boys, mainly." She blinked her eyes. "You got a scholarship in engineering?" she blurted.

Jenn nodded her head. "Pretty lucky, I guess." She took another bite of her sandwich. "Not bad," she said. "But I used to work at a place that made a better turkey sandwich."

"Hmm. Never worked, myself," Lee Ann said. "Well, gotta be going. I'll see you around." She stuffed the remnants of her lunch into the paper sack and started toward the trash can. Then she detoured past the table where Mr. Crewcut was sitting and stopped to talk.

Jenn leaned back against the wall behind her. A sudden wave of homesickness overcame her as she thought of Lorna and the diner where she'd worked for more than two years. She thought of her mother and brother and the squalor in which they lived and felt both blessed and guilty as she took a deep breath of the clean air. Abruptly, she rose and carried her garbage to the trash can. Deep in thought, she barely noticed the young man who was sitting on the wall next to it. When she glanced at him she remembered that he'd been part of their orientation group, although she couldn't remember his name.

"Hi," he said.

Jenn was startled. "Oh! Hi," she replied.

"Your name is Jenn, right?" He smiled deeply. "From California?"

She was embarrassed she couldn't remember his name. "Right," she said.

"I'm Brig Hales," he said as he hopped down from the wall. He thrust her hand toward her.

"Hi, Brig," she said as she shook his hand.

"How'd you like orientation?" he asked with a smile.

"It was okay," she said. "Answered most of my questions, anyway."

He nodded his head. "Want to go get some ice cream for dessert?" He pointed vaguely in the direction of the ice cream shop.

"Sure," she said. "I had some rocky road yesterday, and it was heavenly."

"Let's go," he said with a loopy grin. "If we hurry, we can get back for the afternoon session." Ten minute later they were sitting in the shade of a tree outside the Aggie ice cream store. Jenn tried to pay for her own cone, but Brig waved it away and paid for both. They sat quietly licking their ice cream until Brig said, "You going to the dance tomorrow night?"

"I don't know. I hadn't really thought about it. Why? Are you going?"

Brig licked his ice cream. "Maybe, if I can find someone to go with me."

Jenn's heart stood still. She was eighteen years old and had never been on a date. She licked furiously at the fudge ripple cone. She was unsure if Brig Hales was asking her to go with him or if she was just imagining it. So many new things were happening in her life that she felt as if she were on overload. She desperately did not want to make a fool of herself by assuming something, but she equally felt a yearning to go to the dance if that was what Brig Hales was suggesting.

He wiped his hand with a napkin and threw it in the garbage can. Jenn stuffed the last of her cone into her mouth and followed him across the parking lot. She replayed the conversation in her mind and tried to come up with something that would let him know she was interested without committing herself. As they crossed the street, she said, "You know, if someone asked me to go the dance, I'd probably go."

They walked several steps further before he said, "Well, then, if you'd like a second date with me, I'm willing."

"Second date?" Jenn said.

"I paid for the ice cream, didn't I?" he said with a laugh. "Tell me where you live, and I'll pick you up about eight o'clock."

Jenn swallowed hard. "I'm staying—that is, I guess I live in Providence," she said. "If you know where that is."

Brig laughed again. "I'm from Paradise, and Providence is on the way."

"Paradise?"

"It's south of Providence. Hyrum is in between."

They again reached the Taggart Center, where the students were gathering for the afternoon session. "What's your address?" Brig asked. Jenn told him, and he wrote it on the palm of his hand with his ballpoint pen. "Eight o'clock," he said with a wink.

A smile spread across Jenn's face. "Eight o'clock," she confirmed.

Ali picked her up at the appointed hour. "I need to stop at Fred Meyer on the way home," she said. "Unless you're in a hurry."

Jenn shook her head. "That would be fine."

"You look uncommonly happy," Ali commented. "Did you have a good time at orientation?"

Jenn nodded her head. They drove west toward Main Street in silence until Jenn said, "Ali, what do you wear to a dance around here?"

Ali glanced quickly in Jenn's direction. "Why?"

"Someone asked me to go to the dance tomorrow night," she answered shyly. "I'm just not sure what to wear."

"Who?"

Jenn felt a little uncomfortable, "A boy from Paradise. Brig Hales."

"Brig's old enough to be going to college?" Ali scrunched up her face. "I guess he is. His brother, Alma, was my age in school, and Brig's about three years younger. He's a nice kid, Jenn." She drummed her fingers on the steering wheel. "We'll find something for you to wear while we're at Freddy's."

FORTY

"*Well, Brigham Hales,* you've grown up to be a fairly respectable young man," Mom Lingfelter said with a grin. He stood just inside their front door looking uncomfortable in his light tan chinos and open-throated, dark-blue golf shirt.

"Yes'm. I didn't know Jenn was living with you," he croaked.

"She'll be down in just a moment," she continued. "Come in and make yourself comfortable," she said, sweeping him into the living room. Dad Lingfelter sat in his recliner, reading the newspaper. He lowered it, slid his glasses back up his nose, and inspected the young man who perched uncomfortably on the edge of the couch.

"How's Alma doing?" he asked.

"Just fine," Brig replied. "He's living in Ogden."

"I don't remember whether he and his wife . . . " The white-haired man tapped his fingertips on the arm of the chair while he searched the ceiling for some hidden answer. "What's her name, Brigham?"

"Carlie, sir."

"That's right. How could I forget it? Anyway, do they have any children yet?"

"She's expecting a baby next month," Brig said. "A little girl." He licked his lips.

"How many of you are still at home?"

"Three," Brig replied. "Me and my two sisters."

"How long has your dad been bishop? Nearly five years, isn't it?"

Brig nodded his head. "'Bout that, I guess." Ali led Jenn into the room, and Brig sprang to his feet, relieved. She was dressed in a navy blue skirt and cream-colored blouse. "You look great," he said spontaneously.

"Thank you," Jenn grinned in return.

Dad Lingfelter walked them to the door. "Now, Brother Hales, what time will you have this young lady home?" he said, with his hand on Brig's shoulder.

"Before midnight," Brig swallowed hard.

"Seems reasonable. Well, have a good time, you two," he said as he closed the door behind them.

Brig led Jenn to his car, opened the door for her, and then scurried to his side. "I didn't know you were living with the Lingfelters," he said once he was seated. "How did that happen?"

Jenn buckled her seat belt before replying. "I met Ali when she was on her mission in California."

"Really?" he said. "Was she a pretty good missionary?"

Jenn nodded her head. "Of course, but she wasn't the one who taught me the discussions."

Brig Hales's head whirled toward her. "You're a convert? How long ago?"

Jenn was uncertain whether she had shocked or excited her date. "Just last year," she replied warily.

"Cool! I'm going to get my papers going in October. My birthday's the fifth of January."

"Great," Jenn said, a little unsure of what all that meant. The car moved smoothly through the little town, and she began to relax a bit. Although it was after eight o'clock in the evening, the sun had just dropped behind the mountains to the west. She folded her hands in her lap and thought of the coincidences in her life that had brought her to this place at this time. "This is sure different from home," she said as Brig slowed to a crawl behind a tractor that was moseying down the road.

"Oh? I guess I'm just kinda used to it," he replied. They drove on silently for several minutes before Brig glanced at her and said, "I guess I'd better get you home before midnight or President Lingfelter will have my head."

"President?"

Brig nodded. "He was released as stake president about five years ago. Everybody in the valley knows him."

"I guess I have a lot to learn," Jenn said quietly. A few minutes later they pulled into a parking lot and walked a couple of blocks to the Taggart Center where they joined the other couples in the ballroom. Jenn watched in fascination and dread at those who were dancing. *I don't know how to dance like that,* she thought. Apparently, Brig wasn't that excited about getting onto the dance floor either. He led her to a chair at the side of the ballroom.

"Want something to drink?" he asked. She nodded, and he disappeared into the pulsating throng of dancers. Jenn noticed her hands were sweaty and her heart was racing. She became increasingly uncomfortable as she watched more closely the dancers on the floor. *Why did I come? Brig's going to want to dance, and I'll look like a fool,* she thought. Jenn began to feel trapped with no way to escape when Brig returned with two cups of punch. Gratefully, she took the plastic cup and sipped. *He won't ask me to dance as long as I'm drinking this.* She cradled the cup in her hands. The music ended, and some of the couples on the floor wandered away toward the refreshment table; others just stood and waited for the music to begin again. She sipped slowly at her punch.

"I've got a confession to make," Brig said during the lull. "I'm not much of a dancer." He twisted the cup in his hands and looked at the floor. "We had a Church dance festival a couple of years ago, and I learned some ballroom stuff, but I'm not real good at . . . whatever they call this dancing."

Jenn smiled, "That makes two of us." She took a bigger swig of her punch. "When I was in elementary school we learned a waltz and a fox trot, I think. That's about the extent of my dancing career." The music began again, and those on the floor began gyrating to the beat. Jenn and

Brig sat and watched the other couples. When the music finally ended, the band leader stepped to the microphone.

"We'd sure like to welcome everybody to the dance. Let me introduce the members of the band." He introduced each of the five members, who stood and waved as their names were spoken. "We're going to take a little journey back through time to a kinder and gentler kind of music," he said. "So, grab your dates and go back with us to that old Andy Williams favorite, 'Moon River.'" He turned to the band members, waved his hand a few times to set the tempo, and then gave the downbeat.

Most of the people who were on the dance floor moved slowly to its edge. A few couples began to dance to the slow, melodic tune. "I think this is a waltz," Brig said. "I think I remember how. Would you like to dance?" He stood and held his hand toward Jenn. She took it, set her cup of punch on the chair, and followed him onto the parquet floor. Jenn felt a shiver run up her spine when Brig placed his hand on her waist. They stumbled a bit until they remembered how to move their feet, but soon they were moving with a quiet confidence to the music. When the dance ended, many of those standing around the edges of the floor applauded the dozen or so couples who had waltzed. Brig led Jenn back to her seat as the band began a louder, heavy metal piece.

"Thank you, Brig, that was fun," she said.

"You're a wonderful dancer," he replied.

"You're not bad yourself."

Three hours later they decided it was time to leave. A few times during the evening the band had played slower pieces of music, and the two of them had danced. They had spent most of the time watching the other dancers on the floor with amusement and awe. They walked out of the student center into a balmy summer night. The full moon had just crested the Bear River Mountains to the east and cast a mellow glow over the campus. They walked for nearly a block before Brig reached for Jenn's hand. "Too late for ice cream," he said. "We'll have to do it another time."

Although it seemed as if the whole town had gone to bed, the porch light burned brightly at the Lingfelter home. Brig led Jenn to the porch and held both her hands for a moment. "Thanks for going to the dance with me," he said.

Jenn squeezed his hands. "Thank you," she said. "It was fun." She wasn't quite sure what to expect when Brig leaned toward her. Just before his lips reached hers, the porch light flashed off and on, and Brig drew back quickly.

He let go of her hands, pivoted, and hurried down the steps towards his car. "I'll call you," he said as he opened the door, jumped into the car, and drove off. Jenn stood for a few minutes, watching him go, and then turned toward the front door. Mom Lingfelter opened it with a smile on her face.

"Did you have a good time?" she asked.

Jenn nodded her head. "Yes, Mom," she said with a smile.

FORTy~OnE

Sunday morning Jenn sat up in bed and stretched. Every muscle in her body seemed to rebel. The previous day had been spent weeding the family vegetable garden, helping clean out the garage, and a half-dozen other tasks. While they worked side by side, Ali had asked Jenn about her date with Brigham Hales and had giggled out loud when Jenn told her about the flashing porch light.

"Every one of us Lingfelters has had that old light trick played on us," she said.

Jenn took a break from weeding to stretch her back, "But it's so . . . so comforting to know that there's someone there looking out for you. Someone who cares," she said wistfully.

"I suppose," Ali said.

Jenn thought about how quickly she had become a part of the Lingfelter family and then wondered if she was being disloyal to her own mother and brother. "I'd better write them after church," she said to herself as she continued to stretch and yawn. Church began at eleven o'clock, and the Lingfelters pulled into the parking lot ten minutes before the services began. Jenn followed nervously behind Ali as they walked into the half-filled chapel. A young girl stood at the doorway handing out programs.

Dad Lingfelter shook hands with everyone as he and his wife led the way toward the front of the chapel. It was clear from their responses and the looks on their faces that the people loved and respected them. Ali took hold of Jenn's elbow and kept her from following them. "They're speaking today, Jenn. We can grab a seat back here." She inclined her head toward an empty bench. They had just seated themselves when a man walked quickly to the end of the bench. He was about six feet tall with sparse white hair and deep brown eyes. He wore a pinstriped, navy blue suite, white shirt, and wine-colored tie.

"Good morning," he said with smiling eyes. "You must be the young lady the Lingfelters have been so excited about." He shook her hand. "I'm Bishop Morgan."

"Nice to meet you," Jenn replied.

"Ali, how are you? Ready for school to begin?"

"Excited to get back, Bishop. It's my senior year, and I can see the light at the end of the tunnel."

He turned back to Jenn. "Welcome to our ward, young lady. If you'd see the ward clerk after the block, he can request your membership." He looked at Ali. "Could you see that she meets with Brother Jensen?"

"Of course, Bishop."

With a slight nod of his head, he left them and walked to the door to greet people.

"He seems like a nice man," Jenn said.

Ali glanced over her shoulder at him. "He is. He's only been bishop for six or seven months, since Bishop Campbell died. But he's wonderful. He's a retired professor from the college. You'll learn to love him in a hurry."

A tall, gray-haired woman slid onto the organ bench and began the prelude music. Within a few minutes the rest of the congregation filled the seats in the chapel, and sacrament meeting began. *Just like my ward at home,* Jenn thought. When the meeting ended, quite a number of ward members introduced themselves to Jenn and told her how glad they were to have her in the ward. Ali led her to the ward clerk's office, and Brother Jensen asked her a number of questions so he could request her membership record. Ali had told her parents that she and Jenn would walk home, and they strolled at an easy pace down the street.

"Ali, I can't believe how kind the people around here seem to be. It's like I've known them my whole life, even though I can't remember their names."

"They are good people—not without faults, as I'm sure you'll find out, but good people nevertheless."

They walked on a few more minutes. Ali was humming the tune to a hymn when Jenn interrupted her. "Can I ask you a question?"

"Sure. I might even answer it," Ali said with a lilt in her voice.

"How come you went on a mission? I mean, I know all the young men are supposed to, but you didn't have to. How come you went?"

Ali stopped walking and leaned against a rail fence at the side of the road. "It just felt right. It was a good time for me to go. I was turning twenty-one, and I'd just finished my sophomore year. I decided to go before I started all those upper division classes." She looked wistfully toward the mountains.

Jenn sensed there was more to the story but was reluctant to probe. She leaned on the fence next to her companion and waited.

"Of course, there was Brad," Ali finally said. "He and I had been dating for quite a while. He was a nice boy. There was a lot of . . . of physical attraction." Her voice drifted off, and Ali rubbed her shoulder on the fence rail while she composed her thoughts. "He wanted to get married," she said in a voice so low that Jenn had to strain to hear it. "I thought I wanted to marry him too. I went to Dad and talked to him about Brad." She stopped and wiped a tear from her cheek. "Ah, you don't want to hear this," Ali said as she pushed away from the fence and started to walk toward home.

Jenn caught her. "What happened?"

Ali took a deep breath, "Well, Dad told me he couldn't make a decision for me. He told me that all he wanted for me was happiness. Of course, I wanted him to make the decision for me, or I wouldn't have gone to him in the first place." She wiped away another tear. "Oh, Jenn, I didn't know what to do. Dad suggested that I fast and pray about it. He

223

told me it was the biggest decision I'd ever make in my life." She started to walk slowly again.

"Well, obviously you decided to go on a mission," Jenn said. "What happened?"

Ali scrunched her shoulders. "You know sometimes we go to someone and ask their advice, and what we really want them to do is agree with the decision we've already made. Reluctantly, I followed Dad's advice. I fasted the next day, and that night I knelt at my bedside and asked the Lord what he wanted me to do." She wiped away more tears.

"And did you get an answer?" Jenn said softly.

Ali stopped walking, bowed her head, and turned toward Jenn. "I expected the Lord to tell me to go ahead and marry Brad. I think that's the decision I'd made, and I just wanted the Lord to say, 'Go ahead.' But I got up from my knees, and something I'd never really seriously contemplated popped into my head." She smiled through her tears. "Of course, the answer was, 'Go on a mission.' All my brothers had served missions, but none of my sisters had. I tried all night long to get that thought out of my head, but it just kept sifting itself to the top of my thoughts. I finally got back down on my knees and asked the Lord if that was the answer. Was I really supposed to go on a mission?" She cleared her throat. "And suddenly I was overcome by this feeling of complete peace. 'There is someone waiting for you to find her,' kept coming into my mind. I went back to bed, and the next morning I told Mom and Dad what I'd decided to do. I put in my papers, and four months later I left for California."

The two girls walked together until they turned the corner half a block from home. *I was the girl she was supposed to find.* Jenn broke the silence. "What happened to Brad?"

Ali turned her gaze upward and said nothing until they'd climbed the steps to the front porch. She led Jenn to a porch swing and invited her to sit down. "I told him what I'd decided to do. He had mixed emotions, I think. He'd not served a mission himself—I don't know why—and I think he was proud that I'd decided to go. On the other hand, he didn't want me to leave." She rocked the swing gently. "He told me—promised me—he'd wait for me to return, and then we'd get married."

Jenn turned in the swing and looked at her friend. "Did he?" she asked.

Ali looked straight ahead and rocked the swing. "No, he didn't. Four months after I left, he wrote me a Dear Jane letter. He was married a month later to a girl named Shauna. I barely knew her." She looked down at her hands that were clasped tightly in her lap. "They had a baby three months after they were married," she said flatly.

Jenn put her hand on Ali's arm. "It sounds as if he is a real winner." She looked into her friend's eyes and asked, "But it still hurts?"

Ali nodded her head. "But it looks like the Lord was right. Of course, he always is, if we just listen to him."

FORTY~TWO

School began, and Jenn found herself studying harder than she'd ever done before in her life. She and Ali drove back and forth to school together, and with some encouragement from her friend, Jenn took driver's education lessons from a private firm in Logan. By the middle of October, she had her driver's license and occasionally took Ali's brother Matt's car to run some special errand. As Ali had said, it was an old Honda, but at least all of the fenders were the same color, unlike Ali's car.

Once Jenn had her license, she began to look for a job and found one at the Sizzler on Main Street. She only worked Wednesday and Saturday evenings, but it did provide a little cash. She had tried to pay the Lingfelters for room and board, but they had refused to take any money. She and Brig Hales had gone on a couple of more dates, but he worked most of the nights she didn't, and so there were not many opportunities.

As Halloween approached, life had settled into a comfortable rhythm of school, work, and church. Her records had arrived, and she was formally welcomed into the ward. When Bishop Morgan learned that she had been teaching Primary, he immediately called her to a position teaching the four-year-old class.

Jenn wrote home weekly and told her mother about life at USU. She resisted the urge to tell much about the Lingfelters and the comfortable surroundings in which she found herself. At first she was reluctant to mention much about the Church and her calling, but after thoughtful prayer, she began including that information in her letters. She had received two letters from her mother and one from Damon.

On Halloween night, Jenn and Ali handed out the treats to the trick-or-treaters who came to the door. Many of them thanked "Sister Lingfelter" and "Sister Cooper" before they turned and left. It was a new experience for Jenn, and she loved it. Ali had begun dating a young man named Jerry Smoot, whom she'd met at USU. He had served a mission in England, and Jenn noticed the two of them seemed to spend a lot of time trying to prove which of their missions was better. As their relationship grew, the time Ali and Jenn spent together shrank.

Jenn and Ali arrived home from school the day after Halloween to find Mom and Dad Lingfelter beside themselves with excitement. "Look what came," Mom said as she fluttered a letter up and down in front of the two girls' faces.

Ali reached out and captured the piece of paper. She scanned it quickly and then let out a whoop. "It's Matt's release information," she said to Jenn. "He'll be home the day before Thanksgiving." She handed the letter to Jenn.

"I'm so dumb," she said. "What happens? I mean, I don't know what this all means."

Mom Lingfelter hugged Jenn. "He'll be arriving at the Salt Lake airport just after noon on Wednesday. We'll all go and meet him," she practically shouted. "Oh, these two years have flown by, haven't they, Hon?"

Dad Lingfelter had tears in his eyes. "I can't believe he's coming home," was all he said before he sank into his recliner.

Ali turned to her mother. "Have you called Andrea?" she asked.

"No, dear. The mailman just barely delivered this before you two walked in. Would you give her a call?"

"Sure, Mom." Ali walked into the den and beckoned to Jenn to follow her. "This will be fun," she said as she picked up the phone and punched in a number. "Andrea is Matt's girlfriend. She's been waiting for him." The phone rang several times before someone answered. "Is Andrea there?"

"Have I met her?" Jenn asked.

"I don't think so," Ali said. She covered the receiver with her hand. "Mom said that right after Matt left she used to come over all the time, but I haven't seen her in two or three months." She removed her hand and said into the phone, "Andrea, this is Ali Lingfelter. We just got some great news. Matt will be home on Wednesday, the twenty-fourth." Jenn could hear sounds coming from the phone but couldn't understand them. Ali's face lit up as she listened. "We're going to the airport to pick him up about noon. I'm sure there's room if you want to come along." There was more conversation from the other end before Ali continued, "Andrea, there will just be the four of us going." There was a pause. "Four—Mom and Dad and Jenn and me." Again there was a pause. "Jenn Cooper. She's a young lady I met on my mission, and she's going to USU. She's staying with us. I'm sure you'll like her. Anyway, I'm sure we'll take the minivan 'cause Matt will be bringing a ton of stuff home. It seats eight, so if you want to go with us," Ali drew one leg up and hooked it over the arm of the chair. "Probably about ten o'clock. That will give us time to get to the airport. Think about it, and if you want to go with us, just give me a call. We'll figure out the details in a day or so. Okay? See you too. Good-bye."

Jenn looked at Ali's face and asked, "Something wrong?"

"I don't know. Andrea didn't seem as excited as I thought she'd be. Oh well. I guess I'd better call the rest of the clan. I'm sure the ones who live close by will want to be there. Jenn excused herself and walked out of the den and back to the front room, where Mom and Dad Lingfelter sat talking more calmly to each other.

"Oh, Jenn, did Ali get hold of Andrea?"

Jenn nodded her head. "She's calling her brothers and sisters now." She climbed the stairs to her bedroom and sat down at the dressing table. Four of Ali's brothers and sisters and their families lived within a half-hour drive of the Lingfelters, and all of them usually appeared on Sunday evenings for a visit. That meant that eight adults and eight grandchildren often arrived at dinnertime. Jenn was amazed that Mom Lingfelter didn't seem to mind. In fact, it appeared as if she expected them and prepared enough food for all twenty people who sat down to eat. She wondered if she would feel out of place with so many of the family going to greet Matt. Old insecurities bubbled to the surface, and she began to wonder if she was just overreacting. She wandered out to the car and retrieved her sociology book from the backseat. When she walked back into the house, Ali was emerging from the den.

"Well, I reached everybody, Dad. I'm not sure Roy can get off work, but it sounds as if everybody else will be at the airport. I offered Andrea a ride with us. I hope that's okay."

"Sure," he said with a smile. "We'll put her in the backseat and Matt up front and he'll still be an arm's length away from her." Ali and her mother chuckled at the joke. "I think the next three weeks will go by quickly. We'd better dust your brother's room and get it ready for him."

"Not quickly enough for me," Mom said.

FORTY~THREE

"*Andrea, this is* Jenn Cooper," Ali said. "Jenn, this is Andrea Mott."

Jenn extended her hand to Andrea and said, "Pleased to meet you." Andrea gave a small nod in return. She was a short, pale girl with flaming red hair.

"Let's get this show on the road," Dad said enthusiastically. The five of them piled into the minivan and headed toward Salt Lake City. During the trip, Ali tried to engage Andrea in conversation, but she seemed quite reserved. An hour and a half later they parked in the parking terrace and stepped onto the moving sidewalk that took them to the terminal. "Everybody used to go down to the jet way. But since 9/11, we have to wait out here by the luggage carousels. Ali, will you check the monitor and see if the plane's on time?"

"Sure, Dad." She wedged her way through the crowd in the terminal to the bank of monitors showing arrivals and departures. Jenn followed her. The two of them scanned the arrival screens until they found Matt's plane. It was scheduled to arrive on time, in about twenty minutes. The two girls returned and reported what they'd found out.

"Twenty minutes," Mom said. "That seems longer than the two years he's been gone." She maneuvered so she could see the escalators behind the security checkpoint. During the next ten minutes the rest of the Lingfelter clan arrived. Jenn and Andrea moved to the back of the growing throng.

"I'll bet you're excited to see him again," Jenn said to Andrea.

Andrea shrugged her shoulders, "Yeah, I guess I am." She noticed the look on Jenn's face. "Well, it has been two years since we've seen each other. We both have probably changed a lot. Matt's probably grown a lot, and I've just been working." Jenn could see the doubt and fear in the girl's face. "It isn't as if we agreed to wait for each other or anything. I mean, I've dated other guys while he's been gone."

Jenn nodded her head. "Still, this must be pretty exciting."

"I guess."

Periodically, Jenn went back to the bank of monitors. After what seemed an eternity, the plane's status changed from "on time" to "arrived." She returned to the group with the news, and a cheer went up from the waiting family. Other people had filtered in in front of Mom, and she had to gently push her way to a spot where she could see. The first passengers from Matt's flight began descending the escalator, and the excitement increased significantly. After the first group of passengers deplaned, several minutes passed before the next passengers appeared. It seemed as if nearly everyone had gotten off the plane and there was no sign of Elder Lingfelter. The family began to murmur among themselves.

"Do you think he got bumped?" Ali asked. At that moment Matt appeared at the top of the escalator. He was dressed in a well-worn navy blue suit with his name tag on the lapel. He spotted his family and broke into an enormous grin. He raised his hand and waved, and the entire family waved back.

There was a family picture hanging in the foyer of the Lingfelter home, so Jenn had seen Matt in the picture. He was sitting down, however, and she had not realized how tall he was. His blond hair was trimmed in missionary style, and he had a backpack slung over one shoulder. As soon as he reached the bottom of the escalator, he practically ran to where his family stood. He engulfed his mother in a bear hug and lifted her off the floor. Then he set her down gently and hugged his father. One by one, he greeted his relatives and then, just as the Red Sea parted for Moses, the crowd separated, revealing Andrea. Matt smiled at her, walked briskly toward her, and shook her hand. Andrea smiled bravely back at the missionary.

"Matt," Ali said, tapping him on the shoulder, "I want you to meet someone." He turned away from Andrea and looked at his sister. "Matt, this is Jenn Cooper. I've written you about her."

Jenn smiled at Elder Lingfelter and said, "Pleased to meet you. I've heard so much about you."

Matt's eyes locked onto Jenn's as if two magnets were drawing them together. "My pleasure," he stammered. The two of them continued to stare at each other until Ali tapped him on the shoulder.

"Matt," she said, "help us identify your luggage."

"Sure," he replied, not taking his eyes off Jenn. "There are the two big, old suitcases I took with me, and two cardboard boxes." Reluctantly, he turned to the baggage carousel.

As they waited, Mom said, "Now, don't forget Thanksgiving dinner tomorrow at three o'clock sharp, not on Mormon Standard Time."

Five minutes later the luggage had arrived, and the family dragged and carried it to the car. They wedged the luggage into the space behind the backseat and then put the two cardboard cartons on the backseat. Jenn climbed in next to the boxes. Ali positioned herself between Andrea and Matt in the middle seat while her parents slid into the front seats of the minivan.

"I told the stake president you'd be home this afternoon, and he said to come over to his house when you get home and he'll release you." Dad guided the car through the prepaid parking lane.

"That'll be great, Dad," Matt said. He leaned forward so he could see past Ali to where Andrea sat. "Man, it's great of you to come to the airport," he said.

"Ali invited me," she said, noncommittally.

"It's so good to see you again." He was speaking in short, halting phrases. "I'm a little rusty on my English," he explained. "I'm kind of translating from Spanish." He twisted around in his seat as far as the seat belt allowed. "And you're Jenn Cooper. Mom's told me a whole lot about you."

"I've heard a lot about you, too," she said. "Your family has been wonderful to me."

"Tell us about your mission," Dad said from the front seat. "Did you meet the people you were supposed to meet?"

Tears sprang to Elder Lingfelter's eyes, and he said, "Oh, yes, Dad. Let me tell you about the Soledad family." For the next hour, Matt told them about his experiences with a remarkable family he'd met in Sucre. He talked about the struggles they'd had coming to church, the problems with the Word of Wisdom, and the breakthrough moment when they'd agreed to be baptized. He described how beautiful these people were and confessed that he'd fallen in love with Glorietta Soledad. There was a stunned silence in the car.

"One of the biggest disappointments in my life is that I did not get to see her baptized," he said, shaking his head sorrowfully.

"Why was that?" Jenn asked from the backseat.

"Because she's only two years old," Matt said with a grin. "But when she is old enough, her father will baptize her."

The car crept up the canyon toward Sardine Summit. "Is it good to be home again?" his mother asked.

Matt gazed out the window as they worked their way through the mountain pass. "Of course," he blurted. "But I hated to leave the people. They've become so . . ." He paused for a moment. "So *especial* to me." He blinked back tears. "When I left home for Bolivia, I knew I'd be seeing my family again. But when I left Bolivia, I knew I was probably saying good-bye to these people for good. In some ways, that was harder." He sank into silence.

Dad stopped to let Andrea out at her home. Matt walked her to the front door and shook her hand. "I'll call you later, after I'm released," he said before returning to the car.

"Do you want to go home first, or shall we go directly to President Hunsaker's home?" Dad asked.

"Might as well get it over with," Matt said with a sigh. "The stake president is on the way home."

Jenn watched as Elder Lingfelter sank down in his seat. She could tell he was weary but also extremely sad to be released from something he'd loved so much. She felt gratitude for Sister Ball and Sister Snow and their untiring efforts to teach her, as well as Sister Lingfelter and Sister Sandberg, who had started her in the direction she had gone. Her mind flashed back to the moment in the hospital when Damon had been blessed and had opened his eyes. *I wish he'd open them a little wider and see what the Church has to offer.* She thought of all the kindness the Lingfelters had shown to her and wondered how she'd ever repay them. She felt tears welling up in her eyes.

They pulled up in front of President Hunsaker's house. Reluctantly, Elder Lingfelter opened the sliding side door of the minivan and walked slowly up the sidewalk toward the front porch. He stopped at the bottom of the stairs, looked back over his shoulder, and with a sigh climbed them and pressed the doorbell. His shoulders sank as he waited for the door to open.

Jenn watched with his family from the car. "He really loved the people, didn't he?" she said.

The door opened, and President Hunsaker put his arm around Elder Lingfelter's shoulders. Then he stepped past the missionary and beckoned for the whole family to come in.

"Maybe I'd better wait in the car," Jenn said. "I think this is a moment for the family to share."

"Nonsense," Mom said. "You're a part of our family now."

When they were seated in the living room, President Hunsaker asked Elder Lingfelter some of the same questions Dad Lingfelter had asked. President Hunsaker then released him, hugged him one more time, and asked him if he'd come to the high council meeting the next Sunday morning and give a brief report on his labors.

"They'd all like to welcome you home," he said with a smile. He shook Mom's hand, then Dad's, and then Ali's. "Now, I don't think I know you," he said, looking at Jenn, a little puzzled.

"This is Jennica Cooper," Dad said. "She's staying with us during the school year. Ali met and taught her when she was on her mission."

President Hunsaker smiled at her. "It's good to have you here, Sister Cooper," he said. "Of course, I don't know how you're going to put up with this old reprobate." He smiled at Dad Lingfelter. "He left some pretty big shoes to fill when he was released." He shook hands with Matt one more time. "You can remove your badge, Elder. You're released."

Matt took hold of the black name badge and suddenly sat back down on the couch and began to cry.

"He loved the people so much," Mom said.

"Good!" the stake president said. "That's when you become an effective tool in the Lord's hands."

They waited for a few minutes, until Matt was able to compose himself, and then they left President Hunsaker's home.

FORT𝒴~FOUR

Matt's talk in sacrament meeting was spiritual and uplifting. All of Matt's brothers and sisters and their children were there. Many of the ward members commented on how much he had grown. Following the block of meetings, he and Andrea walked home together while Ali and Jenn followed a discreet block or so behind them. The rest of the family had gone on ahead to get dinner on the table for the whole family for the second time this week. Thanksgiving had been a noisy celebration, made even more raucous by Matt's return.

"What do you think's going on with them?" Ali asked.

"I don't know," Jenn said, with a tinge of jealousy in her voice.

Ali raised an eyebrow but said nothing until they'd walked another half block. The weather was colder, and the two of them were wearing coats and had their hands stuffed in their pockets. "I've asked Jerry Smoot to come to dinner," she said. "He tried to get away from his ward to hear Matt's talk, but he's the elders quorum president, and the times conflicted."

"You've been dating him quite a bit," Jenn said. "Is it getting serious?"

"Well, after he gets baptized by fire with the whole Lingfelter army, he might not want to get any more serious," she said with a smile. "But, yes, I think it's getting serious."

"Congratulations!" Jenn said cheerfully.

"We haven't set a date or anything, but we've been talking." She looked at her brother a block in front of them. He and Andrea had stopped walking, and their conversation had grown quite animated. "I wonder what's going on?" she asked again.

Suddenly, Andrea whirled and marched off down the street toward her home, and Matt walked briskly toward his house. Ali and Jenn sped up their pace and arrived home shortly after Matt. The Lingfelters had set up tables in the living room, family room, and dining room to accommodate the more than forty people there for dinner. When Ali and Jenn walked in, Matt was nowhere to be seen. A flurry of activity was going on as bowls and plates of food were being delivered to all of the tables. Dad Lingfelter clapped his hands above his head.

"Let's have a blessing, and we can get started," he said loudly. The din quieted, and he asked his oldest son to offer the prayer. When the prayer ended, everyone played musical chairs to find a place to sit. Matt was still among the missing.

Ali nodded her head toward the stairs and beckoned for Jenn to follow her. Together they climbed the steps and knocked on Matt's door. "Who's there?" Matt's muffled voice asked.

"Ali," she replied. "Can I come in?"

"Sure," he said. "Why not?"

"Maybe you ought to wait out here," Ali whispered to Jenn. She pushed the door open and walked into Matt's room. The door stayed open a few inches, and Jenn could hear what was being said inside.

"What's the problem, little bro? Everybody's waiting for you to come down and eat. You know, the guest of honor thing?"

"I don't feel much like eating," he replied in somber tones.

"What's up?"

"Andrea and I broke up," he said flatly. "Not that there was much to

237

break up from since I got back."

"I'm sorry," Ali said. "I know how much you liked her."

"Yeah, well, I guess things have changed in the past two years." The room grew silent for a minute or two. "Sis, I don't know whether I've changed or she's changed or what, but there just isn't anything there anymore. You know what I mean?"

"Yes, I do," she replied honestly.

"What about you?" he asked. "Any romance going on in your life?"

"Maybe. In fact, Jerry Smoot ought to be here any minute. I've invited him for dinner so he can meet the whole herd."

"You're a brave woman," Matt laughed. "Or a dumb one. I'm not sure which."

"That remains to be seen, I guess." Jenn could hear Ali moving toward the door. "Come on down, bro, and I'll introduce you to him when he gets here."

"I suppose I'd better," he said resignedly. "Sis, can I ask you a question?"

"Sure, shoot."

"Is Jenn serious about anyone? I mean, she's so beautiful that I can't believe someone hasn't snatched her up already."

Jenn felt her cheeks grow hot. *I shouldn't be eavesdropping.* But she couldn't tear herself away from the door.

"Brigham Hales has dated her a few times, but he just received his mission call, so I don't think he'll pose much of a threat. Why? Are you interested?"

Matt stammered, "Sis, when I saw her at the airport, it was as if time stood still for me. I know that you can't base a marriage on physical attraction, but I've never been hit that hard—ever."

The doorbell rang, and Jenn was not sure anyone would hear it through the cacophony of dinner. She hurried down the steps and answered the front door. Jerry Smoot stood there with a bemused look on his face.

"Hi, Jenn," he said. "Ali invited me to dinner. I hope I'm not too late. The bishop needed to talk to me for a minute after church."

"You're right on time," Jenn said, opening the door for him. "Everybody just sat down. I think Ali's waiting for you. I'll get her."

"I'm right here," said Ali. She and Matt were standing at the bottom of the stairs. "Jerry, welcome to the nuthouse. This is my brother Matt. He's the reason for this gathering. The Lingfelter family dinner is in session." She grabbed him by the arm and led him into the dining room.

Matt looked after them for a moment and then turned to Jenn. Their eyes locked again. "Would you like to accompany me to dinner?" Matt asked.

"I'd love to," Jenn said. "But I don't think we'll find two chairs next to each other." She tucked her hand under his arm, and the two of them walked into the dining room.

Later that evening, all of the guests had left except for Jerry Smoot. He and Ali were sitting in the living room, talking quietly. Dad and Mom were in the family room with Matt. Jenn had slipped away and was sitting in her room writing a letter to her mother. She described how life was going at school and work but avoided saying anything about her church activities. She could hear laughter from the family room. Suddenly President Hunsaker's words sprang into her head. *He really loved the people, didn't he?* "What's the matter with me," she said softly. "Why am I afraid to tell Mom what the Church means to me? Don't I love her?" With that decision made, she began to explain to her mother and brother what joy she found in serving in the Church. The more she wrote, the more she felt that she had to tell them. She was still writing when Ali poked her head in to say good night. She slipped into the room and closed the door behind her.

"How much did you hear this afternoon?"

"Probably more than I should have," Jenn said.

"Is it just a one-way street?" Ali asked. "Or do you have feelings for Matt?"

"Ali, I've only known him for five days. I don't know what I feel."

Ali sat down on Jenn's bed and drew her feet up in front of her. "He's a good young man, and you're a fine young woman. Worse things could happen, but I don't want either one of you getting hurt. With both of you living in the same house, it could get sticky. There's no porch light inside the house. So just be careful, okay?" She slid off the end of the bed. "I can't believe how precious you've become to me," she said as she started to close the door behind her.

"Ali," Jenn called out.

"What?" she said, sticking her head inside the room.

"Did Jerry survive?"

"Yes, he did. I think we might make an announcement soon."

"That's great," Jenn said with a smile. "I'm happy for you."

"Thank you."

As the door closed, Jenn turned back to her letter and finished telling her mother how much the Church meant to her. She folded the letter, slid it into an envelope, and put on extra postage to cover the twelve pages she'd written.

BENEDICTION

Bishop Morgan hung up the phone. "I'm sorry for that interruption, Sister Cooper," he said. "It was rude of me to make you sit there while I took that phone call."

"That's all right, Bishop," she replied. "It gave me time to think about the answer to the question you asked."

He made a tent with his fingers and rested his chin on his thumbs. His lips were pressed against his fingers. He studied Jenn for a moment and then said, "You've lived in the ward over two years. You've been a wonderful Primary teacher; the children love you. I'm so happy this day has finally come." He cleared his throat. "You and Matt Lingfelter have dated for nearly two years. I have to admit, I didn't know how it was going to work out with the two of you living in the same house. Quite frankly, I was a little worried that there might be more temptation than either one of you could handle, especially after Ali and Jerry Smoot were married and she moved out. It left just you two young people there alone."

Jenn smiled and said, "We thought about having a porch light installed in the family room."

The bishop chuckled. "I suppose with President and Sister Lingfelter there, you had pretty good chaperones." He looked down at the open temple recommend book in front of him to the spot he'd marked and repeated, "Are you honest in your dealings with your fellowman?"

Jenn looked the bishop straight in the eye. "Yes, Bishop Morgan, I am."

The bishop finished the other questions, had Jenn sign her name at the bottom of the page, and then signed his name. "When are you going to the temple?" he asked. "If I remember correctly, you and Matt are getting married a week from Friday."

Jenn took the recommend from his hand. "Actually, my mother and brother will be here this Thursday. The Lingfelters say they have room to put them up as well. I'm going to receive my endowment on Friday. So is my brother, Damon. He's been called to serve in the Russia St. Petersburg Mission. He leaves next month. He joined the Church about a year and a half ago. We're still working on my mother, but at least she's quit smoking."

The bishop stood up from behind his desk. The sun behind him still made his white hair seem like a glowing halo around his head. "May God's choicest blessings be with you," he said.

Jenn shook his hand and smiled as she said, "I'm sure they will, Bishop. After all, I'm his daughter, you know."

ABOUT THe AUTHOR

Richard M. Siddoway was born in Salt Lake City and raised in Bountiful, Utah. A professional educator for more than forty years, he serves today as the principal of the Electronic High School, a Utah internet high school operated by the Utah State Office of Education.

He earned his bachelor's degree in biology and his master's degree in educational systems and learning resources, both from the University of Utah. He served three terms in the Utah House of Representatives and has served in a variety of callings in the LDS Church. He is currently president of the Bountiful Utah Stake.

Brother Siddoway is the author of eight books, including *The Christmas Wish, Mom and Other Great Women I Have Known, Christmas of the Cherry Snow,* and *Degrees of Glory,* published by Cedar Fort.

He and his wife, Janice, have eight children and twenty-two grandchildren.